"I couldn'... my eyes, I saw you."

Darcy's words whispered against her skin.

Silver felt herself melt under the seductive pull of his words.

"All I could think of was holding you, touching you, kissing you."

He pulled her flush against him until she could feel every hard, hot inch of him.

She knew she was playing with fire, but she couldn't resist. Pulling his head down to hers, she opened her mouth, allowing her tongue to tease, to stroke before pressing her lips to his.

She *had* to get him out of her system. "Darcy, we're going to exorcise this tension between us with pure, red-hot sex. Just a good roll in the hay."

"Since we're in the office, we'll have to save the hay for another time," he teased.

Her eyes narrowed. "There can't be another time. This is it."

"In that case, I'm going to make sure I do a damn fine job!"

Meg Lacey first discovered romance in the sixth grade when she wrote her own version of *Gone with the Wind.* However, her writing career didn't last. Instead, she went into theater, earned her degree and, over the years, has been an actress, director, copywriter, creative dramatics teacher, mime, mom, college instructor and school bus driver. Currently she is president of her own television and interactive media company, writing and producing in all media from film/video to print. Meg lives in Ohio, where she is currently working on a number of fiction and nonfiction projects.

Books by Meg Lacey

HARLEQUIN TEMPTATION
734—SEXY AS SIN
865—A NOBLE PURSUIT

HARLEQUIN DUETS
13—MAKE ME OVER

SILHOUETTE YOURS TRULY
IS THERE A HUSBAND IN THE HOUSE?
DID YOU SAY BABY?!

MILLION DOLLAR STUD
Meg Lacey

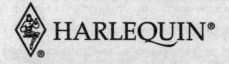

HARLEQUIN®

TORONTO • NEW YORK • LONDON
AMSTERDAM • PARIS • SYDNEY • HAMBURG
STOCKHOLM • ATHENS • TOKYO • MILAN • MADRID
PRAGUE • WARSAW • BUDAPEST • AUCKLAND

My husband and daughters—
for their laughter, excouragement and always
being there when necessary. And who never hesitate
to kick me in the behind when I need it.

ISBN 0-373-25979-4

MILLION DOLLAR STUD

1

RICHARD D'ARCY KRISTOF, heir to the Kristof family fortune, strode into a private library at his country club, removed his bow tie with a jerk and quickly unbuttoned his collar. "That's better. I hate these monkey suits." He took the glass of smooth aged bourbon his older cousin, Nicholas Demetries, handed him, and downed the contents in one gulp, handing it back for another shot.

Nicholas chuckled and refilled the glass. "Rough night, Cousin?"

Darcy scowled. "If I had to dance with one more debutante, or listen to one more proud parent telling me how lovely their...*whoever*...is, I would have jumped off the balcony."

The Tremont twins paused in setting out the poker chips and cards. "Wouldn't have done you any good," Tommy said. "Not if you were thinking suicide. The balcony is only five feet off the ground."

"Yeah," Terry agreed. "Worst that would happen is you'd break a leg and end up in the barberry bushes."

Nicholas, tall, handsome and immaculately dressed in summer formal attire, clasped his cousin's shoulder. "Then all those lovely debutantes you're trying to avoid would be banging on your door trying to give the 'millionaire stud' some comfort."

"God forbid." With a twist of his lips, Darcy sat down at the table and drew the deck of cards toward him. "And don't call me that. You know how much I hate that idiotic—"

Nicholas smiled. "The press has to sell their stories any way they can, Cousin."

"Tell you what, Darcy," said Tommy. "If you need help with that mob of women who're always chasing you, I'm at your service."

"Me, too," echoed Terry.

Darcy began dealing, snapping the cards off and zipping them across the table to the respective players. "Be my guest. I haven't met the woman yet who could intrigue me for more than forty-eight hours. Most of them bore me stiff." He doubted a woman existed who could capture his mind as well as his senses, but that didn't stop him from enjoying them every chance he got.

"Are you talking about in bed or out of it?" Tommy gave him a horrified look. "You don't actually *talk* to them, do you?"

Terry nodded as he considered his cards. "Yeah, what're you doing talking to them, anyway? That's a mistake I never make."

"You're right, Terry." Tommy grinned. "Take our advice—much better to look at them. That way you won't get bored."

Darcy stared at the twins, then shrugged, feeling the tightness in his shoulders. The tension had been building over the past few months, along with his sense of dissatisfaction. Lately, Darcy had felt confined by the aimlessness of his life. But he didn't know what he wanted instead. He picked up his cards, fanning the hand. "At the moment, everything bores me."

"Ah, poor misunderstood rich boy," Nicholas said, mock sympathy dripping off his tongue. He ducked at Darcy's feigned punch. "Wish we all had your problems."

Darcy slid him a glance, then an unwilling grin. "Keep it up, Nick."

Nicholas winked. "Somebody's got to keep your feet on the ground."

Terry gulped his drink, then, his words slurring a bit, said, "Are we going to talk all night or play cards? 'Cause if we're going to talk, I'm going back to the dance."

For a few minutes they played in silence, focusing on the cards and their bets. But then Darcy tossed back another drink and threw in his hand. "Sorry. I'm just not in the mood to play tonight. Let's take a rain check, okay?"

The Tremont twins looked at each other, then back at him. "What's got into you lately?" they asked in perfect unison.

Darcy lifted a brow, his voice tightening. "What does that mean?"

"Oh, screw this," Tommy said, grabbing his brother's arm and raising him to his feet. "Let's go back to the dance. I got my eye on this redhead...."

Nicholas waved the twins to the door, giving Darcy a narrow glance as he did so. When they'd left, he said, "What *is* the matter with you, Darcy? You've been picking fights with everyone lately. Are you having some kind of problems I don't know about?"

"Yes, I...no...hell, I don't know."

Nicholas stared at him. "Is it money? Do you need an advance on your trust?"

"No. I've got plenty of money."

"I'll say." Nicholas chuckled, clasping his hands as he prepared to listen. "Okay. Then regardless of what you just said, it must be a woman."

Darcy sent him a narrow glance. "A woman?" There hadn't been a woman for weeks, not since Susanne Westingham had seduced him in the pool at the Overtons' pool party. Or was it the other way around? Darcy frowned. Sometimes it all ran together.

"I know your parents have been pushing you very hard to settle down."

"With a *suitable* bride," Darcy reminded his cousin. "Which means lots of money and connections. The way they talk about it, I'm supposed to vet them before I even date them. I wouldn't be surprised if they asked me to check their teeth."

Grinning, Nicholas took a sip of his drink. "Well, you can't quite blame them. There's a lot at stake from a family point of view."

"Fortune, reputation, heritage, et cetera, et cetera, et cetera..." Darcy shuddered.

"Afraid so."

"Ah hell, Nick, I'm bored to death. It's all so damn predictable."

Nicholas rolled his eyes. "How could your life be predictable, Darcy? You've got the means to pick up at any time and go anywhere, do anything you want."

Knowing how fortunate he was, Darcy had the grace to blush. "I know, but sometimes I want something different." He felt like the spoiled little kid who wished for a pony, then when he got it, wished for a horse instead.

"Like what?"

"I don't know." Darcy fiddled with his empty glass. "Don't you get bored with it all? The same people, the same places. Doing the same type of things. No real challenge, no real enjoyment. You run from place to place, but it doesn't change." He thumped his fist on the table. "Lord-in-a-box, I'm bored to death, Nick. I need an adventure. Something to take me out of here."

Nicholas shook his head, then focused on his cousin for a long, intense moment. "Darcy, maybe the problem's not on the outside. Maybe the problem is..." He took a breath, then plunged on. "Maybe the problem's with you."

Darcy tossed his head like a restless horse. "Of course it's with me—that's what I'm telling you. It's with who I am."

"That's not really what I meant."

"Sometimes I wonder what it would be like to be nobody. Know what I mean?"

Nicholas picked up the cards, inserting them neatly into their wooden holder. "No, I don't."

Leaning back in his chair, Darcy spread his hands wide. "Nobody. Man, wouldn't that be a lark? To just be an ordinary guy? No living under the microscope, no gossip. No women trying to trap me into marriage, no idiots trying to borrow money or start a fight to prove I'm not any better than they are—nothing like that. Just normal."

Nicholas hooted with laughter. "Come on, as if you could ever be a normal guy."

Darcy's eyes kindled as he sent his cousin the famous Kristof stare, the one his grandfather had used to stare down the enemy during World War II, or so family legend said. "Sure I could. Why couldn't I?"

"Because you've got money and a lifestyle that most people envy and will never achieve—and you're on the most-eligible-bachelor list for every woman from Virginia to New York to Palm Beach, and have been since you turned eighteen." Nicholas shook his head. "You couldn't be normal."

"Want to bet?"

"Bet what?"

"I'll bet that I can live the life of a perfectly ordinary citizen for one month."

Nicholas rubbed his chin for a moment, finally saying, "What are you betting?"

"I'll bet my car on it."

"You'll bet your car?" Nicholas lost his sophisticated air as his jaw dropped to his shoes. "You love that hunk of metal more than you've ever loved a woman."

"That's because it's a hell of a lot more fun and much less trouble. But I'm not worried. I won't lose."

"We'll see," Nicholas commented. "So you plan to waltz out of here and become an ordinary guy, is that it? And where are *you*, the gossip rags' poster boy, going to pull off this little miracle?"

Darcy was puzzled for a moment but then brightened, snapping his fingers. "Let's find a map."

"A map? Why do you need—"

"I need a place to go. It has to be somewhere where no one knows me." He walked over to the bookshelves and started pulling out travel literature the club kept handy for members. "Here we go, a map of the U.S." Darcy walked back to the table and spread it open. Putting one hand over his eyes, he stretched the other over the map, took a deep breath and stabbed with his finger. "All right," he said, studying the spot. "Cecil, Kentucky—good a place as any."

"Cecil? It sounds as if it's in the middle of nowhere. "

"No, look, it's in... I'll be damned. It's in Bluegrass country, a little southwest of Lexington."

"Lexington is the home of horse racing, Darcy. What makes

you think people aren't going to recognize you there? Your family owns a horse farm, for God's sake."

"Since I don't really work the farm, I'm better known in Virginia horse circles—by sight, anyway. No one will connect me with Darcy Kristof of WindRaven Farms, because no one will be expecting to see me as Darcy Kristof. They're going to see a man, period."

Nicholas frowned. "This has disaster written all over it."

"You worry too much."

"You pay me to worry."

Darcy grinned. "Then you're really going to earn your money, aren't you? Now here's the deal. I escape and have an adventure for one month, without anyone but you knowing where I am." He stared into the distance. Maybe this was just what he needed to shake things up. Either that or a new woman. Of the two ideas, the adventure was probably safer. He only hoped it would be as much fun.

"This is the stupidest thing I've heard you say in a long time. If you want to change something, why the hell don't you take over some of your business and family responsibilities? That would be a challenge."

"And put everyone out of work who's there to do it for me?"

"Darcy..." Nicholas sighed. "It's time you got involved with your life."

"That's what I'm trying to do."

"By running away and having an adventure?"

Darcy shrugged. "Why not? Who's it going to hurt?"

"I still think—"

Darcy leaned forward, interrupting him. "Nick, promise you'll tell no one where I am. Not even my parents."

"They won't ask. They're in Europe at our uncle's villa."

"That's right. I'm supposed to be there next week, aren't I?"

"Yes, for Aunt Rosalind's birthday."

"You'll have to make up some story for me, Nick. Come on, be a sport. Do we have a bet?" Darcy extended his arm and stared at his cousin. "I pass as an ordinary guy for one month or I hand over the keys to the Jag. And if I win, your new, very expensive boat is mine to use for the next six months."

Nicholas was silent for a moment, then grasped Darcy's hand. "Ah what the hell, you're going to do it anyway. You've got a bet." He poured them each another tot of bourbon from the crystal decanter. "What in hell are you going to do in Cecil, Kentucky?"

"I'll get by. Don't worry." Darcy downed his drink.

"I still think this one the most crack-brained—"

"Cool it, Nick. You're my lawyer, not a mother hen." Darcy headed for the door, turning to give his cousin an affectionate smile. "Don't worry. Nothing's going to happen. I'm just going to have some fun, that's all."

"All right, but whatever you do, don't seduce all the local farm girls. Your family won't take kindly to that, especially if I have to clean up the mess."

"I don't spend my entire time thinking about women."

"You don't have to—they think about you."

"I can't help that," Darcy exclaimed. "Besides, when did you have to clean up a mess beyond Christina Petrou? Which wasn't entirely my fault. It was just fun, till her parents got involved."

"All I'm saying is be a bit circumspect, all right?"

"I won't do anything anyone could misunderstand." Darcy exhaled, getting his quick flare of temper under control. "Unless they ask for it, of course."

Nicholas gave him a sardonic look. "Oh, now that'll be a comfort to me while you're gallivanting around Cecil."

Darcy laughed. "Trust me, if I see a good-looking babe, I'll turn the other cheek. Or at least I'll try."

"Ah hell, go," Nicholas said, picking up his drink. "But call if you need me."

Darcy waved as he left the room. "See you in a month."

HAVING MADE HIS DECISION to leave, Darcy didn't waste time in getting on his way. Monday morning, just after dawn, he hefted a large duffel bag into the seat of the old pickup truck he'd borrowed from one of his grooms, and hit the road. He felt an unaccustomed feeling of freedom. When was the last time he'd had an adventure like this? Never, he thought. His adventures had always included exotic locales, first-class accommodations and expensive equipment. At the moment he had five hundred dollars in his wallet, a few changes of clothes and a couple of his favorite books. He was ready to roll.

He ignored the interstates and took back roads, meandering through the familiar rolling valleys of Virginia, then the mountains of West Virginia, passing through small towns that brought a smile, and over rivers and creeks with names that celebrated pioneer discovery. He slipped unnoticed into Kentucky, into the eastern Appalachian hills, and finally into the majesty and promise of the bluegrass region—the grazing land, rolling wooded vistas and wide valleys that surrounded his final destination.

SILVER BRAYBOURNE TOOK a firmer grasp on the lunge lines as her horse walked in a tight circle. "All right, now," she crooned, "just settle down. You know what this is all about." Lucky Hand wasn't a young, inexperienced horse, but one who needed retraining if he was ever to reach his potential. And Silver thought this horse had plenty of potential. The problem lately was convincing her father.

"That's right, let's smooth it out." She jammed her old baseball hat down on her head as she studied the stallion's gait, paying close attention to the movement of his back legs as she let the line out a bit. She'd had the horse for about two months, but had only been working him hard for one. "We've had a lot of winners come out of Braybourne Farm. I expect you to do your share." The horse glanced her way as if he understood. "You're a winner. I just know it, and I'm going to prove it, no matter what anyone says." After all, they'd bred and trained a number of winning racehorses, even if they hadn't produced a Derby winner. But she could change that if she managed this farm. She lightly cracked her whip, smiling as the horse responded. Daddy was just getting cold feet, not up to taking a risk. She'd convince him otherwise or she didn't deserve to be a Braybourne.

Silver blinked sweat from her eyes and wiped her forehead on the sleeve of her old cotton shirt. Damn, it was hot. She couldn't remember when it had last been so hot in Cecil. June in Kentucky was generally pleasant, but this year was already promising to be a scorcher. She hoped it wouldn't be dry, too. The past few years had been hard on their crops, not to mention their horses. They couldn't afford to take any more losses.

"'Scuse me, Miz Braybourne," a voice interrupted her. "Doc Winters sent me over with some of that new liniment you was asking about."

Silver glanced over her shoulder at the young man giving her an admiring glance from behind the fence.

"Hi, Jamie. Just put it in the office for me, okay?"

"You gotta sign for it. Doc Winters said you gotta sign for it."

"Why don't you sign for me, Jamie? I'm fine with that."

"The doc wouldn't like it. He's got a new office manager who says he's gotta clean up his act, and she's making the doc's life miserable."

Silver laughed. "Well, I'm almost finished anyway, so bring the paper on out here. I wouldn't want you to break the rules on my account." That was her job. Breaking rules, pushing to see how far she could go, before someone hauled her back to the gate. Unfortunately, most of the time she was pulled up short before she'd even gotten onto the field. But that didn't stop her from trying.

Jamie slipped into the paddock and picked his way over to Silver, taking care to avoid the big black stallion at the other end of the line. He held out a professional-looking clipboard. "Here you go, Miz Braybourne."

"You can call me Silver, Jamie. You used to." She sent the young man a teasing grin. "Before you remembered that I changed your diapers when I baby-sat for you."

Jamie blushed and scuffed his toe in the dirt. "I wish you'd forget about that."

Silver held the lunge line in one hand as she scribbled her name with the other. "Can't, Jamie. You had such a cute little backside."

Silver's grin expanded as Jamie turned every shade of red. "Ah, geez!"

A high-pitched cackle erupted from the fence, followed by a halfhearted command, "Girl, you leave that there young man alone. Ain't no call to embarrass him that way."

Silver handed the clipboard back to Jamie, smiling at his muttered "thank you" as he walked to his pickup truck. She looked over her shoulder at Travis O'Neill, whom her grandfather had nicknamed Tater when he was just a little sprout. "Tater, where've you been? Dad was down here looking for you a little while ago."

"He found me," he replied, resting his elbows on the fence.

Silver stared at him. There was something about his tone of voice.... She slowed her horse to a walk. "Is anything wrong?"

Tater climbed stiffly onto the fence, perching on the top rail. "What could be wrong, girlie?"

She walked to the horse and removed the line, leading him by the bridle over to Tater. "Besides the fact that we're in hock up to our ears, you mean?"

"Nothing new in that, Silver. Braybournes been either in the money or out of it ever since your great-great-great-great-grandfather settled Cecil."

"I know, but we were getting ahead until Brett made that stupid investment."

"Your brother didn't make it by hisself, ya know. Your daddy okayed it."

"I know. If he'd asked me, I could have told him—"

"Point is, he didn't. So I'd let it go if I was you, and do your best to help turn things around, any way you can."

"I'm trying, Tater, but my father doesn't always listen to me. For God's sake, I know as much, if not more, about horses than any of my brothers ever did, and he listens to them. No questions asked. And now with Daddy's accident..."

"Well, you know how it is with a man and his sons." He

held up his hand to shut her up. "Now, I ain't sayin' it's right, just that's how it is with some people."

"Uh-huh. And much as I love my brothers, what did those three sons do? Each of them managed the place for a while, then moved on to something else. I'm the one who stayed."

"You'll be moving on yourself someday, Silver. Some man'll sweep you right on out of here."

"What?" Her chin came up. "No, that won't happen."

"You'll get yourself hitched and—"

"Think again. The only male I'm interested in—" she jerked her head toward her horse "—is this one, 'cause the man hasn't been born yet who can sweep me off my feet." Silver kept hoping she'd find one, but so far all the men she'd met seemed so tame. So familiar. So boring. If she ever met one who wasn't...look out! She didn't see much chance of that, however, not in her social circle.

Tater eyed the stallion and chuckled. "Silver, girl, I don't think that there male is what your pa has in mind for your future."

Silver grimaced as she started on her biggest gripe. "No. I'm supposed to be the Braybourne debutante, go to all the parties and play the dating game."

"I always said you could do anything you put your mind to, girl."

"Oh, I've got the debutante moves down pat. I know when to smile, when to flutter my lashes, when to tease and flirt. But on the whole, I'd rather muck out the stables."

Tater laughed. "Ah, Silver, the man that takes you on is in for a hard ride. You'd swear something is black even if it's as white as a church steeple."

She looked down at her jeans and old, comfortable riding boots. "Did you ever try to stuff your feet into a pair of heels, Tater? Take it from me, you might as well be wearing a piece of wood balanced on a nail. My toes go numb."

"But you look right pretty when you wear 'em."

"Forget the flattery."

"Don't you have something to do today?"

"Today? I don't think...wait a minute, what day is it?"

"It's Monday."

"Oh damn, Mama and I are going to that charity tea. I for-got." She glanced at her watch. "Eleven-fifteen? It's not that late, is it?"

"It surely is."

"Oh, Lord, I have to get going." Taking a good grip on Lucky Hand, she started to walk away.

"Wait a minute, Silver." Tater caught up with her and grabbed the bridle. "I'll rub him down and feed him. You get on up to the house and put on your fancy duds."

"Well, I...he's my responsibility."

"So's that charity project you been helping your mother with."

"I know, but—"

"Go on, git. The horse and the farm will still be here when you get back."

DARCY PULLED HIS PICKUP to the side of the road and stared at the sign on the outskirts of town. Cecil, it proclaimed in elegant letters. *Now the adventure really begins,* he thought, wondering where it would take him. Good or bad, he was here, and he'd have to play it out. What the hell, it wasn't life or death, it was just...what? A way to find something he was missing in his life? He'd been thinking more and more about that lately, with his twenty-ninth birthday coming up. Then he shook his head. What a crock—he had everything. He just temporarily needed something new, that was all. An adventure.

The afternoon heat was kicking in with a vengeance, made worse by the sticky black vinyl seats of his borrowed truck. He'd give anything for a shower and a long cool drink about now. *Right. Enough thought, time for action.* He leaned over, started the truck, then glanced in his mirror and pulled back onto the highway that headed straight to the heart of Cecil, Kentucky.

It was a pretty little town, full of old, well-restored homes, ri-otous gardens and charming shops laid out on either side of a broad main street shaded with majestic elm trees. He looked for a likely place to stop to get a drink and find some conversation that would clue him in on job prospects around Cecil. Unfortunately, everything looked too genteel to get the kind of gossip he needed. Then he remembered his own farm and it dawned on him to look for the local feed and grain store. People there were bound to know what type of work was available.

Darcy found the feed store on the other side of the town, near the outskirts. It was a large enough business to feature gas and diesel tanks, storage areas and a large grain operation. The main building had a broad porch where a couple of old men were seated on wooden chairs, engrossed in a game of checkers.

"This is more like it," Darcy said aloud, eyeing the men.

He pulled into the front parking area, slid out of the truck and stretched, aware of the two men giving him curious glances. With his trademark saunter he headed for the steps, pausing on the top one to ask, "Can I get a cold drink inside?"

"Yes, sir," drawled one of the sparsely thatched, gray-haired gentlemen. "They got one of them cola machines right inside the door."

"They've also got those fancy sodas in there, too, Tater," said the other man, who was wearing an old John Deere hat pulled low over his forehead. "Remember when they put them in there?"

"That's right, I remember 'cause..."

Positive these two geezers might go on this way for a long time, Darcy gave them a grin and small salute. "Thanks." He sauntered inside the building, feeling their eyes on his back. He knew the men's conversation would shift to him as soon as he disappeared through the door. Darcy pulled some coins from his pocket and made his selection at the soda machine. He took a long, cool drink before strolling back toward the doorway.

If I'm really lucky, these two old guys will open up and talk to me. Tell me just what I want to know. Unlike his father, who had an exaggerated sense of his own worth, Darcy generally found it easy to approach individuals in all strata of society, and for the most part it was easy for them to approach him, too. Unless he got on one of his arrogant high horses. Then everyone who knew him ran for cover, as the Tremont twins had last night.

Cold drink in hand, he strolled over to the railing and leaned against it. He watched the checker game, wondering how to start the conversation, when one of the men—Tater—saved him the trouble.

"Just passin' through, are ya?" Tater asked.

"No, sir," Darcy replied. "I'd like to find a job and stick around for a bit. Decide whether to move on or not."

The other man jumped his red king over Tater's black one. "Ah, you one of them migrant workers then?"

Tater glared at the board, then glared at his companion. "'Course he ain't no migrant, Lawrence. What in Sam Hill's the matter with you?"

"Well, I didn't mean no disrespect, I just meant—"

Darcy interrupted before the squabble got more intense. These two men seemed to have a long-running routine, and he wasn't sure he could stand still and listen to it. "I don't know as much about working crops," he said diplomatically, "as I do working horses."

"Ah." Tater nodded. "You a horseman?"

Darcy nodded in turn. "Yes, sir." It was true he'd ridden and been around horses all his life. Even if he didn't do any of the breeding and training work on his farm now, his grandfather had made him work on the farm every summer until he was thirteen. He'd avoided it ever since, but what the hell—a horse was a horse! How bad could it be for a month? "Know of any horse farms around here that might be hiring?"

Tater narrowed his eyes and leaned back, giving him a slow, steady once-over. "Well, I might. I just might."

"Ain't you looking for somebody to help out for a while, Tater?" Lawrence asked.

Darcy met Tater's gaze with his steadiest stare, hoping the man liked what he saw, fully expecting that he would. After all, Darcy had been rebuffed by very few people in his life. The strange thing was, he was just now starting to wonder if he'd earned that reaction or if it was given in sheer deference to his wealth and position.

The man's eyes, bright and sharp, seemed curiously out of place in his grizzled old face. "That I am, Lawrence."

Talk about luck. Darcy was tempted to ask for a job, but restrained himself. His stomach clenched as he waited for Tater to make up his mind.

A long moment later, the old man rubbed his chin and exhaled. "Might be we could give you a try. I gotta warn ya, though, the pay won't be great. But we'd be talking room and board."

"We?"

"Harden Braybourne of Braybourne Farm. Harden had an accident awhile back and he's decided we need some more help." Tater grinned, revealing a large gap between his front teeth that gave him a peculiarly boyish look. "The operation's not as big as it was, but we ain't as young as we used to be, neither."

"Getting older happens to everyone, I hear," Darcy said with a smile.

"Gotta tell you, Son, I'd be a lot happier if t'weren't happenin' to me." He stood up and extended his hand. "Name's Travis O'Neill. Most folks call me Tater."

"Darcy...uh, Rick Darcy." He shook the man's hand. "Just call me Darcy. Everyone does."

"Okay, Darcy. Hop in your truck and follow me back to the farm. I'll show you around and you can tell me about yourself. Then we'll see."

"Didn't you say Harden was lookin' for a temporary manager, Tater?"

Tater nodded, saying slowly, "So he told me this morning."

"Oooeee!" Lawrence hit his knee with the heel of his hand. "Silver Braybourne ain't gonna be happy about that, is she?"

Tater gave his friend an annoyed glance. "You know, Lawrence, you talk a mite too much sometimes."

Darcy was intrigued. "Who's Silver Braybourne?"

Tater clamped his hat on his head. "Sylvia is Harden Braybourne's daughter. Silver's her nickname."

Lawrence laughed. "Name fits her. She's fast moving, with a temper as hard and shiny as a new quarter. Oh boy, I'd love to be a fly on the wall if you hire this young stallion to—"

"Lawrence, like I said, you talk too much." Tater headed for his own pickup, moving at a clip that belied his years. "Saddle up there, Rick Darcy. I got chores to do."

"Yes, sir." Darcy dashed down the steps behind him and leaped into his truck to follow the man to Braybourne Farm.

Tater O'Neill's truck picked up speed on the way out of town, leading Darcy up and down gentle hills, past some surprising, jutting limestone cliffs, then through a woods. Just when Darcy was wondering why this was still considered part of the bluegrass area, the woods parted to reveal wide pastures and farms. Tater turned into a driveway. A white gate swung open automatically to reveal a long road that led to a white house, barn and stable complex, all decorated with dark green trim.

Darcy stared at the sprawling farmhouse. It was slightly shabby, but charming gable windows and a big front porch with flowering vines climbing up the posts made up for that. This place was nowhere near as luxurious as what he was used to, which in itself was a surprising relief. Here he could really be a normal guy.

His stomach clenched again with anticipation. Something momentous was going to happen; he could almost see the hand of fate.... Then he shook his head, marveling at his idiocy. His cousin would probably tell him that anyone could imagine anything in order to justify doing exactly what they wanted to do. As Darcy stopped the truck near the stables and looked around, he had to agree. He didn't know what awaited him here, but he was about to find out. He set the brake, jumped from the truck and followed Tater inside the dim barn. The air was cooler in there and filled with the mingled scents of hay, feed and horses.

"Well, Darcy..." Tater waved his hand. "This here is home."

Darcy's eyes quickly adjusted to the darkness and he looked around. The stables were neat and well ordered, with the names of each horse printed on a decorative board above its stall. As Darcy took stock of his surroundings a few horses came to gaze curiously over their gates. Fewer than he might have expected from the number of stalls. He glanced at Tater.

"We had a few hard years here and had to sell some of the stock. Hell of a shame." Tater reached to scratch behind the ears of a glossy chestnut mare. "We had one colt that had wings for feet. He might a' done the Derby job for us, but...what is, is."

"Tater? Tater, have you seen..." A big voice echoed through the stables, followed by a tall, powerfully built, silver-haired man. His left arm was in a cast and he leaned on a cane as he limped down the stable corridor toward them. He stopped and stared at Darcy, his sharp gaze slicing into him.

Tater stepped forward. "Harden Braybourne, this here's Darcy, Rick Darcy. Just got into town. Says he knows horses and is looking for work. I brought him out to talk about his qualifications, before we go further."

"Hmm..." Harden nodded, his gaze sweeping over him from top to bottom. "You got the look of a horseman, young fella."

Suddenly a bit nervous, Darcy met the man's firm stare. "Thank you, sir."

"Been around them long?"

"All my life. My grandfather was one of the best horsemen I ever knew. I hope I take after him." And not just in his handling of horses, either. The thought surprised him.

"Well, do you?" Harden asked in a dry tone.

"I'm working on it," Darcy said.

Harden gave a bark of laughter. "Well, that's honest, at any rate." He gave him another long, penetrating look before he said, "Let's go into the manager's office and you can fill us in on your experience. Tater probably told you we need some help."

"Yes, sir." Darcy reached to steady Harden as he turned and stumbled.

"Don't do that, boy, I'm not that old. I had an accident is all."

Darcy pretended to kick something to the side, plastering his most diplomatic expression on his face. "There's a rock here. I didn't want your cane to land on top of it and send you sprawling to land on top of me." He grinned. "You're a pretty big man."

Tater winked at Darcy as he opened a door to the left. "Right in here."

Darcy followed the two older men inside, and with an unaccustomed knot in his stomach, prepared to cross his fingers and give a brief and slightly embellished story of his life and career to date. As he answered Harden's probing questions, he silently thanked his grandfather for working his butt off on the horse farm when he was a young boy. He must have absorbed more knowledge than he thought. A half hour later he and Harden were shaking hands. Darcy was hired as temporary manager of Braybourne Farm.

"You understand it's just till I get back on my feet and can take over again," Harden said as they emerged from the office. "Should be a couple of months on the outside. Meanwhile, Tater and Billy and Ed will be helping you."

"Don't forget Silver," Tater murmured.

Harden frowned. "Silver is going to get married soon."

"She is?" Tater exclaimed. "Says who? Silver didn't tell me nothin' about that and I just seen her this—"

"Well, there's nothing definite, so I wouldn't go asking her about it," Harden cautioned. "But I got it on good authority that John Tom Thomas is that far—" he held his fingers one-eighth of an inch apart "—from popping the question." Harden set his face in a mulish expression, blustering, "I can't see any reason she wouldn't accept him. He's well-off, from a first-rate family, good-looking and—"

"He puts me to sleep every time he opens his mouth, Daddy." A female voice floated through the stables.

Surprised, Darcy looked toward the doorway, but the light

was behind the woman who stood just inside. All he could see was a tall slim silhouette with a cloud of platinum-blond hair that glowed like a halo. He stared at the hair. This must be why she was called Silver. He glanced over at Harden, who was now looking a bit flustered.

"Damn you, girl. Where'd you come from? Why don't you make a bit of noise instead of sneaking up on people?"

The woman walked forward, her gait as smooth and fluid as a prime show horse...or a Vegas chorus girl. She had the body for Vegas—the long long legs, slim hips, full high breasts just suggested by an expensively cut summer suit the color of orange sherbet. Lord, but Darcy loved cool women with hellfire and heat underneath. Darcy didn't know why she gave him that impression, but she did. Maybe it was the direct, challenging look she gave him, or the slight pout on her full lips. *Cool, cool ice ready to melt.* His gut twisted and his mouth watered. He wanted to lick her all over. The surge of lust took him completely by surprise and he glanced at the two older men, hoping his desire wasn't written on his face.

"I didn't sneak. I roared up and parked my car right outside behind that old pickup truck. Whose is it, anyway?"

Darcy hid a grin. She could see him perfectly well, but she wasn't going to acknowledge him until she was forced to, a time-honored feminine play to get the upper hand. Funny, he didn't think he looked like much of a threat, but maybe that moment of sheer sexual awareness hadn't been one-sided. As intense as it was, he sure as hell hoped not. Ready to play, he nodded his head in mock deference.

"It belongs to me, Miss Braybourne. I'm sorry if it's in your way. I can move it."

"I parked right behind you, so you'll have trouble getting out to leave."

Darcy grinned. That was subtle. "I'm not going anywhere." He'd thrown the first card. Now he waited to see if she'd pick it up.

She arched a perfectly shaped eyebrow. "Why's that?"

Harden jumped in. "This is my only daughter, Silver...uh, Sylvia. Honey, this is Mr. Darcy—"

"Darcy."

"Uh, Darcy, who's come to help us out for a while."

She lifted her lids slowly, letting the long sweep of lashes flutter a bit before meeting his gaze. A slight smile played over her tempting lips. "Call me Silver, Darcy. Sylvia always makes me feel as if I'm in trouble."

Tater chuckled. "You been in trouble since the day you was born, missy."

"Now, Tater. You'll give Darcy the wrong impression of me."

"Oh, I don't think that'll happen," Darcy said.

"Why not?"

"'Cause I've got a good idea what you're all about."

He did, too. He gave her a slow once-over. Silver Braybourne reminded him of the more successful debutantes he'd grown up with, the ones who made getting their own way an art. He was a bit surprised to find her kind here on this slightly run-down farm, but you never could judge by appearances. Darcy knew many illustrious families who'd slid into genteel poverty. His gaze met hers again.

Silver's eyes glinted. "You think so, do you, Mr. Darcy?"

Again Harden jumped in. "How was the charity tea? Did you and your mother have a good time?"

"We had watercress sandwiches and fruit salad. What does that tell you?"

Darcy chuckled. "Southern fried chicken not on the menu, huh?"

Taken by surprise, Silver smiled at him. "Not even close." She turned back to her father. "However, we did give the children's hospital a big check from the money we raised in our Southern Ladies recipe book sale."

A nice respectable organization with a nice respectable purpose. *Figures*, Darcy thought, almost sighing as he looked at Silver. Regardless of the impression she'd initially given him, Silver was just another dull debutante type—same as all the rest. Why had he thought even for a moment that she was different? Because he was in a different situation?

"So," Silver said, "you're here to help out, you said?"

"Yes, I'm—"

"Silver, why don't you walk me back up to the house?" Harden said.

She patted his hand. "We'll go in a few minutes, but right now it would be extremely rude of me to walk away when Darcy is talking to me, now wouldn't it, Daddy?" She smiled at Darcy, tilting her head like an inquisitive bird. "You were saying?"

"I'm the new—"

"Tater," Harden interrupted again, "why don't you give him the back room to stay in for now."

"Okay, Harden."

With an annoyed glance at the two older men, Silver stepped forward until she was practically chest to chest with Darcy. The sheer intimidating intent of the move tickled the hell out of him. He wondered what she'd do if he slid his arms around her waist and pulled. Tempting, very tempting.

"You were saying?"

Darcy gave her his most innocent stare. "I don't remember."

Her voice dropped to a smooth whisper that had the kick of moonshine. "You said you're the new...what?"

Darcy stepped a little bit closer. "The new manager."

"The new manager of what?"

"This." He waved his arm, as if the king of all he surveyed. "It's just temporary, of course, till your father improves."

Silver let out her breath in a snort that reminded Darcy of an ill-tempered pony. He waited to see what would happen next, half expecting her to come after him with teeth bared. "*You* are the temporary manager at Braybourne Farm?"

Darcy glanced at Harden and Tater, who were standing as still as statues. "Your father just hired me a few minutes ago."

"I see." She glanced over her shoulder at Harden, and Darcy was glad the man was made from strong stuff. Then she turned her attention back to him. "And you, what—magically appeared from thin air?"

He laughed. "No, I got into town this afternoon and ran into Tater. He said you needed some help here, and I was looking for something to do."

"Something to do? Tennis or golf is *something to do*. Running a horse farm is a bit more complicated than that."

Harden interrupted with a firm, impatient tone. "Silver, Darcy knows all that, or else I wouldn't have hired him."

Silver turned and stepped toward her father, while Tater took the opportunity to back out of range. "Oh, I don't know, Daddy. I think you would have hired anything that had the right equipment between its legs."

Harden stiffened, gripping his cane. "Wait a minute, what do you mean by that?"

"I mean this is a boys-only club, isn't it? No girls allowed. Well, sorry, but this girl's here—and she's staying! You know you promised me that—"

Clearing his throat, Harden attempted to regain control. "Sylvia, we will not discuss this at the moment."

Silver propped her fists on her hips. "I don't know a better time."

"Well, there is a better place, young lady. You do not air your grievances in front of the hired help." Harden turned and started for the stable entrance. "It's not proper."

The hired help. Darcy wasn't sure if he should be amused or insulted by that comment. He'd never been called that before. He glanced at Tater. Although he could actually remember having referred to some of his people that way, he'd had no idea until just now how arrogant it sounded.

Silver stalked after her father. "Daddy, don't just turn around and walk away from me."

For a moment, Darcy wasn't sure what to say, so he said nothing. Neither did Tater. Finally Tater sighed. "I guess I ain't meant to understand women. I'll take a horse any day."

Darcy chuckled, which seemed to break the tension the

Braybournes had left behind. Tater gave him a reluctant grin in return.

"Come on, Darcy, I'll show you where you can bunk for a while. It's not luxurious, but it's cozy."

2

TATER LED THE WAY back through the barn and stopped at the door next to the manager's office. Surprised, Darcy said, "You want me to live in the stables?" He'd been positive Tater was going to lead him out the far end of the building.

Tater seemed taken aback. "What's that?"

Darcy recovered fast, aware that he must have sounded snobby. "I mean, I'm surprised that your manager's residence is in the stable."

"This ain't really the manager's place," Tater said as he opened the door and stepped aside to let Darcy into the room. "We have a house on the property, but we had a fire about a year ago and still haven't finished renovating it. Always seemed to be somewhere else to put the money." Tater looked around. "This here room's where the groom usually stays, but it's just sittin' here empty at the moment. You don't mind sleeping in the stables, do you?"

Darcy blinked as he met Tater's hard stare. If he'd been asked that question a few days ago, he would have wondered if the person asking had lost his mind. But now he waved his arm in an expansive gesture. "No, sir, of course I don't. If it's good enough for the horses, it's good enough for me."

Exhaling, Tater clasped Darcy's shoulder. "That's the attitude, boy. Had me worried for a minute. But I always say that bedding down with horses is a lot safer than bedding down with a woman."

Grinning, Darcy said, "Safer, but not as interesting." A picture of Silver Braybourne immediately formed in his mind, her eyes heavy with sleep, hair tousled, the silk strap of her nightgown sliding off her shoulder. Given his choice between a horse and Silver, he'd take Silver anytime.

"Some women have a knack of getting in a man's blood, heating it until it boils over."

Recalled to his surroundings, Darcy met Tater's wise old eyes, and realized he probably knew exactly what thoughts had been racing through his mind. "Those are the kind of women I try to avoid. It's too much like commitment."

"Sometimes it ain't so easy. You gotta have eyes in the back of your head to see 'em coming."

Darcy smiled and changed the subject. "This'll do just fine," he said, looking around the room. "So where do you live, Tater?"

"I got me a little place just the other side of that big hill behind the house. My daddy left it to me. He worked for the Braybournes, too, an' so did my granddad. Braybournes and O'Neills have been together since the beginning, I guess. I watched all four of those little ones grow up, Silver and her three brothers." He smiled, staring into the distance at an image only he could see. "I put Silver on her first pony and taught her to ride. She was a little stick of a thing as a kid, but that little gal was the prettiest rider I ever seen. Fearless, she was." Tater shook his head. "But impulsive."

"It seems to me she hasn't changed a great deal."

Tater winked. "Sure has changed on the outside, though, boy."

Darcy grinned. "I noticed."

Nodding, Tater said in a dry tone, "I noticed you noticing."

"Hopefully her father didn't," Darcy said, sharing a wry look with the older man. "Don't worry, I'm just looking. With a woman like that, it's practically my civic duty."

Tater held his gaze for a moment longer, then changed the subject. "I expect Harden will send down some sheets and such. Bathroom's over there, an' you got a closet, readin' chair and light. You even got a little refrigerator and one of them microwave things over there in the corner. Most of your meals you'll take up at the house with the family. Can't have no real cooking in here, ya know."

"Do you eat with the family, too?"

"When I want. But most times I cook for myself." Tater looked around and rubbed his hands together. "So, you're all set, right and tight?"

Darcy walked him to the door. "Yes, sir. I'll get my things from the truck and make myself at home."

"I'll finish my errands and I'll see ya tomorrow morning, then."

Darcy watched Tater leave, then stepped outside, walking over to his truck to roll up the windows and collect his bag. He stopped for a moment and glanced toward the riding rings and track. The heat was still a force to be reckoned with, and the late afternoon sunshine shimmered off the ground.

He took his time on his way back to his room, stopping to visit each horse as he tried to familiarize himself with his new domain. The last stall contained a black stallion that seemed determined to ignore him. Darcy sensed a wild spirit in the horse, one that called to him. But no amount of coaxing would bring the black any closer.

"Suit yourself, then," he said. "You'll have to make friends sometime."

The horse snorted.

With a grin, Darcy turned and went into his room. He threw the duffel bag onto the chair and went straight to the bathroom. He closed the door and stripped, dropping his clothes on the floor before stepping into the shower. The water sluiced over his skin, washing away the dust he'd gathered on the road. He stood for a long moment, face to the spray, and just enjoyed himself. He was very pleased with the way things had turned out.

Stepping out of the stall into a steamy bathroom, he caught sight of his reflection in the foggy mirror. *Well, here you are, Kristof. You wanted to be just a normal, everyday guy.* He grabbed the towel and wiped off, then knotting the towel around his waist, opened the door and stepped into his room.

"Oh, I'm sorry," Silver gasped, standing frozen in position near the door. "I knocked, but didn't realize..."

Darcy stood, stunned for a moment, then recovered as he

noticed both her shocked expression and the bundle of bedding and towels she held in her arms. He thrust his hands through his hair, slicking it back. "I take it this is an official hostess visit?"

Silver struggled to get her flushed features under control. "What else would it be?"

Darcy glanced from her to the bed, knowing just how to annoy her for maximum result. "Hope on, hope ever."

"Hope *never*, is more like it."

"Now, now, Silver." He winked. "Never is such a long time."

Silver scowled. "I brought you some sheets and a blanket."

"I don't think I'll need a blanket."

"Suit yourself."

"I generally do."

Silver cleared her throat. "I brought towels, too."

Darcy looked down at the damp towel covering him from waist to midthigh. "Now, towels I'm really going to need. This is my only one." He glanced up, catching Silver as she focused her attention on his hips. If she kept staring at him, she was going to see more than she bargained for.

She jerked her gaze up to meet his. The atmosphere suddenly turned steamier than his recent shower as they stared at each other. Neither said a word as Darcy's eyes roamed over her face, over those high cheekbones, catlike eyes, tilted nose. He stopped at the lips. She had a mouth shaped for giving pleasure, the top lip a perfect bow, the bottom one plump and sensuous. As he stared, her teeth worried her lower lip for a moment before releasing it. He wanted to catch that ripe, moist lip between his own teeth and nibble until she opened wide. He tried to keep his thoughts hidden, but the way the towel was creeping up in the front, he was pretty sure she had a good idea what he was thinking.

Silver tightened her grip on the bundle in her arms and exhaled. "Well, I—I should..."

Darcy followed her lead, trying to bring the situation back to some type of normality before he said the hell with it and threw her on the bed. "It's nice of you to deliver these in person. I would have come and gotten them."

"My mother asked me to bring them down right away. She wanted you to feel at home."

"That's very kind of her." He sent her a teasing look. "And what a dutiful daughter you are to respond so promptly." He didn't know why he was continuing to goad her. Was it to see if she was still as impulsive underneath that ladylike exterior as Tater had indicated? All he knew was he wanted her to lose control, not give him that smooth, practiced smile designed to keep him at arm's length.

"Don't push your luck."

He grinned. "I generally have a lot of it to push."

Silver glanced away. "And the ego to go with it, it seems, Mr. Darcy." Was that a smile at the corner of her mouth?

Darcy stepped closer and cupped her chin, turning her face back to him. "Please, just call me Darcy, remember?"

"Your name could be Quasimodo for all I care."

Absently, his thumb caressed her chin as he watched her. "You can call me that if it makes you happy."

"That wouldn't make me happy. The thing that would make me happy is for you to go somewhere else."

He dropped his hand. "Why? You need help here, from what I've seen. So I'm here to help."

"We need help, yes, mucking out the stables. Not a new manager. The only new manager that's supposed to be here is me. That's why."

"I don't think your father sees it that way, does he?"

She didn't answer him for a moment. Then she warned, "I've got my eye on you."

"How convenient." His lifted his brow. "And how very forward of you, Ms. Braybourne."

She gave him a look that was partly suspicious, partly nervous. "What do you mean, convenient?"

He smiled. "What do you think I mean?"

She licked her lips, his eyes following every move. "I think you're flirting with me."

"When I start flirting, you'll know it. I'm very good at flirting."

Silver took a sudden step backward, hugging her bundle tighter. She didn't realize how close she was to the wall, and she cracked her head against the knotty pine.

"Oh." Darcy winced. "That must have hurt."

"No, it didn't."

"Your eyes practically crossed." He stepped closer. "Here, let me see if there's going to be a goose egg." He smiled into her eyes, stunned to see they were the brilliant light green of spring grass. He reached for her, tipping her head so he could feel for swelling. Her hair fell forward and he fingered a strand. "I wondered what this would feel like. It looks like spun silk."

"You shouldn't be—"

"Now, now, easy..." he crooned to her, as if she were a contrary horse. His fingers pressed here and there, caressing as much as searching. He was so close he could sense her beginning to tremble, much as a mare might before a stallion. Involuntarily, his hands pressed down as he stepped a bit closer to her.

"Ouch."

"Sorry. Is that where it's sore?" He closed his eyes for a moment, imagining her in his arms. Unconsciously he stepped even closer.

As his body touched hers, Silver seemed to come back to life—and regain her attitude. She lifted her head and slapped his hand away. "Yes, that hurts. Stop pushing on it."

Stepping back slowly, he smiled. "I think you'll live, but you might want to put some ice on it."

"Thank you." She hugged the towels closer as her eyes darted down his body. "And you might want to put on some pants. Your towel is slipping."

"Oops." Darcy grabbed his towel like a lifeline and attempted to regroup by growling in a soft suggestive tone, "You really want me to put on some pants?"

Do I? Silver would have much preferred to glide her hands

down his sleek, sexy skin than tell him to cover up. "Well, if you don't, I think it's going to get mighty drafty soon."

He grinned. "I don't mind a bit of a draft. It's a hot day."

Silver gritted her teeth at the superb male confidence in that grin. The fact that he was such a prime specimen only made it worse. Darcy reminded her of her black stallion. The elegantly sculpted muscles, the breeding and the wild untamed spirit equaled beauty in Silver's eyes. Combine that with black hair that curled just a bit at the edges, eyes as dark as coal, tanned skin and a strong, finely chiseled face, and it was enough to make a woman go weak at the knees. Her eyes swept over him. Under other circumstances she'd give her grandmother's pearls to make love to the man. Or more accurately, to have a bout of the hottest sex she could ever imagine. Instead, she flattened him with her stoniest stare—or at least tried to.

Darcy grinned. "Ah well, if you insist." He walked over to his bag, rummaging inside to extract a pair of jeans. Turning back, he toyed with his towel, and said, "You might want to turn around so I don't shock your maidenly sensibilities."

Silver decided to call his bluff, mainly out of contrariness. She folded her arms and leaned back against the wall, hoping she looked perfectly at ease. "You won't shock me. I'm used to looking at masculine appendages." Of course, they all belonged to stallions—but a penis was a penis was a penis, wasn't it? Just because the one in question belonged to the most exciting man she'd ever met shouldn't make a difference. She knew her reasoning was completely faulty, but couldn't back out now. It was a point of pride.

Darcy stared at her for a moment, his eyes bold and challenging. Then, he turned around, dropped his towel and stepped into his jeans. Casually, he turned back to face her, holding her gaze as he slowly buttoned them.

"Covered enough for you?"

The jeans sat low on his hips, exposing his tanned, rippling stomach muscles. Silver was tempted to slip her fingers inside, just to see if he really had himself reined in as tight as he was pretending. She stared for a moment longer. She could feel the ache deep inside her as she contemplated her next move. Playing games with this man had an element of danger that could get to be a habit.

Her eyes met his. "Quite satisfactory, Mr. Darcy."

"We're back to mister, are we?"

"What can I say? I'm polite."

Darcy stepped a bit closer. "I don't want you to be polite."

Her voice faltered a bit. "Why not?"

"Because you're much more interesting when you're rude."

"I am never rude."

He chuckled. "You practically told me to get out, that I wasn't wanted here."

"I told you I don't want you here as manager."

Gaze sharpening, he verbally pounced. "But you want me."

"Well, of course I want you." At his sudden wolfish grin she realized what she'd said. "I mean, I want your help. As you pointed out, we need help."

"Help. Of course."

She placed her hands on her hips, ready to annihilate him. "Look, you egotistical ass. I don't deny that a few minutes ago, when you were...I might have become...'preoccupied' with you—"

"Preoccupied?"

He gave her such an innocent look that she wanted to deck him. Instead she thrust the bundle of towels and sheets toward him. "Never mind. That's not the point."

"Pity," he said with an elegant lift of his shoulders as he took the linens from her. "So what is the point?"

She inhaled, then exhaled, hoping to calm herself. "The point is my father's getting older, and even before his recent accident, whether he admits it or not, it was getting tougher for him to work with the horses, not to mention the rest of the farm. And you may have noticed that Tater isn't a babe in arms, either."

Darcy turned aside, tossing the linens onto the bed. "I noticed that."

"Then you can see what the problem is. It's hard to get the

regular work done, much less the training and the breeding we need to move forward with the horses we've still got. And make no mistake, Braybourne Farm still has what it takes. We might not have ended in the big money, but we've had winners, lots of them. And we've had them since the first Braybourne settled in Kentucky." She lifted her chin. "We'll have them again."

Darcy turned back to her, his expression becoming serious. "You love this place, don't you?"

"It means everything to me."

"That's nice."

Taken aback, she stared at him. "What's nice?"

"Caring that passionately about something."

"Well, naturally. Why do anything if you're not passionate about it?"

He smiled.

A few moments earlier that smile would have made her want to open to him as eagerly as a mare to a mate. Even now her impulse was to lead this man over to that bed so fast he'd be crying for mercy! Instead, she stepped back.

"Listen," she said. "Just because you're a passably good-looking man, don't think I'm some little exercise girl who'd be impressed by that. Regardless of what you seem to think."

"You're not, huh?" His eyes held hers with a challenging gleam. "What if a time comes when I decide not to listen to you?"

"You—you..." Silver heard herself sputtering like a worn-out tractor. "You have no choice but to listen to me."

"There's always a choice. It's just that sometimes there isn't any maneuvering room."

Silver lifted her chin and glared at him. "Well, you certainly aren't going to maneuver me into something I don't want to do."

"Oh, I don't know."

She shook her finger under his nose. "You will not get around me with what you consider excess charm."

"I don't want to get around you." He held her gaze. "What makes you think I don't have another position in mind?"

"Why, you...how dare you!" Even as he enraged her, she felt the lick of excitement race along her nerve endings.

He grinned. "Are you afraid you might enjoy it?"

"The sheer arrogance of that remark makes me want to fire you on the spot."

"I don't think you can do that, Silver. Since your father hired me, I believe he's actually the one to fire me."

"I'll speak to him about it."

"And you're going to tell him what? After all, nothing happened. It's not as if I kissed you or anything." He dropped his gaze to her mouth. "What would you have done if I'd kissed you?"

"Slapped you with a harassment suit." Which was stretching the truth, but as usual when she was angry, she lashed out regardless.

"Theoretically speaking, what if I kissed you and you kissed me back—with a great deal of passion, of course?"

She couldn't look at him. "I wouldn't." Another lie.

"Silver?"

She glanced back, practically mesmerized by his reproachful dark eyes. "Oh, all right, I'm human. Maybe I would kiss you back. I don't know why, except..."

"Except?"

Reluctant to answer, she looked away again. She might not understand herself lately, but she certainly wasn't about to open her heart and mind to a man who'd only butted into her life an hour before.

One finger under her chin turned her back to face him. "Except maybe now you're wondering what it would be like to have an adventure? To make love with a stranger? Not the familiar young blueblood your father wants you to marry."

"No. I've never... I'm not marrying him. That's my father's idea, not mine." She scowled. "Why am I even having this conversation with you? This is none of your business."

He smiled, as sweetly as the big bad wolf looking for a snack. "I don't know. Why are you?"

"You started it with all your talk of flirting." Love with a stranger. She tingled at the thought. What woman didn't have a few fantasies—maybe of a chance encounter with a dark stranger, and steamy, uncomplicated sex? That didn't mean she acted on them.

After a long, searching moment and an even more searching look, Darcy stepped away from her to indicate the pile of sheets and towels. "Thanks for bringing these down."

"My pleasure." She threw her shoulders back, adjusted her pearls and tugged down her jacket, attempting to restore herself to the elegant woman she'd tried to present when she first came into his room, which was pretty damn hard under the circumstances. "I have to go."

Darcy walked over and opened the door.

Silver walked past him, then stopped. "Oh, by the way, my mother asked me to invite you up to the house for dinner if you don't have other plans."

"I hope she isn't going to any trouble."

"No. There's always plenty for one more. Mother's used to cooking for a big family and can't seem to stop."

He hesitated, staring at Silver for a moment. "In that case, I'd be delighted."

"I'll pass that along. I, um...okay, I'll see you." Feeling awkward, she stood there for a moment, then turned and stepped away.

"Silver?"

"Yes?" She glanced over her shoulder. Darcy stood in the doorway, shoulder leaning against the doorjamb, hands in his pockets. He was an animal in his prime, confident and seemingly at ease with the world and his place in it.

"What time?"

Her mind went blank as her eyes feasted on his chest. "Time?"

"For dinner."

She met his gaze, noticing the devils dancing there, tempting her closer, beckoning her. "Seven." Then Silver nodded and got out of there as fast as she could without looking as if she was running for her life.

Rick Darcy. She stared at the dusty black pickup parked outside the stables. Where had he come from? Her father had told her a bit about him, but not much. Why didn't her father realize that managing Braybourne Farm was all she'd ever wanted to do? Since she was a little girl, she'd dreamed of what she would do when the farm was hers.

She turned from the pickup and stared at her home. She'd gone to the University of Kentucky, not far from here, and done the things expected of her—studied hard, joined a sorority, cheered the Wildcats on to victory, met the right people, then later got socially involved in the surrounding community—all in an effort to show her father how perfectly she would perform as the head of Braybourne Farm, given the chance. When her brother Brett had left a year ago she'd felt it was her time. Or so it had seemed. Her father had started turning to her more and more to talk over decisions. Silver felt as if she was making great strides. Until Harden fell from the horse and had decided to settle her future.

Settle her future! For God's sake, she was only twenty-six, but to hear her father tell it, she was well on her way to mummification.

And now there was Rick Darcy.

She glanced over her shoulder at the dusty truck, imagining him behind the wheel, the image so strong that she shook her head. Not that Daddy would ever encourage her to look seriously at him—he was rather feudal on some issues, and breeding and family lineage were among them. She could respect his views because he was her father, even as she disagreed with the principles behind them. But her own inclinations might be the real problem, she thought. She hadn't the vaguest idea why she was responding to Darcy so immediately and strongly, but she was. Maybe it was because she sensed he was different, much different from the men she knew. At her first sight of him standing in their barn this afternoon, feet planted as if he owned the place, he'd immediately gotten her back up. The fact that he had the hot come-and-get-me-or-it's-your-loss-baby type of good looks was as annoying as it was enticing.

Swearing under her breath, she headed toward the fence that separated the drive from the landscaped grounds around the house, then stalked up the flagstone path. At least she'd recovered her cool enough at the end of their encounter to give Rick Darcy a good warning. He'd know better than to mess with her from now on. She kicked at a clump of dirt, muttering, "Why did Daddy have to hire him, anyway?"

With a frustrated huff, she stopped to cool off near one of the old, towering oaks that shaded the house. She had the unnerving feeling that things were spiraling out of her control. She didn't like that. Regardless of how she often chafed at the restraints of tradition, she liked making plans and knowing where she was going and when she expected to get there. But now, as she looked at her home, she felt an element of uncertainty, of expectation. It no longer seemed a safe haven—not since Darcy had arrived on the scene. She rubbed the area between her brows, trying to erase the tension that had collected there. There was no reason for her to get bent out of shape. Her father had reassured her that the man was temporary, just until Harden's health improved. But Silver had doubts that her father would ever return to his former capability, which made someone like Darcy even more of a threat. The thought saddened her. Her daddy had been such a big, marvelous presence in her life for so long. It was difficult to watch age creeping up on him, even though the process had been very gradual until this recent accident. His strength of will might still be powerful, but his body was beginning to decline.

She leaned back against the tree trunk. For the first time she looked at her childhood home and wondered if she was strong enough not only to save it, but to bring it to the glory she imagined. Suddenly, doubt crept in where previously there had been only confidence—thanks to a man with raven coloring and a bold, marauding attitude.

Silver sighed. Memories rushed through her mind as she

studied the place. It was a clapboard ranch house that had been added to over the years. It wasn't an architectural gem, but it was home—and had been since Cecil Braybourne settled in the area and decided to build a shack and put down roots. The roots had grown with each generation, until the entire farm seemed to be embraced into the landscape.

As she stared, her mother came out of the front door onto the broad front porch. She had a colander in one hand, a saucepan in the other and a dish towel slung over her shoulder. Silver smiled affectionately. Her mama was as small and seemingly delicate as her father was large and outspoken. To the outside world, Agatha Sweet Braybourne might have seemed a push-over with her polite manners and soft-spoken voice, but Silver knew better, as did her friends. Aggie, as Silver's father called her, was as malleable as a hunk of diamond. Silver felt the power of her mother's personality when Aggie walked to the edge of the porch and looked across the yard at her.

"Well, young lady, are you planning to become part of that tree or just hold it up?"

Silver automatically straightened from her slouch. "Neither one, ma'am—just thinking for a minute."

"Well, come over here and help me snap these green beans while you think."

"Okay." Silver strolled up the path and climbed the steps, walking over to the porch swing. She joined her mother, who immediately set the saucepan in Silver's lap and placed the colander in her own. Silver grabbed a handful of beans and started snapping. For a moment they sat and rocked gently, saying nothing, listening to the sleepy sounds of a late summer afternoon in the country.

Silver began to relax as her fingers performed the familiar homey chore. "Mama…"

"Hmm?"

"How did you first meet Daddy?"

Aggie grinned. "I accidentally crowned him with a baseball."

"What? I didn't know you played baseball." Somehow she

couldn't picture her mother with a baseball bat. She was more the horse and tennis type.

"I didn't. Harden was eleven years old and so full of himself that my little eight-year-old self just couldn't stand it. We were at school and he was playing baseball with some friends. The ball had rolled off the field and over to where I was watching. He pointed at the ball and said, 'Hey, throw it back, you dumb girl.' Showing off for his friends, you know. So I picked up that ball and threw it as hard as I could." Aggie laughed. "Well, I had more strength than aim. That ball took off like a bullet. Unfortunately, it slammed right into his forehead instead of his hand. He went down like an old oak."

Staring at her mother in amazement, Silver gasped. "My God, Mama, what did you do?"

"I sent one of his friends for the teacher and sat down beside him and pulled his head into my lap. He had a knot already starting to swell. So I smoothed back his hair, kissed his cheek and told him he'd better not die on me 'cause he had to marry me when we grew up."

Silver blinked and snapped another bean. "Was he conscious? What did he say?"

"He said, 'Over my dead body, you dumb girl.' And I said, 'If that's what it takes, Harden Braybourne, consider it done.'"

"And Daddy just went along with this?"

Aggie smiled that secretive smile that only another woman can really recognize and understand. "Now, Silver, when did you ever know your daddy to go along with someone else's idea? It took me twelve years to convince him that it was his idea in the first place."

Silver laughed. "How'd you know Daddy was the one for you?"

Aggie shrugged. "Sometimes you just know, honey."

Silver thought about that for a moment. "Are you sure?"

"Well, I did, so I have no reason to think otherwise. Why are you asking?"

To avoid her mother's searching gaze, Silver looked down at

the growing pile of green beans in the saucepan. "No reason, just curious."

"This wouldn't have anything to do with John Tom Thomas, would it?"

"What makes you think that?"

"Because I know how much your father would love to see you settled, and I know how much John Tom would love to have it be with him."

Silver glanced up. "How do you know that? Did John Tom say something to you?"

Her mother handed her another pile of beans. "The man announced to everyone that *you* are his next fence to jump. And he has no intention of taking a spill."

Silver winced. "Surely he put it more romantically than that, Mama."

Aggie chuckled. "'Fraid not, honey girl."

"Oh, Lord. Where did he announce this?"

"At the club the other night, when you were helping Aunt Violet out to the car." Aggie sighed. "I wish that woman would switch to another drink and stay away from the mint juleps. They just don't agree with her."

Giving her mother a dry look, Silver commented, "She says the mint settles her tummy."

"Well, mint is good for that," her mother agreed, eyes twinkling. "It's the alcohol that upsets it."

Silver indicated the stable. "Remember that horse we had who raided the herb bed and ate all the mint one year?"

"Sweet and Spicy, wasn't it? Oh, your daddy was furious because we couldn't have fresh mint juleps for your brother's wedding reception."

Silver stared across the yard, thinking about the gelding they'd sold many years before. Her pleasant nostalgic feeling passed when she saw Darcy emerging from the stables. Her stomach clenched. She could use a bit of mint, or something stronger, right about now, she thought, as she watched him stride across the gravel drive. The man had a way of moving that was almost poetic. Silver waved her hand, vaguely indicating his direction as she glanced at her mother. "I, uh, invited him to dinner tonight like you said."

"What?" Her mother leaned forward a bit, peering toward the stables. "Oh, Mr. Darcy, you mean?"

"Darcy. He wants to be called Darcy." Silver could feel the heat flood her face as her mother sent her a curious glance. "That's what he told me."

"Darcy's a nice name."

Silver shrugged, pretending a nonchalance that she was sure her mother would poke holes through in a minute. "It's okay, I suppose." She didn't dare look up, concentrating instead on the beans, as if her life depended on breaking each one cleanly.

"My, my, my..."

Her mother's comment recaptured her attention.

"That young man sure has a behind to die for."

Shocked, Silver whipped her head around to stare at the older woman. "Mama. You're too old to be looking at his *behind*."

"Now look here, Miss Saucy Mouth. I may be a bit older, but I'm not dead, and I believe in saying what's on my mind."

"Since when? You always come at a subject round about, so you can take people by surprise."

"Well, that's true, but I'm thinking of changing my approach. I've decided that your father has been getting his own way for too many years. He's becoming a bit difficult lately."

"You won't get an argument from me, Mama." Silver glanced over, but her mother still had her attention focused on Darcy, who was now climbing into his pickup truck.

"I didn't get to meet this Darcy before Harden hired him. But now that I look at him, I can say your father does have an eye for talent. I wonder if he's as good in the 'saddle' as he looks?"

"Mama, for God's sake, what's gotten into you?" Just thinking about her mother referring to Darcy and mentioning sex made Silver squeamish. Next thing she knew, she'd start thinking about her parents in bed together, which might give her nightmares for the rest of her life.

Her mother wagged her finger vigorously. "Don't pretend to be prudish, Silver. If you can't look at that young man and see a work of art, then I'm very worried about you."

"Well, of course I can—"

"Besides, we live on a farm, honey lamb. No one understands sex better than someone who lives on a farm."

Silver arched her brows. "Our own little sex education clinic, you mean?"

"Absolutely. You not only learn about the passion to recreate, but you learn the value of good breeding, too."

"Oh please." Silver tried to change the subject. "This isn't your subtle way of yammering at me about marrying John Tom Thomas after all, is it? Because this conversation is along the same lines as Daddy used a few days ago." She cleared her throat. "The breeding part, I mean."

"Of course not. I do not yammer," her mother huffed. "But now that I think about it, I don't really understand what you've got against the man. He's certainly got the right stuff. And if I remember clearly, you had a crush on him all the way through high school."

"That was high school. Right now he just seems so...so tame." An image of Darcy flashed into her mind.

"Tame?"

"Proper. Broke to saddle, to use John Tom's own riding metaphors."

Fixing a penetrating gaze on her, Aggie smiled. "You want a wild stallion, do you? Like that black monster you're trying to train right now?"

Silver flushed. "I don't know what I want. I'm all mixed up." But she *did* know what she wanted—a man who could take her breath away, a man with an element of danger instead of the ingredients of soft white bread. A man she hadn't known since she was in braces.

"Hmm." Her mother gave her a wise look and a hug. "Don't fret, honey. I'm sure something will happen to help you figure it out. It always does. And when it does, just go with what feels right."

Silver leaned her head on her mother's shoulder for a moment. "Maybe I'm being silly, Mama."

"Maybe."

"I mean, John Tom is handsome, friendly, has good manners...."

"That's true. But on the other hand, Silver, that description could fit any number of males, including our dog."

Silver chuckled at her mother's dry expression, but said nothing for a moment. She didn't want to marry John Tom. She didn't want to marry anyone. Not yet. The man who could make her change her mind was somewhere out there, she supposed. *Perhaps even closer than you think,* a small voice whispered. But marriage wasn't her focus at the moment. Braybourne Farm was.

"Your daddy and I just want to see you happy, Silver. We're not getting any younger, you know. But that doesn't mean we want you to rush into something that wouldn't be right for you."

"I know, Mama." She turned to face her mother. "I can't promise I'll choose the right person—when I finally choose, that is—but I'll try not to disappoint either of you."

Her mother stroked her cheek. "Honey, you're missing the point. Try not to disappoint *yourself.*" Aggie patted Silver's hand, then stood up and took the saucepan from her. "I need to see to the chicken," she said, headed toward the door. "You did tell your Darcy that supper's at seven?"

"He's not my Darcy, Mama."

Her mother grinned. "Just a figure of speech, honey lamb. But it sure is something to dream about, isn't it?" She hesitated for a moment before opening the screen door. "You remember what I said now."

Try not to disappoint myself.

Silver looked toward the stables. Easier said than done. Her life had changed since she'd left the house earlier that day. She bit her lip. She couldn't decide if it was changing for the better or the worse.

3

REMEMBER YOU'RE Rick Darcy. Nobody important, just everyday, ordinary Rick Darcy. So don't forget and do something dumb. With that thought planted firmly in his mind, Darcy took a deep breath and knocked on the screen door of the Braybourne home at exactly 6:55 p.m.

It would be so easy to slip, as he had earlier with Tater. Then he'd either be out on his ear, or treated with the same wary deference most people used when they knew his background. All of a sudden it was vital that he remain here. It didn't really have a damn thing to do with Silver Braybourne, nothing at all. He didn't want to examine that possibility too closely, though.

"Well, hello. You must be Darcy." From inside the dim hallway, a soft feminine drawl got his attention. A moment later the door was pushed open by a warmly smiling woman. "Welcome. I'm so glad to meet you. I've heard so much about you already."

"Uh-oh, that could be good or bad depending on who was doing the telling."

"Not at all. I'm Agatha Braybourne, by the way. Most people call me Aggie. It's not such a mouthful."

Caught by her tangible Southern charm, Darcy smiled back. He took the small nosegay of flowers he'd been holding behind his back and presented them to her. "Delighted, ma'am."

Aggie accepted the bright blooms, and her smile expanded as she stepped back to let him into the house. "Isn't this lovely of you. Will you just look at what this young man has brought me, Silver?"

Darcy watched as Silver strolled up the hallway. She looked different now, more casual, her suit, heels and pearls replaced by sage-green slacks and a sleeveless cotton sweater. She still looked cool and delicious to Darcy's hungry eyes. "Hello, again," he murmured.

Her eyes glinted as she glanced from the nosegay in her mother's hand to him. "Flowers?"

"It was nice of him to think of me, don't you agree, Silver?"

"Very nice, Mama."

"Why don't you show Darcy into the dining room? I'll put these in water, then round up your father and we'll be ready to eat." Aggie bustled away, pausing at the kitchen door to say, "I hope you like Southern fried chicken, Darcy."

"I love it."

"Those flowers seem a bit familiar."

Darcy slipped Silver a sideways glance. "How so?"

"They remind me of the ones growing in the flower patch alongside the stables."

Darcy grinned. "Really? Fancy that."

"What an unbelievably cheesy thing to do—pick flowers just so you could charm your way into my mother's good graces."

"Surely you're underestimating your mother. I think it would take more than a few flowers."

Silver glared at him. "Just so you remember that."

"Yes, ma'am."

"And don't call me ma'am."

"Whatever you say."

"Of all the annoying..." Silver turned on her heel, still muttering under her breath as she led the way through a wide archway off to the left. "Come on, dinner's on the table."

Darcy grinned and followed Silver into a spacious airy room with large windows that overlooked a beautiful backyard garden. He was surprised to see a number of pricey antiques, from the cherry table and chairs to the sideboard covered with old silver. Whatever money problems the Braybournes might have at the moment, clearly that hadn't always been the case.

Harden entered just then and sat at the head of the table, his posture as erect and proud as Darcy's own father's would be in the same situation. His wife took a seat at the other end, directly across from him. The familiarity of the scene gave Darcy a shock for a moment. He nodded in Harden's direction. "Sir."

Harden inclined his head and waved his hand toward a chair. "Sit down there, boy. Sit down."

Darcy waited and held a chair for Silver, then took his own. He gave the laden table an appreciative glance. "This looks delicious."

"I'm glad," Aggie said. "Harden, you'll say grace, won't you?" After the brief blessing, obviously not one of Harden's talents, Aggie smiled and picked up a platter of fried chicken and passed it to Darcy. "Now we won't stand on ceremony. You just dig in and help yourself."

The next forty-five minutes were spent in light conversation as they passed chicken, green beans, mashed potatoes, homemade jams and biscuits around the table. Darcy couldn't remember when a meal had tasted so good. Finally, the table was cleared, and Aggie brought in a cream pie topped with curls of chocolate. Silver followed with an antique silver coffeepot. To Darcy's great appreciation, Aggie placed a huge slice of the pie in front of him, while Silver poured a cup of strong, rich coffee into his china cup.

Darcy gave the dessert an appreciative look before sliding his fork through the mound of whipped cream and into the dark chocolate pudding beneath. After tasting a bite, he nearly rolled his eyes with pleasure. "Damn— Excuse me, this is delicious, Mrs. Braybourne."

"Aggie."

"Aggie."

"Well, I wish I could accept the compliment, Darcy, but I didn't make it. Silver did. It's her special recipe."

"A special recipe?"

"I call it Braybourne Bourbon Pie."

Darcy licked his lips. "It's the best thing I've ever tasted. And I've tasted the—" He caught himself before he told her about the various chefs who'd worked for him over the years. "I mean, it's absolutely delicious."

"Why do you look so surprised?" Silver demanded. "I'll have you know that I'm an excellent cook."

"Yes," Harden said, with a proud smile. "My Silver will make some man a very good wife."

"Daddy..." Silver said warningly.

"And I know just the man."

"Daddy, please don't—"

"He's itching like a racehorse at the gate."

"Harden." Aggie's smooth voice broke in. "Stop teasing Silver in front of Darcy."

"I wasn't teasing," Harden blustered.

Silver was unable to hold back any longer. "Well, you should have been."

Darcy cleared his throat and changed the subject. "I've been admiring your garden, Aggie. My mother would be so envious she'd be asking for cuttings."

Aggie beamed at the compliment. "You know, Darcy, I've been working on that garden out there ever since I came here as a bride."

"It's beautiful."

"Silver, why don't you take Darcy outside and show it off for me."

"What? No." She shook her head and her mother looked surprised. "I'd rather not."

"Sylvia," Harden boomed, "don't speak back to your mother like that."

"Excuse me, Mama," Silver said automatically. Then she set her jaw, sending her father a lightning-bolt stare. "Really, Daddy, there's no need to—"

Aggie started to interrupt, but Darcy stood up instead and got everyone's attention. He was anxious to escape an uncomfortable situation—and afraid he'd accidentally stick his foot in his mouth again. It had been hard enough watching every word as it was. "I'd really like to see the flowers, Silver, if you wouldn't mind. Maybe walk off your pie a bit before I turn in."

Silver hesitated for a moment, then pushed her chair back and rose to her feet. "If you'd like." Darcy fought back a grin.

The resignation in her voice would have done justice to an aristocrat on the way to the guillotine. He followed her through the archway and into the hall, admiring her fluid stride as she led the way out of the house, onto the front porch and around to the side garden.

Silver stopped, waving her arm. "This is the garden."

Darcy chuckled. "So I see."

Dusk was falling, and the garden glowed with serenity as it waited for night. All around were the sounds of chirping crickets and the low guttural cry of frogs in the nearby ponds. Darcy could feel the peace seeping into him. It was the same sense he remembered as a child strolling with his grandfather over the fields and through the woods of Virginia. He really missed his grandfather.

Sighing, Darcy strolled over to a stone bench and sat down. He patted the seat, inviting Silver to sit next to him. When she didn't move, he added an incentive. "Afraid?"

Silver stalked over and plunked herself down. "Of you? Hardly."

"I thought I might make you nervous, is all."

"Why would you think that?"

Placing his hand on her bare arm, Darcy gently slid his fingers down until they reached the back of her hand. He hid his satisfaction when she jumped, then shivered. "No reason." As she snatched her hand away, he changed the subject. "What type of flowers are these around the bench here?"

Silver looked up. "I'm not sure. My mother is the gardener, not me."

"You sure do make great desserts, though." He needed her to look at him, to reassure himself that she was really as affected by him as he thought, regardless of her attempts to prove otherwise. The truth was always in the eyes, or so books said.

She glanced at him. "Thanks. I'm glad you liked it."

Her light green gaze seemed darker and more mysterious, or was that just a trick of the fading light? He lowered his voice. "I like a lot about Braybourne Farm."

Her bottom lip trembled slightly. "Like what?"

"Oh, the location, and the opportunity, and the people..."
His finger touched her mouth and moved slowly over her bottom lip until he reached the corner. "You have a pie crumb right here." He plucked the bit of crust onto his finger, then put his fingertip to his mouth. "Umm, even the leftovers are delicious."

Silver exhaled. "I don't know what you're up to, but—"

"I'm not up to anything, except I'm a man, you're a woman, it's a beautiful night...."

"Let's clear this up right now. I'm not interested in a relationship with you or anyone else."

He leaned forward. "I'll bet I can change your mind."

Silver tried to annihilate him with a look, but her gaze wouldn't cooperate. Instead there was a hint of longing, overlaid with an edge of excitement. "Oh, now you've decided to *bet* on changing my mind?"

"I like to gamble now and then. What about you?"

"I like to bet on winning propositions."

Darcy chuckled. "Me, too. That's why I offered it."

She gave a flirtatious look, one so instinctively female that Darcy could swear she was unaware she was doing it. "Okay. Say it again."

"I'll bet I can change your mind about getting involved with a man."

Her lashes swept down, then lifted as she smiled, the provocative pout making Darcy itch to possess her. "Not possible."

"Is that a challenge? I can't resist a challenge."

"That wasn't a challenge."

Darcy grinned, leaning forward to drop a kiss on the tip of her nose. "No? Who're you trying to convince? You or me?"

"Getting involved with people you work with can be messy."

Darcy laughed. "But it could be fun. Don't forget about fun."

Her mouth firmed. "There's more to life than fun, Darcy."

"Like what?"

"Like love and honor and—"

"Who's talking about love? I'm just talking about a way for two healthy adults to have a good time for a little while. After all, you said it yourself—I'll be moving on at some point."

"That's the plan."

"So?"

She shrugged. "So that's an even better reason not to get involved with you. You don't have any staying power."

"You don't want me to stay?"

Silver shrugged again. "I don't know. It's a real Catch-22, isn't it?"

Darcy drew back and winked. "Don't worry, Silver. I'm very good at finding my way around obstacles. Especially when the reward is something I want."

"Set your sights on something else. The only thing I want is to train a championship horse and start winning races."

Darcy smiled and took the plunge. There was something about this woman that brought out his competitive spirit. "I'll bet I can help you with that, too." He'd never done the hands-on training, but one of the top experts in the country worked at his family's Virginia farm. If needed, he'd call him up and quiz him.

Silver hesitated for a moment before meeting Darcy's gaze with a cautious one of her own. "That's a bet I might consider taking you up on. I don't have a lot of time."

"I have an idea. If I help you with one, then we automatically put the other to a test, too." He put every bit of arrogance he could muster into his challenge, positive she had too much spirit not to jump at it, if for no other reason than to take him down a few notches.

Silver stared long and hard. Finally, she nodded and extended her hand. "Let's see what you're made of, Rick Darcy."

Darcy rose from the bench and bent low to capture her hand in his. Jolted at the contact, he impulsively brought her hand to his lips, turning the palm over to press a kiss in the center. Just a quick taste, he promised himself. His lips touched her briefly with a feather-light touch. It wasn't enough. He looked up at her and was lost as he met the challenging amusement in her eyes. He'd show her. Stepping closer, he dipped his head and licked her bottom lip, her taste melting on his lips like sweet meringue.

"Oh." Her moan was all he needed to tell him he was on the right track. He licked her top lip, thrilling when she opened her mouth to allow him access. He deepened the kiss as he pushed aside the fabric of her top to caress her shoulder. Her skin had the smoothness of rich cream. He followed this first caress with his lips, working his way toward the tender hollow at the base of her neck. Her head tilted back and she arched into his embrace, her full breasts pressing forward.

He grabbed her waist, lifting her from the bench, pulling her against him. Her hands slipped around his neck, and a small cry of anticipated pleasure escaped her lips. He breathed in the smell of her, spicy perfume mixed with sexual arousal. Her scent surrounded him, invaded him, and he realized he was starving. His lips sought hers again as his hands moved up her body.

Silver's fingers plunged into his hair, pulling it hard as she ground her mouth against his. He felt her response—breasts tightening, hips lifting. One more moment and he'd be lost. Desperate, he tore his mouth from hers.

"Silver. Silver, if we don't stop right now..."

She went perfectly still.

"Silver?"

As he watched, all of the color seemed to drain from her face. "Silver, are you all right?"

"Yes," she said curtly, in a tight tone of voice.

He glanced back at the house, dim now in the evening light. Luckily, the curtains had all been drawn. "Sorry. I don't know what—"

She glared at him. "Oh please. You're not going to say you don't know what came over you, are you?"

"I...well, yes."

She pushed him away. "That's the lamest excuse in the

book. At least let's be honest. Let's just say our hormones temporarily got the better of us. But it's over now and it won't happen again."

"It won't?" Darcy frowned. This wasn't the way the scene was supposed to go. He was the one who was supposed to be logical and magnanimous. She was supposed to be begging him for more. He was completely confused.

"Absolutely not. Let's chalk it up to an interesting experiment and leave it at that."

Darcy stared at her, at her lips still swollen from his kisses. "You want to forget this ever happened?"

"Of course. It won't be a problem."

His eyes narrowed. "It won't, huh?"

"No."

"You won't look at me and remember what happened here, what you felt like in my arms, how I tasted? You won't remember any of that?"

"Mr. Darcy!" She batted her eyelashes at him, the consummate Southern belle. "I swear, you sound a bit upset. Please don't take it personally. I'm sure you're a good lover, sugar, and if you hadn't stopped, well, I would have really enjoyed myself. However, you did stop, and now that we have our wits about us, I'm sure you'll agree that ignoring this entire incident is the best thing for both of us."

Darcy backed up and shoved both hands through his hair. "Well, it might be, but—"

"But nothing. Let's just say we got that part of our bet over with, and it ended up a draw."

"A *draw?* You call it a draw when you melted in my arms? I don't think so."

"I'm stunned. I wouldn't have thought you'd be such a sore loser."

"I'm not a sore loser, because I very rarely lose. When I play *anything,* I play to win. And I keep on playing until I do."

"How you do carry on. It was only a kiss, after all."

"For now," Darcy promised. "Just for now." A bit confused, he backed away, feeling that she'd somehow turned the tables on him without him having the vaguest idea how it had happened. Scowling at her little smile, he turned on his heel and stalked back to his new home at the Braybourne stables.

SILVER COULDN'T SLEEP. She glanced at the clock on her bedstand: four o'clock. It would be dawn in another hour or so. Only a kiss, she'd told Darcy. That was like saying the great Secretariat, winner of racing's prestigious Triple Crown, was only a horse. After Darcy had lifted his lips from hers, it had taken every ounce of self-control to give him her best Scarlett O'Hara imitation. All she really wanted to do was sink down to the ground, preferably with him on top of her.

She threw back her light blanket and got out of bed. Wandering over to the window, she knelt on the window seat and pressed her forehead against the glass. The moon was full. She could make out the stables in the cool blue moonlight. Unfortunately, from this angle she couldn't see the front door, nor could she see whether Darcy's pickup truck was parked outside. But she could see his window at the end of the stables. It was dark, with the blinds drawn.

Well, of course it is, you idiot. He's sleeping. Probably sleeping peacefully, just as you should be doing.

She studied the stable again, noticing that the weathervane on top of the cupola needed adjusting. She'd have to see to that. Her eyes wandered back to Darcy's window.

I wonder if he sleeps nude?

She squeezed her eyes tight and took herself firmly to task, before shoving back her heavy fall of hair. She glanced at the clock once again. The luminous dial now read 4:10. Silver sighed, then yawned. She'd tossed and turned all night, her dreams full of disturbing images. Her biggest curse from childhood on had always been her imagination. Of course, it hadn't helped that as a little girl her brothers used to tell her bloodcurdling tales when her parents weren't around to stop them.

But tonight's dreams had nothing to do with monsters. In one she'd found herself standing on the edge of a wide canyon. The trail to the left led along the top of the cliff to safety, while the one to the right snaked seductively over the edge and into the unknown. Agonizing, she'd weighed her options, then started down the path to where a man beckoned. When she changed her mind and tried to scramble back, it was no use. She began to slip, to slide, to fall....

Silver glanced back at the stables. Licking her lips, she stared intently at Darcy's window once again, hoping—for what? She didn't know. But she was tempted to find out. What had she always longed for? A man as wild as a stallion, as bold as they come, standing outside convention...a man like Rick Darcy. The thought thrilled and terrified her.

Who was Rick Darcy?

Her father had told her what little he knew of Darcy's background, but still she wondered. In a community where everyone knew most everybody, when someone like Darcy showed up, you couldn't help but wonder. He liked to gamble, he'd said. She stiffened, biting her lip, suddenly wondering how much access he would have to their books and finances. She hadn't considered how easy it might be for him to swindle them. Lord knew, there was barely enough money now, but if they were careful, and if her new horse lived up to his name... Then she relaxed. Her father wouldn't turn everything over to Darcy, would he? No, of course he wouldn't. She was being ridiculous.

She glanced again toward the stable. And still felt an uneasiness that refused to go away when she thought about the man now living inside.

Under the circumstances, going back to bed was out of the question. She might as well get dressed and get a head start on the day. She rose, performed her morning grooming rituals, then walked over to her armoire for her clothes, the same armoire that her great-grandmother had used. Tradition held sway in her bedroom, from the furnishings that had belonged to various generations of Braybournes to the shelves of childhood books that still graced a corner of the big room. But to Silver, tradition did not represent avoiding risks, as it did to some people. Life was about risk, and she was getting ready to take her biggest one.

She stood, tucking in her blouse before tugging on her riding boots and then quietly letting herself into the hallway. She crept along the carpet, taking care not to wake her parents, whose room was at the far end of the hall. Reaching the front door, Silver emerged onto the porch, shivering as the cool night air hit her bare arms. It would be warmer in the stables.

As a matter of fact, with Darcy in there, she thought whimsically, it would be downright hot! She swallowed a chuckle. At least she still had a sense of humor. Now, if she could only find a way to deal with the man without reacting like a hormone-ridden teenager, she just might make it through with everything intact—including her dignity.

She marched down the stone path and through the picket gate onto the drive, then set a straight path for the stables and the horse paddocks beyond. Attempting to be quiet, she tugged open the stable door just wide enough to slip inside. She stood for a moment and absorbed the atmosphere. She'd moved confidently through these stables since she was able to walk, and no one, she decided, would ever come between her and this place. She walked slowly down the broad aisle, smiling at the sleepy nickers of the horses, walking over to stroke a velvet nose and to caress a curious ear. Finally she came to her destination—a large stall at the very end of the stables, next to the haymow and tack room, kitty-corner to Darcy's room. She glanced over her shoulder at Darcy's door, but it remained closed. It was way too early for anyone to be about. She glanced at her watch. It was scarcely 4:30. Braybourne Farm generally started stirring around 5:15 or 5:30.

Grabbing a bridle from a hook near the stall, she stepped closer to the half door. Resting her elbows on the door, she whispered to the black horse, "Hello, big fella. How's my fella today?" She gave the horse a moment to get used to her presence before opening the latch to slip inside. "Oh, you're a beautiful boy, you are," she crooned, watching as the horse turned his face in her direction. She extended her hand, letting the stallion sniff her scent, then ran her palm down his nose, caressing him as she spoke softly. The horse nuzzled her ear for a brief moment, then seemed to remember that he was a huge powerful animal and that such displays were not in keeping with his image.

Silver chuckled as she scratched his ears. "Oh, you big phony. I know you're not as bad as you pretend."

"I wouldn't count on that if I were you."

At the sound of Darcy's voice, Silver let out a gasp and whirled around, bumping into the horse's shoulder. The stallion gave her a bad-tempered nicker as he shuffled out of the way.

"Damn it," Darcy exclaimed. He unlatched the door and reached inside to grab her arm and pull her backward as the horse continued his restless movements. "Be careful."

Silver let out her breath in a whoosh as she slammed into his broad chest. "The only thing I have to be careful of is you." *That's the truth*, she thought as she inhaled the pleasant male scent of his warm skin.

"No. You have to be careful around twelve hundred pounds of bad-tempered horseflesh."

She glanced at the stallion. "Lucky Hand is not bad tempered."

"You couldn't prove it by me. I think he wants to take a bite out of something."

"Not me," she said, looking back at Darcy. "But you might be this morning's breakfast if you don't take your hands off me. Lucky Hand is very protective."

"So am I." He wrapped his arm around her and pulled her through the opening, closing the door behind her. "And I'll take my hands off you when I'm good and ready."

"Starting right now," she hissed, "I'm putting you on notice. There are some things I won't tolerate, and being manhandled is at the top of the list."

He smoothed his palm down her back. "You call this being manhandled?"

"Yes. What do you call it?"

He stepped a bit closer. "Rescuing."

"If and when I have need of your services, I'll ask for them."

He smiled, his teeth a flash of white in the dim light. "Which services would those be, darling?"

"You...you egotistical ape!"

"Now, now, let's be nice. Remember, we don't want to upset the horse."

"You listen to me. I do not intend to play these games for the duration of your employment."

"Good," he said with a grin. "I like a woman who knows what she wants and gets right down to business."

"Stop trying to get around me with your charm." *Maybe this guy is a con man, after all, trying to get me off guard and make me fall for him,* she thought as she tried to apply reason to a situation where emotion was more likely to rule.

"You think I have charm?"

She glared at him. "Some people might say so."

"You just did."

"Well, I didn't mean it."

"What did you mean?"

She lifted her chin to its haughtiest level. "Will you let me go? I have to see to my horse."

Darcy glanced over her shoulder. "Your horse looks just fine now that he has his stall to himself again. But you, you're another story." His fingertip traced the delicate skin beneath her eyes. "There are a few shadows here."

"I couldn't sleep."

"Funny," Darcy whispered, "neither could I. What were you thinking about?"

"I wasn't thinking."

"Dreaming, then." He smiled, a rakish smile that made her stomach flip over. "Did your dreams wake you up?"

"No, my nightmares did," Silver said, her sarcastic tone suggesting he was the subject of those nightmares.

"Ah well, it was too much to hope that you'd dream about me, I suppose."

"Absolutely."

He trailed his finger down her nose and over her lips. "I wasn't so lucky. When I closed my eyes you were there."

Oh, lord, why did he have to say that? She was just beginning to feel as if she could hold her own in the face of the man's overwhelming magnetism, and then he had to go and say something that was guaranteed to start her nerves jumping again and her blood pumping.

"I'm sorry to hear that." She forced the words through her lips.

"All I could think of was holding you as I did last night, touching you, kissing you." He followed his words with action.

"Does this Neanderthal approach work with all your women?" she gasped.

He grinned. "Pretty much."

"Then you haven't met the right type of women."

"Darling, I've met all types of women. I haven't seen a lot of difference between them, besides the obvious physical ones, that is."

"Well, you've never met one like me, take my word for it."

Pressing her back against the stall door, he asked, "What makes you so different?"

"What makes me different is that if you don't let me go this very minute, you're going to get my knee in your crotch."

"That would definitely get my attention."

"I'm sure it would."

With a bold move, he cupped her buttocks, pulling her flush against him, until she could feel his hard bulge pressing into the V of her jeans. "On the other hand, you aren't exactly in the best position to execute your threat. So I think I'm safe."

Silver knew she was a damn fool to respond, but she couldn't let his challenge go unanswered. Besides, the man brought out something wild and untamed in her. She slipped her hand into his dark, curling hair. "You're safe, hmm? Then perhaps I'd better change my approach."

She rocked her hips against him, realizing she was playing with fire, but unable to resist. Pulling his head down to hers, she opened her mouth slightly to allow her tongue to stroke and tease, before pressing her lips against his. She was drowning, the foolhardiness of her action now fully apparent as she succumbed to a wave of emotion. The man shook her to the core, bringing long-suppressed sexual feelings to the surface. Her hands caressed his bare shoulders, then his chest, her fingertips tingling with excitement as she kneaded and stroked.

Lucky Hand's head butted between them, forcing them apart for an instant. But Darcy ignored him. Sweeping Silver up into his arms, he headed for the nearest door. Turning the doorknob, he shouldered his way inside, kicking the door closed with his heel.

He looked down at the woman in his arms, taking in her flushed cheeks, her mouth swollen from his kisses. *Maybe this is what I've been needing—a good, hot, sweaty bout of sex. Not a total change in my lifestyle.*

He leaned back against the door, reluctant to put her down, adjusting her weight in his arms until she clasped her legs around his hips, like a cowgirl seeking a perfect ride. He kissed her again, slow probing kisses, his tongue plunging inside to duel with hers, back and forth, in and out, echoing the movement their bodies were aching to complete. She clasped her arms more firmly around his neck, anchored her legs more securely and held on, giving back as good as she was getting.

After a long moment he lifted his head and stared at her. Her green eyes were glazed, the pupils huge and vulnerable. With his gaze roaming her face, he took time to memorize each feature, drawing out the process until he thought he'd go mad with wanting her. And he did want her—more than he'd wanted anyone. He'd been intimate with a number of women, but couldn't remember any of them creating this mingled feeling of excitement and tenderness. There was something different about Silver Braybourne. Something that should have set off all his alarms of self-preservation from the moment he met her.

Generally, when he wanted something he ignored all warnings, but not this time. To his horror, considering his state of arousal, his innate sense of honor started to get the better of him. His conscience stirred, and for a brief moment he considered letting her go. After all, he was only going to be here for a short time. How fair was it to interrupt her life? He didn't want her to cherish false hopes about any future. Women were funny that way. Even though he might think it was all fun and games, females had a bad habit of making it personal. Personal was something he tended to avoid. If he stopped now and vowed never to touch her again...

Darcy lowered her until her feet touched the ground. "Silver, I need to—"

"So do I." She gave him a decisive nod. "Look, I consider myself a practical woman, Darcy. I like to take action and solve problems. Maybe we should just get this sexual attraction out of the way so we can concentrate on other things." A hint of desperation crept into her matter-of-fact tone as she trailed her hands down his chest to the waistband of his jeans. "What do you say?"

Those words made Darcy put his noble impulses behind him. This was a woman who obviously knew what she wanted and went after it—a bit more directly than most. Still, she was the same spoiled, single-minded society butterfly type he was familiar with. The venue might have changed, but not the basic personality. He didn't know why he was attempting to invest her with other attributes. Wishful thinking, maybe? He cupped her buttocks and pressed her harder against him. "When you put it that way..."

Silver looked him deep in the eyes. Her determined face suggested she'd just made an executive decision. "This is what we're going to do. We're going to exorcise this...this tension between us with sex. Pure, red-hot sex, something we both obviously need. There's no need to complicate it with any emotion. Just a good fast bout in the hay. Like a stallion and a mare."

"I get to be the stallion, right?" Darcy chuckled at her expression before glancing around the room. "But we're in the manager's office. So we'll have to make do and save the hay for another time."

Her eyes narrowed. "There won't be another time, Darcy. This is it. We're going to get this out of our systems so we can both move on."

His eyes narrowed in turn. "In that case, I'm going to be sure I do a damn fine job."

He would, too. She obviously expected the best and she was going to get it. He prided himself on delivering satisfaction, and on remaining friends with his former lovers. While the friendship was oftentimes difficult, he could completely guarantee the other.

He led her around the huge oak desk to the chair and sat down, pulling her into his lap. His hand swept up her side from hip to breast, and her neck arched at the languid caress. He kissed her throat, his tongue sliding over her skin to nip her at the base.

"You taste delicious...like cotton candy," he murmured.

"Mmm, more," she breathed.

He tugged her top from her jeans and unbuttoned it to reveal her lacy white bra. She was built like a goddess, with ripe, full, firm breasts. He stared for a moment and her flesh reacted to his gaze, firming and swelling over the low-cut cups of her bra. He filled his hands with her, thumbs stroking over the top curves, before his fingers dipped into the deep valley between. He leaned forward, replacing his fingers with his lips. Teasing, tasting, tantalizing, he stroked his tongue over her flesh, pulling down her bra with his teeth before closing his mouth over her. He nibbled and pulled her erect nipple, then switched to her other breast, repeating the same caress, finally unfastening the front hook of her bra. She tightened her hands in his hair, pulling him closer, then arching to get closer still.

His hands slid down over her ribs to her waist, and her stomach muscles clenched as he unsnapped her jeans. He ran his finger along the waistband before slipping inside to tease the concave dip of her navel and finger the lace of her underpants.

Silver lifted her hips and resettled herself astride his lap. Ready to ride, she started to rock her hips, pressing even harder against his erection. Her hands left his hair and made their way south, molding his shoulders before splaying over his chest to pinch his nipples. They moved lower still, roaming over his button fly. Then two fingers slid under the placket.

"Do you sleep nude?" she whispered.

Darcy jerked as her finger touched him. "Yes."

"I thought you might. You don't seem the type for pajamas."

He groaned as her finger circled his tip. "Nude is more comfortable."

"How did you know I was in the barn?"

"I heard you, so I got up and threw on some jeans."

She undid a button. "I was very quiet. You couldn't have heard me."

"I did." He held his breath as she moved to the next button. "I was thinking about you."

"Good thoughts?"

He smiled, his eyes holding hers. "Oh yes, very good thoughts. So good I was aching and couldn't sleep."

She leaned forward and licked his lips. "Before, when you asked me if I'd dreamed about you, I lied. You were there, in my dreams...."

He arched back, lifting his hips until the full length of him rested against her V and her lower stomach inviting her to touch. Silver smiled as her fingers slipped another button from its hole. Suddenly a loud crashing sound echoed outside the room. She froze.

"What the—" Darcy began, swiveling his head in the direction of the door.

"It sounds like the stable doors," Silver answered.

The crash was followed by Harden Braybourne's yelling, "Okay, Tater, back it right in here. That's it."

Silver darted a look at the clock on the wall: 5:00 a.m. "It's my father. I don't understand. He never gets in here before 5:30."

"Watch it, Tater. You're going to run into Strawberry's

stall," Harden continued to yell. "Straighten the wheel. I don't want those bales of hay to fall off."

"Oh, my God, he's going to take one look at us and know what we were doing here. How am I going to explain?" Silver slid off Darcy's lap, hooking her bra and buttoning her blouse as she looked around for a way out. "He can't find me here with you."

"Since your father is on the other side of the door, the only way out is the window. We can jump through, or stay here and brazen it out."

She sent Darcy a stare that could have withered an entire corn crop. "Staying together here is not an option. Not with you looking like that, and me like this. The window's a better idea."

"I was kidding. If you go out the window, what am I supposed to do?"

"You can say you wandered in here to make some coffee or something. Or you heard a noise and you came to investigate. Use your imagination."

"How about I'm getting an early start to the day?"

"It would be more convincing if you were wearing a shirt, shoes and some underwear, don't you think?"

"I don't think your father gives a damn about my underwear."

An unwilling chuckle burst forth, hastily suppressed. She pulled up the blinds, opened the window and removed the sliding screen. She handed it to Darcy. "Here, replace this after I leave."

He took the screen. "Are you coming back? Or are you going to keep going until you reach the county line?"

"And leave you a clear field to take over permanently as manager of Braybourne Farm? Don't bet on it. I'll be back in ten minutes. I've got work to do."

"The only thing I'm betting on is making Lucky Hand a winner." He grinned. "Oh, and having you, of course."

He cupped her chin and dropped a quick kiss on her lips, a kiss she instinctively returned before she came back to her senses. She tore her lips away from his and climbed through the window, stepping down into a bed of marigolds.

"You can lie to yourself about this attraction between us all you want," Darcy said through the open window. "But don't ask me to believe it." Then he cut off any reply by fitting the screen back into the window and lowering the blinds.

4

SILVER AVOIDED TRAMPLING the marigolds as she moved away from the window. Ducking down next to a tall, flowering hedge, she took stock of her situation, wondering what the hell she was doing.

When she left her bedroom a short while ago, she would never have believed she'd be squatting in her mother's flowers half an hour later, trying to avoid being caught in mischief by her father. She felt as if she were nine years old again. Except this time the forbidden adventure was totally different. She blew her hair out of her eyes. *Was it ever!* Now, as then, her problem would be trying to put on a normal, everyday face so no one would suspect what she'd been up to. At the moment she wasn't sure how to do that. She could probably manage to face her father, and even Tater. But suddenly she wondered how she would react toward Darcy the next time she saw him. How could she face him and not give herself away? She felt herself blush.

She hadn't been embarrassed about their physical activity. Her mother was right; living on a farm, you thought differently about matters of sex. It was instinct. After all, hadn't Silver always thrilled to see the mares bred, to watch the stallion completely aroused, ready to take apart anything that got in the way of his having the female? And the mare, trembling, anticipating, as urgent as he to couple. It was electrifying, and always had been to Silver. It set her heart pumping and her mind fantasizing.

And now there was Darcy.

Darcy, with the power of his sexuality, his frank hunger, his inevitable expectation that females would fall at his feet for his attentions. Well, he wasn't far wrong about that. There was an appeal about him that transcended his looks. Virility emanated from him. No wonder she'd been swept away. She might be practical, but she was also impulsive. If she'd really stopped to consider her actions, she never would have let down her guard in the first place. After all, she was a Southern belle to her fingertips. She knew how to flirt, tease and play the game—better than any, to listen to her ex-boyfriends. If she'd used her age-old female weapons correctly, she'd have ignored his challenging innuendos and taken aim with her fluttering lashes, megawatt smile and coy expressions, bagging the man on her own terms. But no, she had to step right up there and throw a challenge back at him. An action she might live to regret.

Oh, well. Nothing to be done about it now. Like Scarlett O'Hara, she decided she'd think about all of this later—maybe tomorrow, next week, three months from now.... Damn, she wouldn't be able to stop thinking about it. Every time she saw Darcy she'd remember.

Silver sighed as she stared into the distance, watching the morning sky dress itself in colors to welcome the day. *Come on, get a grip.* It would have been sex, just sex. No big deal—natural animal-kingdom stuff. *Get past it. Stiffen that Braybourne spine and go about your business.*

Having given herself an appropriate pep talk, she stood and stepped around the bush, emerging onto the stone path that led to the stable's entrance. She looked down at herself as she walked, checking to be certain her zipper was closed and her clothing aligned. In a quick panic she checked her blouse, convinced she'd buttoned it incorrectly. No, it was fine.

She glanced up and almost stumbled over her own feet when she saw Tater watching her. He was standing by the door of the stables, staring at her as he casually pulled on a pair of old leather gloves. She hesitated for a moment. How long has he been there? she wondered. He couldn't have seen her climb through the window, could he?

Head tilted consideringly, Tater called, "What're you up to, girl?"

Taking a deep breath, Silver strolled toward him, hoping she looked nonchalant. "Nothing. What makes you think I've been up to something?"

"Because you got the same guilty look on your face as when you gave all your father's riding boots away to the thrift store."

Silver gave him an astonished look. "You're making that up. I don't remember that. Daddy would have blistered my hide."

"That's because I managed to get them back before he found out."

"Oh." Silver smiled at the old man. That was typical of Tater. He'd always been around to rescue her from complete disaster. He considered it a sacred charge, given his long family association with the Braybournes. He was more like a favorite beloved uncle than an employee. Too bad he hadn't been around to rescue her from herself earlier this morning.

"Well?"

"I don't look guilty, Tater. This is my thinking look."

"What're ya thinking about, girlie?"

She cast about for an answer, replying lamely, "Oh, this and that." She changed the subject. "Hey, what're you up to, running around so early?"

"Me and your daddy had to get that load of hay this morning from the Thomas farm. They needed to move it out first thing. Are you sure you're feeling all right, Silver?"

"Yes. Why?"

"You just don't look the same to me."

She needed to divert him before he really began asking questions. "Actually, if you want to know what I was thinking about, it was Lucky Hand."

Tater gave her a suspicious look, as though he wasn't convinced, but then shrugged and asked, "What about him?"

"I want to enter him in the Rosemont Cup next month."

"Are you nuts, girl? That horse is still as wild as bedamned."

"Only because he'd been poorly trained before. You know we've been making progress with him."

Tater lifted his hat and scratched his head. "We'd have to make a lot more than what I've seen to race him. That's why we got him for nothing in the first place."

"We didn't get him for nothing. We won him."

"Might as well been less than nothing for all the good we'll get out of him. He don't want to run 'less he wants to run. Racehorses gotta run all the time—not just when they're in the mood, don'cha know?"

Riled now, Silver strode toward the stable doors, saying over her shoulder, "You come see me work him this morning and then tell me that." Lucky Hand was a winner. She knew it in her bones.

Tater followed her around the truck blocking the door and into the stables. She was still arguing with him when she looked over and saw her father talking to Darcy. Darcy was still clad only in his jeans, but he seemed perfectly at ease as he shared a laugh with Harden.

"Well, good morning, sleepyhead," her father called. "I'm waiting for my coffee."

She frowned, feeling as if he'd just delegated her to housemaid. Never mind that she came into the manager's office every morning and put a pot of coffee on, and that her father always had his first cup there. Darcy didn't know that. She marched toward them, with Tater right behind her. "You know, Daddy, you aren't helpless. You could go in and make a pot of coffee if you wanted."

Harden chuckled. "Well, sure I could, darlin', but you make it so much better."

"Don't try to get around me with your sweet-talking ways. That might work with Mama, but it won't work with me."

Harden gave a full-bellied laugh. "Well, hell, Silver. It doesn't work with your mother, either, or so she says."

Darcy jumped in. "You know how it is with females, sir. They just have to be contrary to get a man fired up."

Harden nodded. "Ain't it the truth, Son, ain't it the truth."

"No one asked you, Darcy." Silver practically spat the words at him.

Harden shook his finger at Darcy. "You'd best be careful. My daughter is a real firecracker when she's got her dander up."

Darcy smiled. "I'm sure she is."

Silver almost choked at the knowing look he gave her. Anyone with eyes could see they were no longer complete strangers. He couldn't go around giving her looks like that without someone guessing something. And she'd wondered how she'd react when she saw him again! The answer to that was simple: when she got him alone, she'd kill him!

She smiled, her expression so sweet she almost gave herself a sugar high. "Is appearing bare-chested a new look for stable managers?"

Her father answered for him. "Darcy heard a noise in the barn awhile ago and got up to investigate. Could be it was that raccoon that's been hanging around, Tater. That little menace is getting bolder every day. Next thing you know, he'll be saddling up and riding one of the horses."

Tater sent a sharp glance at Darcy, then his eyes darted back to Silver. "A noise, huh? Did you get a look at the...'coon, you say it was?"

Darcy flushed a bit as he glanced at Tater, then focused his eyes firmly on Harden. "No. I'm not even sure it was a raccoon. I only heard some shuffling noises and then some banging, like something being knocked over."

"Next time," Tater said, his voice dryer than dust, "maybe he'll turn on a light so's he don't wake you up."

Darcy grinned. "Hope so. Now, if you'll excuse me, I'll finish getting dressed." With that he turned and disappeared into his room.

There was no way Silver wanted to be left alone with her father and Tater, so she made her own escape. "I'll get the coffee started, Daddy."

Her father blew her a kiss. "Thanks, darlin'."

Silver stopped. "You're in a mighty good mood this morning, aren't you?"

"I'm in a good mood every morning."

Silver and Tater both rolled their eyes. "With any luck," she said, "a lightning bolt won't descend from the heavens and strike you down for lying."

Harden sent her a sly glance. "I was over at the Thomas farm this morning, Silver. And I have to tell you, if ever a man was upside down and head over heels, it's John Tom."

Hoping to avoid the conversation, she joked, "He'd better see a doctor about that condition, don't you think?"

"He'd much rather see a minister, I'm thinking."

Setting her jaw, Silver planted her fists on her hips. "Look, Daddy, I am not interested in John Tom Thomas. I wish you'd get that through—"

"Well, he sure is interested in you. His mama told me all about it this morning."

Silver grasped her head in her hands. "Enough, please, enough." Even if she had been interested in him, the episode with Darcy this morning would have proved to her how wrong it would be to encourage John Tom. She wanted someone who could make her tremble—not someone to keep her safe and cosseted.

"I told his mother to tell John Tom to stop by this morning."

"Why?"

"I thought it would be a good idea."

"It isn't, Daddy. It's a horrible idea." Unable to get a response from her father, Silver turned to Tater. "Don't you think it's a horrible idea, Tater?"

Tater looked from her to Darcy's door, then back again. "It ain't my business, but it might be a good thing all around."

"I can't believe you'd say that."

Tater shrugged and walked away to get started on his day's work. Silver watched him go before turning back to her father. "You won't always have it your own way, Daddy. You can't just bully people into doing what you want, regardless of how often you tell them it's because you love them."

Her father smiled. "When you've lived as long as I have, you see things more clearly than when you're young."

"No. You see things the way you do because you're just too stubborn to change once your mind is made up."

"I only want what's best for you, honey lamb."

"Then for God's sake, Daddy, let me do what I need to do. Quit smothering me. Let me breathe."

Her father stared at her for a moment before turning on his heel and heading somewhat unsteadily for the manager's office. "I'm going to make the coffee myself."

"Daddy, where's your cane?"

"I threw the damn fool thing out. It got in my way."

"Still, you need to—"

"Who's smothering who?" her father growled over his shoulder.

She watched him limp away, now feeling guilty in more ways than one. "I'll be in with Lucky Hand, if you need me."

Her father stopped and turned around. "We've got to have a talk about that horse a bit later, Silver. Right now, I have to do something about my morning coffee."

His martyred tone prompted her to ask reluctantly, "Do you want me to make it for you?"

"No, no need," her father said, standing as firm as if he was ready to defend his homeland to the death. "I'll make it."

Silver hid a smile. "Eight scoops for a full pot, Daddy."

Harden dismissed her with an ill-tempered wave and disappeared inside the office.

Silver stood still for a moment, enjoying the quiet. Darcy had disappeared, Tater had disappeared and so had her father. For now she had the stables to herself. She was queen of all she surveyed. A soft nicker from her right disabused her of that notion. She turned to look at Lucky Hand, who was poking his regal head over his stall door, demanding her attention. At her glance, the horse jerked his head in an imperial manner. Grinning, she decided she was just a humble peon after all, bowing before a king.

"I suppose you're looking for your breakfast, aren't you?"

The horse answered with a small whinny, still managing to sound as if she'd better get her butt right over there or else. Chuckling, she headed for the stall and patted Lucky Hand's soft nose. "All right. I heard you. It's coming right up."

She busied herself for the next half hour getting fresh grains and refilling his water bucket. Then, with her horse happily munching, she grabbed her rake to clean the stall, replacing the soiled hay with fresh bedding. She concentrated on her work, paying no attention to her father shouting directions as Darcy and Tater began unloading the hay from the truck. When the job was done to her satisfaction, she slipped a halter on Lucky Hand and tied him to the rail to begin grooming him. It was one of her favorite activities. She delighted in smoothing the brush over his sleek black coat, making him shine like ebony. Her horse liked it, too, even though he pretended to accept it as if it was his due. It was their time together, hers and Lucky Hand's. But this morning there was another presence in the stall with them, whether she wanted him there or not. Darcy.

As she stood there, her hands sliding over the sinewy muscles of her horse, she tried to put her experience with Darcy into perspective. There was no reason to beat herself up. All she'd done was take the moment and go with what seemed natural. She knew that if they hadn't been interrupted she would have made love to him. But, she told herself firmly, she only would have done it so she could better concentrate on her job. The man was a distraction, and the best way to deal with a distraction was to get past it.

Silver shifted her weight, a bit uneasy with what she knew was not a lie exactly, but certainly not the whole truth.

Truth was the man was a prime, grade A, certifiable hunk of raw sex. Just looking at him made her hungry.

"Hungry?" Darcy drawled.

"What?" Stunned, she jerked around to find him standing at the door. God, the man couldn't read minds, could he?

He gave her a funny look, then held up his hands. "I brought you a breakfast bar and a cup of coffee."

"Oh, that's nice."

"I thought you could use some energy after all your morning activity," he teased as he opened the stall and stepped inside. "I know I'm exhausted."

She put down the brush, taking the mug and fruit bar. "Darcy, don't start."

"I'm talking about the work we've been doing. I just un-loaded a truckful of hay." His eyes twinkled. "Were you think-ing of something else?"

"I...never mind." She took a sip of coffee. "Wow, this is pretty good. Daddy made this?"

"No." Darcy grinned. "Tater. After one taste, we poured your father's coffee out the window into the flowers."

Silver chuckled. "Poor little marigolds."

"Tater swore he could hear them groaning."

"Daddy didn't see you do it, did he?"

"No. He went back to the house after he realized he couldn't unload the hay bales with his cast on."

Silver nodded, practically inhaled her breakfast bar. Darcy was right—she was starving. They sipped their coffee in si-lence for a few moments, the feeling of companionship taking her by surprise. When he wanted to, she thought, Darcy could be as easy to be around as he was on the eyes.

"He's a beautiful horse."

"Yes, he is." Silver smiled. "He knows it, too."

"That's just a male preening his feathers."

"Well, some males have a lot to preen about."

"Oh?" He stepped a bit closer. "Tell me more."

She slapped her empty cup into his hand. "I'm talking about the horse."

"So am I, of course."

"No, you're not. You're talking about..."

He put the mugs down. "What?"

"You know perfectly well what. I've already told you there will be no—"

Darcy put his fingers on her lips, silencing her. "Now it's my turn to tell you." He stepped closer, until she could feel the heat of his body. "It won't end here. It would be best if it did, but it can't. Not now. I've got the taste of you on my tongue, your scent in my pores and the feel of you on my fingers." He pressed a hard kiss on her lips. "There will be a next time, Sil-ver, and then a time after that. So you might as well get used to the idea."

"For a man who just got hired and has yet to prove himself, you're mighty arrogant, aren't you?" she drawled.

"I proved myself a little while ago. And if you're honest, you'll admit it."

"We're not talking about your potential sexual prowess. I'm talking about you. I haven't the vaguest idea who you really are. Or what you really want here. This doesn't seem like the right sort of place for you, but I'm not sure why. So I'm not positive you're completely trustworthy."

"If you hadn't thought you could trust me, you wouldn't have let me near you."

"That was just lust. And you know it."

He said nothing, just looked at her with eyes that peered into her soul. He was right. She'd said she didn't really trust him, but on some level she must. The man was a total contradiction. He was well-spoken, obviously educated, but drifting from job to job. His hands were strong, but well cared for, not the hands of a worker. Her thoughts spun as her eyes locked on his waiting gaze. Yes, Darcy was a jigsaw puzzle. It only made him more fascinating.

After a moment, he smiled and pushed a lock of hair behind her ear. "Besides, what's wrong with lust? You have to start somewhere."

She couldn't answer him. She could only stare, caught by the powerful desire he created in her. What was wrong with lust? Not a damn thing. *Stop thinking with your anatomy and use your brain*, she chided herself. This man could take away everything she'd been working for during the last year, everything she'd always dreamed about. She'd already made one mistake where he was concerned. She wouldn't make another, tempting as it was.

Silver shook her head, her voice firm. "No, my decision stands. It won't happen again."

"Well, it hasn't really happened yet," Darcy said, his gaze penetrating, "but I intend to do something about that."

"Oh you do, do you?" She couldn't prevent the thrill of excitement running up her spine any more than she could prevent her flirtatious response.

He nodded, saying in a soft whisper, "Are you up for an adventure?"

She tilted her head, studying him, not quite trusting the gleam in his eye. "What?"

He ran the tip of his finger over her bottom lip. "You're a gambler at heart, Silver Braybourne. It's written all over you. So, let's make another bet."

"What kind of bet?" The feel of his hand almost caused her knees to buckle.

"I'll bet I can change your mind about our making love before the week is out."

Silver could feel the recklessness wash over her. It built until she extended her hand, grasping his firmly in a hearty shake. "You're on, Rick Darcy." Now she vowed to resist the man if it killed her. And it damn near might.

He grinned, then lifted her hand to his mouth, brushing his lips over her knuckles. "A woman after my own heart."

Silver shivered as his lips lingered for a moment. She closed her eyes, wanting him to lift his lips from her hand and press them against her mouth—just once before she swore off him forever. She jumped when he leaned forward to blow softly on her cheek. "What're you—"

"Just a bit of hay not ready to leave that luscious skin, is all."

Jerking her hand from his, Silver brushed it over her face. "Thanks," she muttered, trying to slow her breathing and return her stomach to its accustomed calm. If anyone else had said that she would have gagged. So why did it sound so right coming from him?

Darcy smiled as his knuckles brushed her chin. "No problem."

He seemed to loom over her in the stall, larger than life, imbued with the same majesty as the powerful stallion standing by her side—such was the power of his personality. A personality that she'd have to put every effort into resisting if she wanted to keep some measure of sanity.

Perhaps sensing her uncertainty, Lucky Hand butted her shoulder with his muzzle. The nudge was hard enough to release Silver from whatever fantasy was overtaking her. She shook her head as if awakening from an enchanted sleep, and turned to her horse.

"Okay, okay, I get the picture. It's time to get moving."

Silver busied herself for a moment, smoothing a loving hand over the horse's long neck as she regained her control. When she turned back to face Darcy, he was just an ordinary man...nothing special about him, no inherent power. All right, so he was one of the sexiest, best-looking hunks she'd ever seen, but that didn't change the fact that he was nothing more than a man her father had hired to help them while they were getting back on their feet.

Silver unhooked the stallion's tether and took a deep breath before saying in her coolest tone, "If you'll excuse me, I've got to get my horse into the ring. We're a bit late for today's training. And you know the most important thing about training is—"

"Consistency. Yes, I remember hearing that."

"Then you know I have to stay on schedule. Things have to happen when they have to happen."

"Absolutely." Darcy stepped back, reaching to open the stall door so Silver could lead Lucky Hand through. "It wouldn't do to be too fast or too slow. It might throw the timing off. Then where would we be?"

He was laughing at her. She didn't have to look at him to know it. It was there in his deep, slower-than-a-slug drawl. Her temper sparked, but she firmed her lips into a straight-down-the-homestretch line and marched forward. She had work to do and she was damned if she was going to let Rick Darcy interfere with her concentration anymore today.

"I have to finish up some things in here, Silver, then I'll meet you in the ring."

Silver threw him a glance over her shoulder as she and Lucky Hand headed for the door. "That's not necessary. We're doing just fine."

"Did you forget about our wager?"

"Are you deaf, or just too arrogant to live? I've already vowed that isn't going to happen, so put it out of your teeny-tiny, one-track mind."

Darcy grinned. "Not that wager, sweetheart, the other one."

She frowned. "What other one?"

He gave her a glance full of pity. "Last night I bet I could help you make this horse a winner and you took me up on it."

"I did? I don't remember...." The events of this morning had crowded out all memory of the night before.

"You definitely did. And I can't wait to get started. I want to see if you're right about how special this horse is."

"I am right. I have to be right."

"Because you can't stand to be wrong?"

Shaking her head with a sharp, emphatic movement, she said, "No, because I'm betting my future on it. All I ever wanted to be, all I ever will be, is riding on this horse."

He gave her a skeptical look. "That's an awful lot to put on a horse, isn't it?"

"You don't understand how important this is. This horse could be the start of something big. Of course, it will take hard work and every ounce of commitment I've got, but that's okay, because..." Her words trailed off, and she tried to drop the subject. "Never mind."

But Darcy wouldn't let her. "Because?"

Silver lifted her shoulders in a self-conscious gesture. "Because there's honor and satisfaction in working really hard to accomplish something that everyone told you was impossible, don't you think?"

Darcy started to say something, then seemed to change his mind. Instead, he scuffed the toe of his boot in the dirt before saying in a diffident tone, "I don't know. I've never found anything impossible."

"If that's so, then what are you doing here? Roaming around the country in a beat-up old pickup truck with one suitcase to your name?"

Looking a bit uncomfortable, he shrugged. "I got here by chance."

"By chance? Well, I'm here by choice. And I'm going to hang on to what I've got with both hands, if it kills me."

"I can appreciate that. I think I'd do the same. But what I said still goes. I'd like to try and help you prove this horse can be the winner you think he is."

"Because of our bet?"

His gaze shifted from her to the horse and back again. "Not entirely, but that will do for now. Anyway, I'd like to try."

Still a bit wary, she met his eyes, and to her surprise, discovered sincerity, a spark of excitement—and a hint of uncertainty that made him seem more down-to-earth and approachable. If this man was acting, she thought, he was a damn fine performer. She glanced at her horse, which was growing impatient at standing still. She didn't want to share Lucky Hand, but having a bit of help might be advantageous. They didn't have long before the Rosemont, and she needed every minute she could get for training, along with her other responsibilities. Maybe it wouldn't hurt to—

"What do you say, Silver?"

"Okay," she said slowly, "but what I say goes."

"Absolutely. He's your horse."

"Lucky Hand can win. I know it. He's been misunderstood, is all. He just needs the opportunity."

"Then it's lucky for him that he ran into you, isn't it?"

Silver threw her arm over her horse and pressed her forehead against his shoulder. "I think it's lucky for both of us."

Darcy envied her. What was it like to be that committed to something? he wondered. So committed that you'd be willing to do anything and risk everything? He didn't know. He'd never been in that position. He'd never really felt that strongly about anything in his life. He accepted what he had without ever thinking seriously about it. It was just there. His cousin had indicated that Darcy's real problem was internal, something he wouldn't change by running away from life's responsibilities. Maybe Nick was right. Maybe it was time Darcy started building his true place as a man instead of just using the privileged position he'd inherited through birth as an excuse to drift through life. A life that was becoming increasingly unsatisfying. Perhaps it was time for him to take a deeper look at himself and find out who he was really meant to be, to find the man beneath the trappings of wealth. With a flash of insight, Darcy realized that together, Silver Braybourne and Lucky Hand might be the making of him.

He watched as she soothed her horse, suddenly feeling twinges of guilt as he considered how he was deceiving her, not only about who he was, but about how much he knew. Then he shrugged it off, reassuring himself that Silver was a big girl. She could take care of herself. She'd be okay. It wasn't as if there was anything more than sheer natural animal attraction between them, plus the thrill of the chase, after all. They both understood the game; he was sure of that. But the horse... His gaze swept over the stallion's powerful lines. The horse was an added bonus.

If Darcy could be part of training Lucky Hand for greatness, if greatness was truly his destiny, then he might learn something about himself as well. He might even discover his path for the future. After all, he couldn't keep screwing around, as he had been, until he ended up a joke—the rich playboy who could do nothing more substantial than carouse and romance women. God, no—he knew too many people like that.

He rubbed his chin, watching as Silver led the powerful stallion through the stable doors and into the morning light. His breath caught as the sun hit Silver's hair, turning it to the bright nimbus of an angel's halo. An angel? No, that didn't fit Silver Braybourne, unless you counted her heart-stopping beauty, which had stunned him from the moment he'd first caught sight of her. But then again, maybe that was really pure devil-sent temptation.

He concentrated on her smooth stride as she paced beside her horse. The way that woman could move was a sin, a perfect sin. If he could have, he would have sold his soul to make love with her a little while ago. He was damn grateful the devil had been somewhere else at that moment, otherwise he'd have been a straight-to-hell goner. Turning on his heel, he headed for the manager's office.

Later, after making phone calls and taking care of other items on the job list Harden had left him, Darcy approached the training ring. He hooked the heel of his boot onto the bottom rail and observed Silver and Lucky Hand. He wasn't sure who was more exciting to watch, the woman or the horse. They both moved with a grace and strength that was pure poetry in motion. And that was what it was all about, he thought, as he watched Silver lead her horse on the lunge line. You had to have both the smooth, steady stride, that seemingly effortless motion that so many people took for granted, and the power. The power that suddenly blasted off into speed as a racehorse tore up the track. Of course, that wasn't what made a winner.... Darcy could almost hear his grandfather's voice instructing him. *A winner has to have heart. A winner has to have that one indefinable quality that could never be taught—the desire to win, win at all costs, whatever the odds, whatever the hardships.* That's what made some horses great and others merely very good. Was there really greatness in Lucky Hand?

He studied the horse, remembering how his grandfather had told him to look for the nuances. Horses had emotions, too, just like people. Now that Darcy thought about it, they were often easier to understand than people. If a horse didn't like you, its ears went back and, if you were in the right place— or the wrong one—you received a nip or even a kick. Simple, to the point. His gaze shifted to the woman skillfully handling the lunge line. Now, if Silver didn't like you she'd—what? Bite? The thought made him smile. A nip from Silver was something he would look forward to.

Darcy climbed the fence and perched on top. All around him were the signs of summer in full swing. It was too early for the heat to swell, but as he felt the sun strike his back, he knew it promised to do so later in the day. No matter; he liked it hot. Of course, he generally liked it hot while he was lying on a beach with a beckoning ocean and a long, tall drink beside him, but he'd adapt. He had a long, tall blonde to look at instead. He grinned, feeling very pleased with himself, drinking in the sweet taste of the day. At the moment life had some real possibilities.

Silver caught his eye as she turned to follow the horse's circle. Careful not to distract Lucky Hand, he nodded to her, then settled down to concentrate on her work. He was impressed. She knew what she was doing. It showed in her patient, even handling, in her encouraging voice that had just the right amount of authority. The horse seemed to know it, too.

Darcy switched his attention back to Lucky Hand. Then it hit him. There was something about that horse that looked very familiar. Alert, his head carried high, ears active, the black stallion was beauty, balance and symmetry delivered in one attractive package. Definitely, something looked very familiar. Where had Silver gotten him? He couldn't remember what she'd told him. But he could swear he knew this animal. Had he seen him race at some point and not realized it? He watched them work awhile longer, waiting until Silver brought the horse to a stop and removed the line before he leaped off the fence and strolled over to join them.

Darcy indicated the lunge line. "Why are you training him like a beginner again?"

Silver bristled for a moment, then took a deep, calming breath before answering, "I thought it best. When we got him, he was a real handful. Not very responsive or respectful of the rider, or the bridle." With a rueful expression, she patted her horse as if she was sorry for telling tales out of school to the principal. "I thought it best to break him of old bad habits by just going back to basics so I can smooth out his gait and work on his obedience."

"Well, that was a good idea."

Silver glared at him. "Thanks. I thought so."

"That sounded... Look, I wasn't trying to be patronizing or anything. I meant it."

"Sorry. I guess I'm a bit touchy where this horse is concerned." She coiled the line and slipped it over her arm. "He deserves better than he's had so far."

"From what I can see, he's got it." Darcy fell into step with her as she walked the horse to cool him down.

"It's the training, you know. That's what it's all about. If the trainer isn't any good, then the horse is behind from the beginning, no matter what his bloodlines or potential."

"My trainer would agree. He always says—"

"Your trainer?"

"Where I was before—the place I was...." Damn, he needed to think before he spoke, not let himself get caught up in a conversation. "Anyway, there was this old guy who was there. One of those old coots who's been around forever, you know what I mean? He was teaching me as much as the horse, or so he said." *All right, back on track now.* "He always said that the horse had to have the heart, but by gum it was up to him to supply the rest of it."

Silver smiled. "That sounds like something Tater might say."

"Tater reminds me of him, now you mention it," Darcy said, sending a mental apology to the trainer at his family's farm, who was thirty-five if he was a day.

"Tater thought I was nuts when I told him I was going to enter this horse in the Rosemont Cup."

"You are?"

"Sure as I was born a blonde!"

"A born blonde? Now that's something you don't see every day." He grinned. "A born-again blonde, perhaps, but not a true one."

Silver stopped and gave him a cool stare. "Well, you've seen one now."

"I don't know, Silver. I'd like to trust you, but I might have to do some exploration to make sure," he said, his gaze skimming down her luscious body.

"My God, you have such a one-track mind." Her quick head shake caused her horse to skitter to the side, immediately drawing her attention back to him. "Shh, shh, now," she soothed, "it's all right."

Darcy glanced at the black stallion pacing at their side. The horse responded by flicking his ears and giving him a look that said quite specifically he'd best not think him too tame and malleable yet or he might end up missing a few fingers. There was just enough temperament in this horse to make him a formidable competitor, Darcy thought, as well as a discipline problem. It reminded him of...of— "Where'd you get this horse, anyway?"

"Daddy won him in a poker game."

He could feel his jaw drop. "What? You're kidding me."

Silver chuckled. "Nope. True as I'm standing on Kentucky earth, Daddy won him in a game. He had a lousy hand, too, he said, but he pulled a Braybourne bluff."

"What the hell's a Braybourne bluff?"

Lashes lowered, the picture of innocence, she sent him a sideways peep. "Well, now, that's a Braybourne secret weapon. We only use it when the situation is desperate. And the great thing is, once we've used it, no one ever knows if it's real or not."

"There's some magic formula you apply?"

"Nope. Simplicity is the key." Giving him a teasing little grin, she slipped the coiled rope to her shoulder and used her free hand to demonstrate. "You look at your cards and make an assessment—what have I got, what do I wish I had, what do they think I have? Then you just up and follow through."

"Carpe diem, eh?" *Ah, the benefits of a good education*, he thought as he met her surprised eyes at his use of the Latin term.

"That's right...'seize the day.' Or as my granddaddy used to say, grab that old day by the throat and don't let it go until you've squeezed everything out of it you can get."

Darcy laughed. "I think I would have liked your granddaddy."

"He was as stubborn as my father, but I loved him to death. What about your family? Are they—"

He cut her off, figuring he'd better steer the conversation back into safer channels. "So your father won this horse in a game? Someone actually bet a horse?"

"Daddy was playing poker with some of his old cronies one night at the Horse and Bridle Club, when some guy he didn't know came up and asked if he could take the empty seat at the table. Well, naturally Daddy and the others didn't object, 'cause..."

Darcy's eyes twinkled. He could just see the scene. "He was fresh pickings?"

Silver's eyes twinkled right back. "Right. And the pot had been changing hands all night. So they told him to pull up a chair, and he did. Daddy said that man played like he meant to lose every penny. Finally, he put up a horse so he could stay in the game."

"What else would you put up, right?"

Silver nodded with a sly grin. "Naturally, everyone had been sipping Kentucky bourbon—just to keep the whistle wet while they played. So when the man put the horse on the table, figuratively speaking, no one thought too much of it. Next thing you know, Daddy won a pot of money and a horse. The next day, the guy had left the horse tied up to Daddy's pickup truck, and disappeared."

"At least he was honorable and paid his debts."

"That's what Daddy thought, until he got the horse home and discovered not the profitable Thoroughbred racer he'd expected, but a problem in the making. There's not much you can do with an undisciplined racehorse, unless you want to spend a lot of time starting from scratch. In which case, there's no prospect of fast, easy money from any wins, only bills for feed and care." She glanced at Lucky Hand. "This guy was hellbent on making everyone's life miserable for a while."

"What's his ancestry?"

"Daddy said the guy told him something about the horse being born and raised in Virginia. But I've been too busy to check his lineage as yet."

"Virginia?" Darcy turned and took a better look at Lucky

Hand, this time studying every aspect of the horse without trying to give away his intense interest. "How old is he?"

"Three years old, I'd say."

He cast his mind back. Virginia... Just then Lucky Hand turned to look down his nose at him. One glance was all it took now that Darcy was primed with a bit of information. That one haughty, watchful glance and Darcy nailed the connection that had been eluding him. *Take a Chance.* He'd swear this was one of Take a Chance's colts. Three years ago they'd bred Take a Chance with Mistress Mine at his farm. He was sure this horse was a result of that union. He swept his gaze over the black again, coming back to see the horse watching him, assessing him. Darcy could appreciate Lucky Hand's caution. Arrogance and charm, that's what the stallion would have gotten from his sire and dam, if he was right. And Darcy was sure he was right.

"So, uh," he said, clearing his throat to break the silence. "What happened after you got him home, besides him being a handful, I mean?"

Silver smoothed her hand over Lucky Hand's neck. "I fell in love," she said simply. "I took one look at him, at his distrust and his pride in not letting anyone know he was afraid, and I fell in love. I looked into his eyes and I knew he was something special. No one had ever helped him see that before. Or at least not recently they hadn't."

"Not every pairing of horse and buyer is ideal. You know that."

"I know. I'm sure some of our horses might be in the same boat." She frowned. "I hope not, though. As breeders, we try to keep a close eye on what happens to our stock."

"You're a small operation, so it's probably easier. Big operations don't always know what happens after the initial sale."

She bristled. "I like to think of us as having a personal touch, not being a small operation."

Shut up before you say something you shouldn't. "Okay, so you fell in love and...?"

"Decided to train him. I thought I could straighten him out.

And I badgered my dad until he agreed that I could try. Then I got this idea that I should race him.''

"But isn't the Rosemont Cup only about six weeks away?"

"Yes, but Lucky Hand is coming along so fast. It's almost as if we've turned a corner this last month, as if he's finally decided he might begin to trust me, to obey without thinking. Besides,'' she said, her expression eager, "I know he wants to race. I can just feel it. And it's a good thing, because we really need the money this race could bring.''

Darcy nodded, trying to keep his sympathy off his face. Silver wouldn't care for sympathy, he knew. She had too much pride. "Your dad and Tater indicated that things were a bit tight," he said, his voice careful and understated. "But to set your sights on winning a race like the Rosemont—isn't that a bit risky?''

Silver grinned. "Aren't you the one who said I was a gambler at heart?''

"Yes, but it's always best to gamble when you have a high probability of winning. There must be another way to get some cash if you really need it so much—''

"Oh, and what do you suggest?''

"Sylvia, Sylvia...'' A man's loud voice broke into their conversation.

"Oh, God...'' Silver groaned.

Darcy glanced over his shoulder to see a tall blond man sauntering their way, with Harden at his side. "Don't bet on it. He looks more ordinary than that.''

Rolling her eyes, Silver groaned again. "He is. Much more ordinary, unless you count his good looks, his money, his position, his connections, his—''

"There you go. The answer to your prayers.''

"John Tom is the answer to many women's prayers. Unfortunately, I'm not one of them.''

5

JOHN TOM THOMAS approached with all the insouciance of a man who had no idea he was about to sink into quicksand. With Harden a step behind, he strolled right up to Silver and planted himself in front of her as if he knew he was the most welcome sight in the universe.

"Well, well, well, Silver, look who's here," Harden said in a hearty voice as he kept a wary eye on his daughter. "I almost ran your young man down in the driveway a few minutes ago, he was so anxious to get here. Right, John Tom?"

"Sylvia." The immaculately dressed John Tom smiled, his full attention on Silver. His voice reminded Darcy of how cloying hot fudge sauce could be.

Silver opened her mouth to speak, then glanced at her father. Instead of blasting him, as Darcy thought she would, judging by the expression on her face, she merely sighed. "John Tom, how long have we known each other?"

"Oh, since grade school, maybe?"

"Right. And how long have I been asking you to call me Silver?"

John Tom smiled. "I like the name Sylvia. It's my mother's middle name. So she approves, too."

Of the name or of Silver? Darcy wondered.

Silver planted a fist on her hip. "Well, big f—" Harden's coughing fit overpowered the rest of her sentence.

Darcy couldn't help laughing, but did it so softly that he was surprised when Silver whirled on him. He wagged his finger. "Uh-uh. Misplaced anger." At his comment, he honestly thought Silver would explode, but he'd underestimated her. After a moment's struggle, she regained her control and turned back to the two men, who were now paying more attention to the horse as they discussed the finer points of equine beauty.

"It doesn't matter what he looks like, John Tom," Harden was saying. "This horse is—"

"I agree, Harden," John Tom interrupted.

Darcy stepped forward as he saw the horse's ears flatten. It wouldn't do to have the stallion beat up on a neighbor. But Silver already had a soothing hand on his back.

John Tom didn't seem to notice as he continued, "I don't know why you've still got him hang—"

"Back up there a bit, John Tom," Silver snapped. "You're going to spook him."

"Don't be silly, Sylvia. I've been around horses my entire life. I know how to handle them."

"That's right, Silv—uh, Sylvia," her father echoed. "John Tom has one of the best farms in the county."

Darcy thought it was time he spoke up, instead of standing like a country bumpkin. "Congratulations. That's a real achievement in this area, isn't it?"

"John Tom," Harden said immediately, "this is Rick Darcy. He's helping us out for a while."

"Oh?" John Tom sent Darcy a penetrating look. "Doing what?"

Darcy was tempted to tell him he'd been hired as a stud service, but he managed to hold his tongue, aware that Silver would probably make him pay for the comment.

"Darcy's helping manage things for a bit," Harden said, with a sideways glance at Silver. "At least that's what I hired him for yesterday."

"That's great, Harden. This way Sylvia will have a bit more time."

"No, I won't."

John Tom sent her a surprised look. "Well, Sylvia, since you're constantly telling me you can't go out because you have to oversee this, or you're behind in that, I'd think a temporary manager would be a huge relief."

"Well, it's not."

"Thanks," Darcy said under his breath as he practically choked on his chuckle. This woman could be so damn contrary. Damn if he didn't want to grab her and kiss her until her eyes crossed.

"Silver, there's no need to be rude."

"I'm not being rude, Daddy, I'm being truthful." She sent Darcy a look that practically singed his eyebrows. "You know how I feel about this temporary manager thing."

"Sylvia," John Tom said, in a very reasonable manner, "surely there are other things you could be doing with your time. More important things, such as..."

Silver's eyes narrowed. "Such as?"

"Well, there's the autumn ball, for example. My sister is on the planning committee and she was saying just yesterday how much taste you have and wouldn't it be great for you to co-chair with her."

"I have other commitments," Silver said flatly.

"What other commitments?" Harden asked pointedly.

"None of your nevermind, Daddy."

Her father planted his feet in the dirt, obviously ready to make a stand. "Maybe I could ask your mother to pick up some of those commitments."

Not to be outdone by her father, Silver planted her feet in a perfect imitation of his stubbornness. "Absolutely not. They're my responsibility."

Harden's jaw jutted forward. "What exactly are you referring to?"

"Sylvia, I'm sorry if I've caused a problem here," John Tom murmured. "I just thought—"

Glancing from one Braybourne to the other, Darcy figured he'd better practice some casual diplomacy before father and daughter came to blows. "I think what Silver means, Harden, is that she has to get Lucky Hand ready for the race."

"What race?"

Tossing her head, Silver said, "The Rosemont Cup." The words hung in the air, leaving behind the impression that any man with half a brain should have realized that intention already without her even telling him.

"Silver, did you fall on your head this morning? What in the hell are you talkin' about—the Rosemont Cup! Of all the—"

Chin lifted, Silver reached up and draped her arm over Lucky Hand's shoulder and faced her father. "I am entering him in the Rosemont Cup," she said, over-enunciating each word.

Darcy couldn't help but respect Silver's strong stand, partially because he'd never really taken such a position about anything. Maybe it was time he started.

Harden's mouth fell open before he closed it enough to snarl, "Are you crazy? Did I raise a loony bird?"

"I know I can win."

"This damn horse can't even get a quarter mile without having a temper tantrum, or just plain refusing to run. What makes you think you can haul his hindquarters around a mile-long track?"

"I know I can because I've been working this horse every day for the last month and a half, and I'm making real progress. I've got six weeks to go, and I'm going to give him every minute of my time."

Harden stepped toward his daughter. "You don't have that much time, missy."

Silver took a step, too, leaning forward until they were practically nose to nose. "Well, I'll tell you what, Daddy—why don't you put your money where your mouth is?"

Darcy chuckled. This woman was a real firecracker when something set her off. Her father ought to know that by now. But still Harden leaped in with no thought for his own safety. Darcy wasn't sure if that was courage or just plain cussedness.

"Now you listen to me, Silver Braybourne—"

"No, sir, I don't think I will. Because you're just going to say something I don't want to hear, and worse than that, you're going to insult the black." She turned away from her father and practically hovered over Lucky Hand, a mother protecting her child. "I can't allow that. His ego is still fragile."

"Oh, for—Silver, he's a horse."

"He's still got feelings, Daddy. He listens to our tone of voice—and how do you know he doesn't understand every single word we're saying?"

"Sylvia, Sylvia..." John Tom shook his head, the picture of patronizing patience. "I don't know where you came up with that, but horses aren't that intell—"

"Butt out, John Tom."

Harden's eyes snapped. "By gawd, young lady, you're not too big to turn over my knee."

Darcy grinned; he couldn't help it. The thought of Harden turning Silver over his knee for a "good wallop," as his nanny used to say, might be as entertaining as watching a good sporting match. He glanced from a flushed Harden to an equally flushed Silver. No. Make that more entertaining. At this rate the winner would probably be even money.

"Now, Harden, calm down. You know your daughter's sense of humor." John Tom had either the nerve or the idiocy to step between the Braybournes. "She didn't mean to be disrespectful, did you, Sylvia?"

"I certainly did."

John Tom laughed and dropped an arm around her shoulders, squeezing her close. "Always teasing. You always did have such high spirits."

Silver's eyes searched for, then found Darcy's. He couldn't help but respond to the appeal he saw there. The appeal that plainly said, *Get me out of this before I kill one of them.* Darcy couldn't ignore a woman in distress. Besides, he didn't like the proprietary way John Tom was touching her.

"Talking of high spirits, Harden," Darcy said, "this horse might be full of them. I'd agree with that, but I don't think he's beyond redemption. I think Silver has the right—"

Before Harden had an opportunity to open his mouth, John Tom said, "Excuse me, but you've been here less than a day, haven't you?"

Darcy could feel the other man measuring him, trying to decide if he was some type of threat to him, or just another hired

hand. *Okay, you want a threat, I'll give you a threat. You're just a bit too cocksure to please me.* "Sometimes a day is all it takes to make a decision," Darcy said, being careful to keep his back to Harden as he deliberately let his gaze slide from Lucky Hand to roam leisurely over Silver.

Silver's eyes widened as she met his. Then an unholy appreciation at his effrontery filled her eyes. "Especially when you see something you think is possible," she stated.

"Everything's possible if you want it bad enough," Darcy answered, his voice low and intimate, aware that the man in front of him was beginning to puff out until he resembled a stuffed fish.

John Tom opened his mouth, then closed it with a snap as Harden said, "Making this horse a winner isn't one of them. The man I won him from said he couldn't get him to race 'cause he was too temperamental. Plus, he paid too much attention to the other horses. The man tried blinders, he tried everything, but he finally had to—"

Silver shrugged off John Tom's arm and stepped around him to face her father. "Maybe he just wasn't any good as a trainer."

Harden surprised her by nodding. "I'll go along with that. From the way the guy was talking, he didn't have much of a clue of what it took to train a horse. I'm not even sure how he got a piece of horseflesh like this. He said something about taking it off somebody's hands as a favor, but I didn't get any more than that."

Darcy turned to face Harden. "Some people see a Thoroughbred and just see dollar signs. They don't think of the effort it takes to train a fine horse." The mystery of Lucky Hand had just deepened. How had this horse gotten into this mess, anyway? He'd have to check it out.

John Tom's brows lifted. "And you're familiar with that, are you?"

"I'd say so," Darcy said, keeping his voice level even as he read the implied insult in the other man's voice.

"How's that?"

Darcy glanced at the tall man, who was now bristling. He knew John Tom was itching to find out who he was and where he was from. He would, in his circumstances, especially if it involved a woman like Silver.

The trick now would be saying just enough without revealing too much, or inviting the guy to question him further. Darcy smiled and said, "I've been around winners all my life."

"That so?"

"It is. So I can recognize a Thoroughbred when I see one, whether he's got four legs or two." After a moment, Darcy pulled his gaze from John Tom's and focused on Harden. "Now, Harden, Silver, this horse has been standing long enough, don't you think? Why don't I walk him out some more to cool him down before we work him again?" He glanced at Silver. "You are planning to give him a good gallop on the track today, aren't you?"

"Yes. I am."

"Right." He began to turn the horse, saying over his shoulder, "You just stay here and visit with your young man..." Darcy used Harden's term and let the pause extend for a moment, just to see what she'd do. To his amazement, she held her tongue, although it was probably choking her to do so. He winked at her and walked away. Lord, teasing Silver Braybourne could become a habit. One he'd be very happy to continue. Not that he could, of course. Four weeks from now he'd be history here. Four weeks in which he might figure out what he wanted to do with himself.

He glanced at the horse walking by his side. *Maybe you can help.* Darcy grinned as the black sent him a look that firmly indicated he wouldn't make it easy on anyone. He'd much rather do it his own way.

Darcy understood the horse's attitude. It had been the story of his very privileged life so far, even if he'd never really admitted it before. But an easy ride wasn't what he'd find at Braybourne Farm, and that was one of the things he was finding so appealing. The other— He smiled as he patted Lucky Hand's midnight-black coat, thinking instead of the woman with moonlight hair. Darcy wasn't sure who would be the bigger challenge, the woman he had to tame or the horse. Damn if he wasn't itching to get started with both of them.

SILVER WATCHED DARCY stroll away, leading Lucky Hand. She'd give her last pair of boots to be with them at the moment. There was a similarity about the two of them that had just now struck her. Perhaps it was nothing more than their darker-than-night coloring. Perhaps it was the swagger when they walked, both of them obviously aware of their male power and beauty. They both had that cocky attitude that promised no one would put a rope on them unless they wanted it. And even then it would have to be on their own terms.

Silver's blood raced at the challenge. Even as she told herself not to get involved with Darcy, she couldn't help but dream. After all, a woman could dream, couldn't she? And a man like Rick Darcy was as much something to dream about as developing Lucky Hand into a winning racehorse. But she had to admit that what would keep her going was the thrill of the journey. To her mind, getting there was most of the fun. The rest was anticlimactic. There was a seductive challenge to bringing both man and beast to heel.

Eyes riveted on Darcy's tight buttocks and long legs as he strolled across the grass, she found herself regretting that she'd decided to follow her head where he was concerned. It would be much more satisfying to follow her desires.

"Well, if you two'll excuse me, I have to leave you alone." Harden's voice broke into her thoughts, his heavy-handed attempt at playing Cupid making her frown. "I've got to make a phone call. I'll be up at the house. Stop by before you leave, all right, Son?" Ignoring his daughter, he gave John Tom a quick clasp on the shoulder and then hobbled away.

It was a good thing he didn't say anything to her, Silver thought, or she might have told him what she thought of his tactics. She didn't want to face John Tom, so she refocused on Darcy, trying to pretend she was actually observing her horse.

John Tom was doing the same. "Who is that guy, Sylvia? He was very familiar with you, don't you think?"

"Familiar?" She glanced at the man by her side. "Oh, God, John Tom, you sound like a nineteenth century novel."

"Okay, then I'll use a more modern term. He looked as if he wanted to get into your pants. How's that?"

"John Tom!" Silver could feel herself turning as red as a fall apple, and forced down a panicked chuckle. If he only knew that a few hours earlier Darcy had not only tried to get into her pants, she'd helped him do it.

"You wanted modern, you got modern," John Tom said, his expression turning sulky.

Silver glared at him. "Even so, what a thing to say."

"He was flirting with you. You saw that, didn't you?"

"You're imagining things."

"No, trust me, I was not imagining things. A man knows when another guy is trying to poach on his territory."

"Territory?" she asked, her tone dangerous, her eyes narrowed.

"That's right."

Her chin lifted and her shoulders squared. "I'm nobody's territory."

"Sylvia," John Tom said, his tone a bit exasperated, "you know very well what's expected of us here."

"Not by me."

"Oh, for... We've been together since we were teenagers."

"Barring about ten other girlfriends on your part, and at least one serious boyfriend on mine. Remember?"

John Tom waved his hand. "None of that meant anything."

"It didn't, huh?"

"No...just wild oats. All men have to sow them."

"News flash—so do women. And I'm not done sowing mine. As a matter of fact, I'm just getting started."

John Tom's face darkened as he glared at her. "Both of our families agree it would be a good thing for us to settle down together."

"Well, I haven't agreed to any such thing."

"Sylvia..."

She whirled to face him. "Will you quite saying 'Sylvia' in that tone of voice? You're treating me like a two-year-old having a tantrum."

John Tom, making an obvious effort to control his temper, folded his arms. "Aren't you?"

"No, I'm damn well not. I am expressing my opinion. Something you, your family and mine seem to have forgotten matters."

He attempted to put his hands on her shoulders. "Are you hurt because I haven't made my intentions clearer before now? Because—"

"John Tom, I swear you have a head thicker than Kentucky limestone," she retorted, slapping them away. "I am not hurt. I am angry that you assume I'll just kick up my heels and...and—"

"Marry me?"

Lord, she couldn't even bring herself to say the *M* word, so she just muttered, "Right—that."

John Tom patted her hand. "You know what? I think you just need a bit of time to get used to it. Marriage is a big step. For me, too."

Either his ego knew no bounds, or his lack of comprehension was larger than she'd imagined. But if she had to choose, she'd bet on the ego. John Tom had always had a high opinion of himself. An opinion reinforced by his doting relatives, his good looks and his money. He was a sought-after bachelor. All the girls Silver had grown up with sharpened their weapons whenever he was around. He just wasn't what she wanted by her side for the rest of her life. Lord have mercy, she wanted to kill the man after ten minutes, which didn't seem propitious for happily ever after. Besides, it hadn't taken more than a few dates with him over the last four months to convince her that the good-looking boy she'd once had such a crush on no longer had any power to make her insides tingle, unless you counted the flutter of her eyelids as she tried to keep them open.

As if triggered by the memory of those dates, a yawn broke

through, her jaws stretching so far open she thought they would break.

John Tom squeezed her. "You're tired. No wonder you're so cranky."

"I am not cranky."

He laughed, a genuine laugh that lighted his face. "No, of course not."

She shook her head as she studied John Tom's smiling face. When he just relaxed, he could be quite charming. Not charming enough for her to want to marry him, but at least to have a conversation without wanting to strangle him. She rubbed her eyes. "I'm tired because I didn't get much sleep last night."

"See? That's my point. You need help."

"I have help. I have Darcy, remember?" Her face set in its most contrary lines as she focused on his quick frown. She might not have wanted Darcy's help, but she had it, and now that John Tom so patently disapproved, she was bound and determined to fight to the death to keep it.

"I might be able to turn someone loose from my farm temporarily."

"There is absolutely no need to do that. And I don't appreciate your butting in, either."

"Sylvia—"

"John Tom." Silver straightened to her full height and flung her arm across her forehead, allowing her voice to raise. "You're giving me a headache. And when I get a headache I start to cry. And when I start to cry, I get hysterical—you didn't know that, did you? And when I get hysterical..." Her voice rose with each sentence until she was screeching like an owl on the hunt.

John Tom clapped his hands over his ears. "Goddamn, you nearly broke my eardrums." Silver almost giggled at his involuntary reaction, but he quickly got himself back under control. "Do you have a headache? I can help with a headache because my mother gets these horrid migraines. Would you like me to rub your neck?"

"No. I just need to get out of the sun and into the shade. I'm going to go into the stables to sit down."

"Oh, good idea." He started backing up. "I'll call you later. I'll just say goodbye to your parents before I leave."

Silver didn't answer him. She was concentrating on looking as if she was a woman in the midst of an attack, instead of one who wanted to attack. From the corner of her eye she watched as he walked across the grass toward the gate that led to the yard. Checking to be certain he wasn't looking back, she sprinted across the pasture to the stables and dashed inside.

Stopping right inside the door, she took a deep breath. She hadn't been putting him on, at least not completely. She *was* getting a headache. She inhaled again, her senses soothed by the scent of hay and horses, by the cool shady interior. She could feel herself begin to relax. The familiar atmosphere always affected her this way. It was the one place she really felt at home. Thanks to her upbringing, she could handle herself in any situation, from high-class social occasions to an informal sit-around-and-grouse session with farm hands. But here in the stables was the place she liked best. Her preoccupation with horses had begun in childhood, turning into the passion for horses that all young girls possessed. Probably something Freudian there, she thought with a chuckle, but when wasn't something Freudian? Sigmund Freud had been obsessed with sex. But in her case that young girl's passion had never faded. It had only grown more intense and committed over the years. Now, when she wanted to make it her life's work, she seemed to be surrounded by men who wanted to mold her into something else. There was one thing she was determined on—no one would force her in any direction that, deep down in her heart, she didn't really want to go. No one. Not her father, not her mother, not John Tom, not Tater, not even—

"It won't work, so you might as well cut the attitude."

Startled, Silver turned her head in the direction of the teasing drawl. She smiled as she heard Darcy talking to Lucky Hand.

"You can ignore me all you want, big guy, but eventually

you'll come around. You know why? Because I can be as stubborn as you are, that's why."

Creeping closer to the stall, she could see Darcy wiping Lucky Hand down, then running his palm down the horse's legs to check for any tenderness. Darcy saw her as he turned to reach for the saddle he'd slung over the half door.

"Lover boy gone?"

Silver thrilled as she heard a bit of jealousy in his voice, regardless of how he'd tried to hide it. "He's saying goodbye to my parents."

"Humph."

To Silver, Darcy's snort sounded very much like Lucky Hand's when he was completely, totally disgusted with the proceedings. Amused, she leaned on the gate, folding her arms. "Pardon? Were you trying to communicate with me or the horse?"

Darcy sent her a dry look. "You're not really going to marry that stuffed shirt, are you?"

Silver could see he resented asking the question. "Why?"

He waved his hand. "Forget I asked. You couldn't consider it. Not after we—"

"Well..." Silver decided to keep him guessing for a bit. The man was too sure of himself. Look how he assumed there would be a next time between them. Did the word *no* mean nothing to anyone anymore? Did all the men in her life have heads as thick as bricks? "It's my father's deepest desire."

"What about you? What about your deepest desire?"

He met her eyes, looking fully confident that she would say he was the answer to her prayers. Which was why she abruptly denied it. "There are some distinct advantages to a union with John Tom."

"You make it sound like a merger."

"I think that's the way my father sees it."

"I'm not surprised. Fathers generally think that way because deep down they believe there's no one in the world really good enough for their little girl. So they might as well make it materialistic. That way they won't have to worry about their darlings being taken care of in the future."

"You sound as if you know something about fathers trying to marry off their daughters."

"Believe it. I've got firsthand experience. Once I barely escaped with my hair."

Silver chuckled. "That bad, huh?"

Sending her a rueful glance, Darcy slung the saddle over Lucky Hand's back and began to buckle the girth. "The only reason I'm still standing today is because the girl was persuaded she was mistaken in her affections."

"By you?"

"I had help."

"What kind of help?"

"My law—uh..." He reached for the bridle before he continued. "My *lawless* cousin, Nick, came to my rescue, guns blazing."

"Cousin Nick sounds like a handy guy to have around."

"He is." Darcy turned back, to finish slipping the bit into Lucky Hand's mouth. Before Silver could probe further, he handed her a riding helmet and reached to open the stall door. "Let's see what this guy can do, okay?"

"Okay," she said, stepping back to give them room to clear the door.

He led the black into the aisle and turned to give Silver a leg up into the saddle. "How long is the track you've got here?"

Settling in, she adjusted the stirrups. "Only about a quarter of a mile."

He walked past her, escorting them out of the stables into the light. "How're you building his stamina?"

"I've been doing it by repetition. But now I'm ready to take him to a longer track where we can work on a sustained burst of speed before the first turn."

"Where's that?"

"Not far, three or four miles. We'll have to truck him. The track belongs to one of our neighbors." She turned the horse toward a pasture to the west of the stables. "I haven't done it yet because I didn't want Lucky Hand exposed to other horses. I wanted to work with him more before I did that."

Darcy held open a gate. "From what I'm hearing, that's a smart decision."

"I thought so."

They walked the field in silence for a few moments, Silver pulling her concentration from the man by her side to the horse. Only an idiot would sit on this much power and speed and not concentrate. She could feel Lucky Hand begin to strain under her hand. He wanted to run. He was born to run. It was just that somewhere along the way he'd gotten off track. She leaned forward and patted his neck, whispering into his ear, "Don't worry, baby, you're going to get your chance. I'm going to see to it."

When they got to the track, she kept him under strict control for a few laps, working him in an easy canter, feeling his stride. *He's improved*, she thought. There was a smoothness to his gait that had been missing when she'd first started working with him. It was as if he was suddenly remembering what he should be doing. Silver knew it wasn't just remembering, though, as much as retraining. Horses responded to repetition and consistency. She'd been working on his stride, on his response to the bit and to the weight on his back. But more than that, making Lucky Hand the competitor he was born to be depended on giving him back his confidence. Bad things happened when confidence failed—to animals as well as people.

After one more lap she turned him loose. His stride extended into a gallop and he started to fly. The air rushed by her, fanning her cheeks. She worked him hard, then steadily backed off, until finally they walked over to where Darcy stood by the fence. His gaze was intense, if slightly puzzled.

She removed her helmet, raking her fingers through her hair. "Something wrong?"

"Huh?" He pulled his gaze from the horse and stared up at her. "Oh, no. Nothing."

"You look kind of funny."

He reached up to help her dismount. She dropped her reins,

so the horse would stand still as trained, then she threw her leg over and slid down. When she reached the ground, Darcy's hands were still around her waist, and she stood trapped between the horse and him.

"Probably the sight of your tidy little behind sticking up in the air."

She chuckled. "That sounds like you."

"Does it? But you don't know me, remember?"

"No. That's right, I don't."

He pulled her a bit closer so she had no choice but to practically snuggle up against his hard body. "But you'd like to, right?"

"Well..." She hesitated because she wanted so badly to say yes. She knew it would be a mistake, but she did want to know him; she couldn't deny it. She found him a complete paradox. That intrigued her as much as, if not more than, his obvious sexuality and heartbreaking looks. "It would be helpful to know you better if we're going to work together, I guess."

"I agree."

"I'm not talking in the biblical sense, you understand."

"Damn, there goes all my hope. Thanks for shooting that down."

She gave him an arch look. "I thought I shot that down earlier this morning."

"Not completely. You just wounded me. I still have hopes of recovery."

"Nothing's changed, Darcy. With my head cool, I realize it would have been a disaster, no matter how I tried to justify it."

"Disasters can bring out the best in people."

"They can also bring out the worst."

"So you won't let me make love to you so you can save me from myself?"

Because she was tempted, she evaded him by joking, "I have never met a man so able to twist and turn a conversation to his advantage in my entire life."

"Not even the resident boyfriend?"

"No, he's just obtuse, not sneaky."

"Sneaky? I've got to tell you, that cuts deep."

"I think you'll survive."

He pulled her even closer, until she had no choice but to put her arms around his neck—anything else was uncomfortable. At least that's what she told herself.

His gaze burned her, setting fires everywhere it touched. "There's more to life than surviving, Silver."

"But surviving is what we're here to do."

"Not entirely. We're here to enjoy, too. And to my mind there's nothing more enjoyable than this." His head swooped down, his mouth taking hers.

If he had forced her, she could have resisted him. But no one could resist this gentle, teasing pressure. No one could mistake the enjoyment of his lips as they rested on hers, never once presuming, just giving her a choice to respond or not.

Not? How could she not respond to a man as skilled as Darcy? Even in the full sun he had the seductive quality of darkness about him. A hot, welcoming darkness where anything was possible and everything was desirable. With a sigh, she relaxed against him. Still he didn't take the kiss further. Instead, he stroked the tip of his tongue over her lips, almost as if he were a cat licking rich cream.

She shivered, tightening her arms as she instinctively fitted her body more closely to his. Silver was still revved up from her exhilarating ride. She could still feel the vibration, the thundering pounding in her thighs, that shivering, almost sexual sensation that came when she let her horse and her spirit fly free. She needed that feeling now. Since Darcy wasn't taking the lead, she did. She opened her mouth and teased until she felt his hunger grow. Her tongue tangled with his as they strained against each other, their breath mingling as their bodies longed to do. His hands were slipping down her back, cupping her buttocks, arching her against him when they were suddenly forced apart.

Shocked, they both stared at Lucky Hand, whose head had butted theirs. Then the horse tossed his mane as if to say enough is enough.

Reluctantly, Darcy let her go. "It's not enough I have to contend with your two-legged boyfriend—now I have to fight off a four-legged monster as well?" He laughed.

Recalled to her surroundings, Silver cast one horror-stricken look around and groaned.

"Silver, don't worry. No one can see us."

"I...you...every time I get near you..."

"I know. It's a bitch, isn't it?"

That surprised a laugh from her. "Yes, yes it is," she agreed as she met his rueful eyes.

"It's not any better for me. I mean, every time I turn around I'm..."

"You're what?" she whispered.

Frustrated, he rammed his hand through his hair. "Damn it, Silver, I can't keep my hands off you."

She giggled, thrilled at his rough tone. "I know. It's a problem."

"A problem? No, it's not a problem. It's a disaster, is what it is. I don't know how to handle this situation. It just dawned on me that you're actually my employer's daughter. I've never had that problem before."

"Your previous employers didn't have daughters?" she teased.

"I've never worked for anyone before, so I'm not quite up on the protocol."

"You've never worked for anyone?"

'No. I mean..." A strange look rushed over his face.

"Did you find the secret for manufacturing money or something, so you didn't have to work for a living?"

"No. No, what I meant was I've functioned kind of independently."

"Independently. Worked for yourself, you mean?"

"Sort of. I didn't have to consider other people, exactly. I just followed my own road, I guess you could say. But now there's you." He shook his head. "I wasn't looking for you. I was just looking for an ad—" He broke off abruptly.

"A what?"

"Never mind, Silver. Because now I think I've really been looking for something else all the time. I think I've been looking for me. Trying to find myself."

Her expression softened. "I'm doing the same."

"And you're not supposed to be part of that."

She was hurt in spite of herself. "I know that. You're not part of it for me, either."

"Besides, I'm trying to get away from the type of women I've been—" Again he broke off.

"Well, don't let me stop you." She jerked her thumb. "There's the road. Hit it, buddy."

"Don't you understand? I can't."

"Why not? We'll get along without you. We did before. We will again."

"Oh hell. Okay then, will you marry me?" he blurted, then turned absolutely white.

Her eyes practically bugged out of her head. "What? No, of course not. We don't want to marry each other. We don't even know each other." God knows where that had come from. She knew Darcy wasn't serious, he was just ticked off, frustrated and impulsive. What would the idiot have done if she'd said yes? Not that she would have. She'd obviously responded as impulsively as he.

"I know." He closed his eyes, gnashing his teeth. "I don't know why I said that. It just slipped out. I don't want to get married."

"Me neither."

"Okay, so we agree, marriage is out. Next solution, how about you just bite the bullet and go to bed with me instead?"

Silver clasped a hand over her breast. "Oh, be still my heart. How could any woman refuse such a romantic proposition?"

Darcy grinned. "See what you're doing to me? I can't even think straight."

Silver reached for Lucky Hand's reins. "How about we get to know each other instead?"

"That'd be good. And we'll make a pact. No touching. Even

if we're tempted. 'Cause every time I touch you I get in big trouble."

After a rueful glance at him, she began walking back across the field. "Okay, you're on. We'll get to know each other."

Falling into step with her, he asked, "How?"

"How what?"

"How do you want to go about it?"

"I don't know. Maybe I could draw up a business plan and get back to you."

He grinned. "Until then maybe we could just talk."

She couldn't help but grin back. "Talk?"

"You're familiar with the concept? Friendly conversation. No shouting or yelling, no ultimatums. Look, why don't we go for a friendly ride later. You could show me around town or something. Maybe we could stop and get something to eat."

"I, uh..." Talking was one thing, but an entire evening spent in his company? Much as she'd love to, she was afraid.

"That is if you don't have other plans with lover boy this evening?"

"Lover boy! I have no plans to—" She caught sight of Darcy's satisfied smile. "I fell into that, didn't I? You mentioned him to force me to accept, didn't you?"

"Me? What makes you think I'd do something like that?"

"'Cause I have a feeling you play dirty."

"I do. And I don't like to lose."

"Neither do I."

"I know, sweetheart, that's what makes you so irresistible. You're like this gorgeous flower that snaps closed when you get too close."

She stopped. "I know we've slipped a bit, but we have to remember what happened this morning."

His eyes swept over her. "Trust me, I've memorized every detail."

"No, when I say remember, I meant remember that I said there'd be no more..." Her voice lacked conviction, but she'd work on it.

He smoothed his hand over her hair. "Mmm...that's right.

You did, didn't you. But then, I always say, who knows what's in a woman's mind?" He played with the end of a lock, leaning a bit closer. "Especially a Southern woman. They're so good at hiding their thoughts when they want to."

She bit her lip. "Darcy." To her relief he shoved his hands into his pockets.

Giving her a businesslike look, he asked briskly, "What time do you want to leave? How's seven? Unless you want to go earlier?"

"Seven would be good. I have too much to do the rest of the day to go before."

"Me, too. It's settled then."

Silver nodded. "I'm going to take Lucky Hand in and hose him down."

"Don't forget to ice his legs. You might even use some liniment. You ran him pretty hard."

Just that little bit of bossiness snapped Silver out of her fog, the fog she was in danger of drifting into every time he touched her. "Of course I won't forget. I've been taking care of horses for a long time. And I've been taking care of this one since he arrived, so I think I know what I'm supposed to do."

Darcy held up his hands, palms out. "All right, all right, I surrender. I spoke without thinking. I apologize."

"Apology accepted," she snapped as she turned on her heel.

"And don't forget his vitamin mixture."

Don't forget the vitamins? Who the hell does he think he is? Urging her horse to move a bit faster, she led him toward the stable, all the time muttering about the bossy, high-handed, egotistical male she'd left standing in the dirt behind her.

6

DARCY SAT AT THE DESK in the manager's office, the surface littered with papers. He made a notation, then neatly filed the paper he was working on in a manila folder. Instead of being bored, he was finding the work exhilarating. Maybe his cousin was right about it being time to use his mind for something other than thinking up harebrained stunts.

After he'd left Silver, he'd spent the rest of the day updating himself on the Braybourne operations. Harden had reviewed some of the ordering methods and forms, then excused himself to catch up on some correspondence. Darcy thought it more likely that Harden had overdone it during the day and had gone to rest. He knew better than to mention that, however.

Tater had given Darcy a full rundown on every horse in the place, including those they had some hopes for, those who were prime breeders and those they might need to sell sooner than expected. Then Tater had gone his own merry way to finish some personal business.

Silver had taken care of Lucky Hand and then disappeared as well, after blowing back into the office once to collect the farm's accounting books. Since Darcy had been on the phone to his own farm manager at the time, having called him collect to ask some questions about the black stallion he thought might be from their stables, he wasn't inclined to ask her to linger. Much as he would have liked to.

There was just something about that woman that got under his skin. It wasn't anything as obvious as her beauty, although that was considerable. No, it was more the challenge of her. The challenge of taming that fire-and-ice personality of hers. He was tempted to call his cousin to tell him about his situation, but decided Nick would freak the minute he mentioned Silver.

The phone rang. Darcy reached over and picked it up. "Hello, Braybourne Farm. Oh, hi. No, John Tom, Silver's not here. I think she's at the house. Oh, you...well, I don't know what to tell you except, yes, if I see her I'll pass on the message. Eight-thirty at the Derby Club. Right, got it."

Darcy hung up the phone and, shaking his head, scribbled a note. John Tom Thomas might be an okay guy, but he wasn't in Silver's league, and the sooner he realized that the happier he'd be. Not that it was any of Darcy's business. He was destined to be in and out of her life in four weeks. It wasn't as if he was going to make any commitment to her.

Commitment. He clapped his hand to his forehead. *Did I really ask her to marry me?* What the hell kind of crap was that? He'd never resorted to that little trick no matter how frustrated he was. He knew a lot of guys who did, not with their own social strata, but with those they could take advantage of. Darcy had always been vocal about the sleaziness of it all, and now what did he do? Open his mouth and say "Will you marry me?"

Darcy squirmed in his chair. He could just see his grandfather looking down on him, trying to decide whether or not to come and give him a big boot in the butt. At this point, he'd have to bend over and let him, because he deserved it. He hadn't meant to say the words, but he'd looked into Silver's brilliant green eyes and the next thing he knew he was a goner. Thank God she knew he wasn't serious. He buried the uneasy feeling that he could be, given half a chance. After all, he knew that was how his grandfather had married his wife, the love of his life. As a matter of fact, Grandy had proposed a few hours after meeting her, Grandmother said. And they'd had a love affair that lasted until his grandfather's death. Besides, family legend had it that love at first sight happened to all of the first-born Kristof sons. And Darcy was not only firstborn, he was an only child, so there was enough potential about the entire thing to make him wary.

He glanced at the clock. Six-fifteen. He'd better get going if he wanted to grab a shower and find something halfway pre-

GIFTS from the Heart

Play and you can get **2 FREE BOOKS** and a **SURPRISE GIFT!**

GIFTS from the Heart

Play Gifts from the Heart and get 2 FREE Books and a FREE Gift!

HOW TO PLAY:

1. With a coin, carefully scratch off the gold area at the right. Then check the claim chart to see what we have for you — **2 FREE BOOKS** and a **FREE GIFT** — **ALL YOURS FREE!**

2. Send back the card and you'll receive two brand-new Harlequin Temptation® novels. These books have a cover price of $3.99 each in the U.S. and $4.50 each in Canada, but they are yours to keep absolutely free.

3. There's no catch. You're under no obligation to buy anything. We charge nothing —**ZERO** — for your first shipment. And you don't have to make any minimum number of purchases — not even one!

4. The fact is, thousands of readers enjoy receiving books by mail from the Harlequin Reader Service®. They enjoy the convenience of home delivery... they like getting the best new novels at discount prices, **BEFORE** they're available in stores...and they love their *Heart to Heart* subscriber newsletter featuring author news, horoscopes, recipes, book reviews and much more!

5. We hope that after receiving your free books you'll want to remain a subscriber. But the choice is yours — to continue or cancel, any time at all! So why not take us up on our invitation, with no risk of any kind. You'll be glad you did!

A surprise gift FREE!

We can't tell you what it is... but we're sure you'll like it! A

FREE GIFT!

just for playing **GIFTS FROM THE HEART!**

NO COST! NO OBLIGATION TO BUY!
NO PURCHASE NECESSARY!

PLAY GIFTS from the Heart

Scratch off the gold area with a coin.
Then check below to see the gifts you get!

YES! I have scratched off the gold area. Please send me the 2 Free books and gift for which I qualify. I understand I am under no obligation to purchase any books as explained on the back and on the opposite page.

342 HDL DNL4   142 HDL DNLS

FIRST NAME	LAST NAME

ADDRESS

APT.#	CITY

STATE/PROV.	ZIP/POSTAL CODE

 2 free books plus a surprise gift

 2 free books   1 free book

(H-T-05/02)

The Harlequin Reader Service® — Here's how it works:

Accepting your 2 free books and gift places you under no obligation to buy anything. You may keep the books and gift and return the shipping statement marked "cancel." If you do not cancel, about a month later we'll send you 4 additional books and bill you just $3.34 each in the U.S., or $3.80 each in Canada, plus 25¢ shipping & handling per book and applicable taxes if any.* That's the complete price and — compared to cover prices of $3.99 each in the U.S. and $4.50 each in Canada — it's quite a bargain! You may cancel at any time, but if you choose to continue, every month we'll send you 4 more books, which you may either purchase at the discount price or return to us and cancel your subscription.

*Terms and prices subject to change without notice. Sales tax applicable in N.Y. Canadian residents will be charged applicable provincial taxes and GST.

If offer card is missing write to: Harlequin Reader Service, 3010 Walden Ave., P.O. Box 1867, Buffalo NY 14240-1867

BUSINESS REPLY MAIL

FIRST-CLASS MAIL   PERMIT NO. 717-003   BUFFALO, NY

POSTAGE WILL BE PAID BY ADDRESSEE

HARLEQUIN READER SERVICE
3010 WALDEN AVE
PO BOX 1867
BUFFALO NY 14240-9952

NO POSTAGE
NECESSARY
IF MAILED
IN THE
UNITED STATES

sentable to wear. Twenty minutes later, stepping from his shower, he stood in front of his limited closet. For the first time he regretted not bringing more of his wardrobe. He shook his head. *Don't make so much of this,* he said to himself. *It's a ride in an old beat-to-hell pickup truck and a hamburger. That's it.*

What about eating at the Derby Club? a mischievous voice whispered in his ear. After all, John Tom had made it sound as if he and Silver had it all arranged.

Maybe Darcy should just show up there with Silver on his arm. No, forget it. He wasn't going to play that game, though the thought was appealing. Not because he wanted to send the message that she was hands-off, but to make the guy realize he'd have to work harder to get her. That could work to Silver's advantage, couldn't it?

The one thing Darcy had figured out so far was the Braybournes were very tight financially at the moment. An influx of money and some security would make all of them breathe easier. From what Harden had indicated earlier, John Tom could provide that. Darcy's realistic side told him he had no right to stand in anyone's way. So when he saw Silver tonight, he'd give her the message and let her take it from there.

Darcy grabbed a clean pair of gray slacks and hesitated between the shirt and tie he'd impulsively packed and a pale turquoise knit polo shirt. He grabbed the polo shirt. The other would make it look too much like a date to suit Silver, or his name wasn't Rick Darcy.

Rick Darcy. It had such a normal ring to it. He hoped he could live up to it.

Meeting his own dark eyes in the glass as he patted a bit of aftershave on his face, he thought he looked pretty normal. He combed his hair back in no particular way, not realizing that his overall style had that careless *GQ* look that many men tried to emulate without ever coming close. He slipped into his boots, then, without another thought for his appearance, left the room.

Darcy strolled over to see Lucky Hand before he left the stables. His farm manager had agreed about the possibility of this animal being from WindRaven Farm's breeding operation. He'd told Darcy he would check the records, do some more digging and see what he could find out. Lucky Hand turned his head and met Darcy's gaze. The horse's eyes were mildly disdainful.

"It's a shame you can't talk. I'd sure like to know how you ended up being sold off in a poker game...because you sure as hell act as if you should be in the center of a winner's circle." Darcy chuckled as the horse snorted and went back to his hay. Dismissed by a horse, he thought. Still chuckling, he turned and headed for the Braybourne house.

As he approached the door, he felt a few butterflies in his stomach. *What the hell. She's just a woman.* He raised his fist to knock.

"Hello there, Darcy." A soft Southern female voice came from right behind him. "My land, don't you look nice."

He turned to face Silver's mother. "Hi there, Mrs. Braybourne."

"Aggie, remember."

"That's right, Aggie."

"I don't suppose you're all dressed up for me?" she said in a mock-hopeful manner.

"No, ma'am." Then he could feel himself flush. "I mean..."

She patted his arm. "Well, I sure hope it's not for Harden."

Darcy laughed, all of a sudden completely at ease with the small dynamo standing in front of him holding a basket filled with cut flowers. "I've got to tell you, Aggie, much as I already respect your husband, I'd rather date your daughter."

"Date, is it?"

"No, ma'am, that was a slip of tongue." He glanced around, looking for inspiration, and found it in the Kentucky hills off in the distance. "Actually, I asked Silver if she could show me around the area, then stop and get a burger."

Aggie inspected him, head to foot. "Son, you're going to give Loretta down at the Burger Shack a heart attack looking like that."

He looked down. "Like what?"

"Like you just stepped out of a men's magazine ad. I think you'd better think of something else for your date than a burger."

Silver stepped through the door onto the porch. "It's not a date, Mama. I don't know where you got such a silly idea."

"I know, Darcy told me it wasn't. That was a slip of the tongue."

Darcy, however, couldn't say a word. He could only stare at the sight of Silver Braybourne dressed in a siren-red dress that barely covered her thighs. His mouth went dry. If she turned around and that dress was backless, he was going under with no hope of coming up for air.

Aggie chuckled. "Now then, you two have a good time on your whatever you want to call it."

Silver tossed her head like a restless horse trying to avoid the bridle. "A friendly, neighborly thing to do for an employee who is new to the area is what I'd call it, Mama. I'd do the same for Tater or anyone who—who..."

Darcy bit his lip to keep from laughing as her mother sent Silver a skeptical look. He thought he'd better help her out, so he said, "I can't tell you how much I appreciate your daughter's kindness."

Aggie transferred her sardonic gaze to him. "I'm sure you can't."

"I, um, I'll be home early, Mama."

"Um-hmm," Aggie said. "But if not, should I have your daddy wait up?"

"Good Lord, no!" Silver wailed, before recovering. "Quit teasing. The last time he waited up for me I was fourteen years old."

"I always trusted you knew what you were about, Silver. Even when it seemed incomprehensible to everyone else." Aggie's gaze slid from Silver to Darcy. "But in this case, I guess you'd have to be a female to understand."

Darcy grinned at Aggie. Damn, he liked this woman. He could see where Silver got her wit and style. He had a feeling Harden hadn't known what hit him when he met Aggie. Almost the way Darcy felt about meeting her daughter. Obviously there was something about these women that got under a man's skin.

"Bye, Mama." Silver leaned down to give her mother a kiss on the cheek, then sailed by Darcy and down the steps.

"Holy hell," he whispered as she passed him. Darcy was frozen to the porch, unable to move anything but his lips. He stared at her back, at the smooth, gleaming expanse of skin that her dress revealed. Man, he wanted to run his hands down her spine and keep on going.

"If I were you, young man," Aggie said, "I'd catch up with her before she leaves you behind."

Darcy made an effort to pull himself together, sending Aggie a slight smile. "You think that's possible?"

"It depends on how swift you are."

His smile widened. "I'm pretty quick off the mark."

"But have you got staying power? That's what wins the race."

He took a deep breath. "I guess I'll have to find out."

He gave Aggie a little wave, then clattered down the steps, but not so loudly that he didn't hear her whisper, "Lord help us."

He caught up with Silver as she neared the gate. Reaching around her, he politely opened it so she could go through into the parking area.

"Thanks," she said.

"Uh, my pickup is right over there. Sorry I didn't get a chance to wash it or clean it out. As it is, I don't think my truck will do justice to that dress."

She brushed her hands down her skirt. "This old thing?"

Darcy considered her for a second. "Now, if that wasn't a classic Southern belle in action, I don't know what was." And wow, this Southern belle was a stunner. The way she could make that dress move, the way it caressed her breasts with each breath, the way the skirt hugged her waist and swirled around her legs all spelled disaster. His disaster.

She sent him a glance over her shoulder that immediately

raised his blood pressure. Her lashes swept down, then lifted to reveal eyes sparkling with mischief. "You haven't seen anything yet."

Wary now, he walked over to his truck and yanked on the door handle. What did she mean by that? Something told him that Silver at her charming best was a dangerous woman. He much preferred it when she was quick-tempered and touchy. He could understand her that way. He meant what he'd said earlier, that Southern women were very good at showing an enchanting surface manner and letting their real emotions boil underneath. That was one of the things that made them so fascinating to Darcy's way of thinking, but it made for one hell of an explosion when those emotions blew. He sent Silver a narrow glance. Instead of complaining about the dusty seats, she seemed perfectly content to be putting her grade A self into an old pickup. For some reason that made her even more formidable. He held the door open. "Your chariot awaits."

"Thank you, sir." Silver placed her hand on his and allowed him to help her into the truck. She flounced around for a moment, settling herself, as he got behind the wheel and started the engine.

He glanced at her, wishing she'd pull that skirt down to less intriguing levels so he could drive without running into a ditch. "Where to?" His voice was a bit sharper than he intended.

She sent him a tiny smile. "You wanted to see the area, so I thought I could show you a few of our neighbors' farms, just to give you the lay of the land. Then I can show you some of my favorite spots, and then the town."

He backed out of his parking place and started down the long drive. "I drove through Cecil on the way here. That's where I met Tater. At the feed store."

"That's okay. You haven't seen the town I know. I can tell you the history of the place. For example, I can point out the site of the first whorehouse in Kentucky—" she grinned "—or so legend says. And the first racetrack, and the first moonshining still to operate during Prohibition."

"No kidding. All three claims to fame right here in Cecil?"

"Yep, the founding fathers were forward thinkers." Silver laughed. "According to my granddaddy, racing, whoring and drinking went together like a three-legged stool. Still do, I'm told."

Darcy nodded. "All enjoyable ways to spend time."

"And some of the cash burning a hole in wealthy pockets."

"Flush pockets are always a license to sin." When he thought of some of the money he'd run through with absolutely no thought but pleasure, he cringed.

Silver gave him a wise, all-knowing look. "The people of Cecil were, and are, a resourceful lot when it comes to sin. We aim to see that everyone who visits our fair community feels taken care of."

"How are you going to take care of me?" He jumped right in with both feet. He couldn't help it. The breeze was playing with her skirt, her long slim legs were beckoning, her lips were wet where she'd moistened them and her breasts were barely tucked into that neckline.

"Well," she cooed, "after we see some of the sights, I thought we could get something to eat."

"I'm putty in your hands. Just point me in the right direction."

"Good, that's just the way I like it."

There was enough satisfaction in her comment to make him a bit apprehensive. There was something different about Silver, besides her outfit. Something that made him nervous. If he didn't know better he'd think she'd marked him as a takeover target, or was out to teach him some type of lesson. But she'd been so adamant about not getting involved that he was sure he was imagining things.

Darcy turned left out of the drive onto one of the main highways that led to Cecil. The road twisted and turned as it wove in and out of woodlands, past some huge limestone cliffs carved by the Kentucky River as it wound its way west. Then the sharp peaks and overhangs became friendlier as wide-open fields welcomed them. Here and there he saw pastures that stretched for miles, all bordered by fences, some painted white, some brown, but all of them neat and orderly.

Everywhere he looked, old fences of limestone ran across the fields as well, walls that had been built by men who'd cut the stones from the vast limestone quarries in this part of the state. A sense of history lived here, a real connection to the past. It was newer than the traditions that lived on in Virginia, but it was just as ingrained, and to Darcy's eyes, remarkably similar. Silver pointed out neighboring farms, giving him an update on their operations, their horses, and practically a blow by blow description of their winning races. She pointed out some of the childhood and teenage haunts of her brothers and herself—the fields where they'd jumped their first horses, her elementary and high schools, the road that led to the local lover's lane.

Darcy grinned at her. "Lover's lane?"

"I got my first kiss at the end of the road, as a matter of fact."

He chuckled. "I'll bet you even had an old swimming hole, too." He could just see a bright-haired young Silver leaping off one of the high rocks into the water.

"Don't smirk. As a matter of fact we did. There's a dandy one not too far from the farm. If you're real nice to me I might take you there one day."

"How nice do I have to be?"

"Real nice. Nicer than you usually are."

"Sweetheart, I've been trying to be nice to you since we first met."

She rolled her eyes. "Trying to be nice and trying to seduce me are two different things."

"Oh? I got the feeling the latter was reciprocal."

"That was so you wouldn't think you had the upper hand."

He sent her a grin that had more than a hint of sarcasm. "Trust me. It worked. Temporarily, at least."

Rather than deal with his last statement, she changed the subject. "Are you getting hungry? I'm starving."

"Yeah, I could eat. We can try this Burger Shack your mother told me about. But she also said that in her opinion I looked too good for the place. And I'm sure you do." He had to work to keep his tongue from hanging out when he said that.

Silver laughed, even as she acknowledged his compliment. "The Shack is one of those places where you can show up wearing anything from farm overalls to an evening gown, and Loretta Devine, the owner, treats you just the same."

"Let me guess, she treats you like family?"

"Like dysfunctional family."

Darcy laughed. "I get the picture. Well, I also heard somebody mention the Derby Club." He should tell her right now about John Tom's message, but couldn't bring himself to do so.

Silver glanced over at him. "Hmm. You might like the Derby Club. It's not a private club, even though it sounds like it. It's just a restaurant and bar, with a horse theme, of course. It's a bit of a hangout for all the local horse people."

"A lot of your friends, you mean?" Now he really regretted mentioning the place. His cousin would tell him he was living way too dangerously as it was. Darcy knew he might be recognized if he got out among horse people.

"Um-hmm."

Darcy could see her mind spinning. What was she thinking? Did she want her friends to see her with him? With a hired hand? That was essentially what he was. Since he'd come to the Braybournes' he'd begun thinking seriously about what people really saw when they looked at him.

"Look, maybe the Derby Club is a bad idea. I mean, I'm just a guy who works for you. If we went there people you know might get the wrong impression."

"Are you calling me a snob?" Her eyes flashed. "Because I'm not a snob. I don't have enough money to be a snob."

He tromped down on the gas. "I don't think money has anything to do with it. I think snobbishness is more a feeling of overwhelming superiority, whether it's justified or not." God knows, he could name any number of people whose entire lives revolved around who they knew and where they'd been last seen.

As the breeze rushed in the open windows, Silver pushed a

lock of hair out of her eyes. "Now, if you were calling my father a snob, that would be a different story." She frowned. "Although he's not exactly a snob, he's just a bit old-fashioned about some things."

"Like the right type of man for his daughter?"

"Yes." A half smile flitted over her lips. "As much as I want to stuff him down a well sometimes for his attitudes, I know he's trying to do what he thinks is best for me. I do know that. The only problem is—"

"That you don't agree?"

"Not even that. It's more that if someone tells me what's best for me, I'm bound and determined to go the other direction." She shrugged. "I'm just contrary, I guess."

"Like a horse who wants a drink of water but kicks over the bucket instead."

"Exactly right." She sent him a saucy smile. "Don't you just hate to do what people expect you to do?"

"Generally." Silver Braybourne was a kindred spirit, he decided, which was one reason he found her so appealing. But not the only reason by a long shot. "So is the Derby Club a yes or no?"

"No. But not because I don't want to be seen with you." She turned to face him, reaching to grasp his arm. "The reason is that the place bores me to death, and I'd much rather take you to Loretta's Burger Shack. I think you'll like the atmosphere there a lot better. I know I will."

Silver considered Darcy from under her lowered lashes as he turned into the parking lot. She glanced from him to the Burger Shack and back again. Even though he'd talked about being a hired hand and was wearing casual clothes and driving a beat-up old pickup, there was something about Rick Darcy that seemed out of place in these modest surroundings. She was trying to see him perched on a counter stool in the Shack and couldn't quite picture it. Maybe the Derby Club would be better.

Her timing was a bit poor, since he'd just thrown the truck into Park. "Maybe you'd prefer..."

He turned to her and stretched his arm along the back of the seat. "Prefer?"

She met his dark eyes, which were warm and glowing. If she needed confirmation that her new red dress was making this man drool, she had it. From the moment his eyes had first swept over her, she'd felt his appetite growing. His fingers touched her hair, casually playing with the ends. Her skin burned everywhere his gaze touched. He trailed one long finger over her jawline.

"Prefer what?" he repeated, his voice warm as hot fudge and twice as rich.

Her tongue stroked her lips as she tried to moisten them enough to form a word. "Prefer a fish sandwich to a burger. Loretta makes mighty tasty fish sandwiches, too."

His finger stroked over her lips. "My, my, my. Cecil, Kentucky, is full of all kinds of tasty things, isn't it?"

Oh help, where's that Southern belle when I need her? "People in Cecil have big appetites." *Kiss me,* she prayed. *Please just lean right over here and kiss me.*

"Yes, you indicated that before."

"Well, it's true." Her eyes widened as he moved a bit closer. They were sitting in the parking lot of the biggest gossip factory in town, right out here in daylight in front of anyone who might want to get a glimpse of Silver Braybourne ready to throw caution to the winds and neck with this dark-haired devil right in front of God and everybody. And she didn't care. She wanted him to kiss her more than she'd ever wanted anything. Silver could just imagine everyone in town shaking their head and asking, "What is the world coming to?"

Get a grip.

She pulled her gaze from his, needing a few moments to break the spell he seemed to weave without any effort. Rick Darcy was a man who'd obviously had his own way with women much too often to suit her. He was a formidable opponent; she freely acknowledged that. Perhaps it hadn't been wise to dress provocatively to try to teach him a lesson about who was in control. Privately, she was dead sure she'd end up making love to him, regardless of what she'd said. And she would thrill to every minute of it. However, it was essential she be the one who would determine the time and the place. She wasn't putting the power in his hands by allowing him to do so.

She waved her hand in front of her face. "We're in for a hot spell, it seems."

Darcy grinned at her as his fingers trailed over her shoulder. "Lord, I hope so."

"According to the Weather Channel, that is." So much for good intentions. She attempted to recite the alphabet backward to keep her head clear.

His fingers trailed down her arm. "I love the Weather Channel."

O-N-M... "Loretta always keeps her air-conditioning at frigid levels."

"I'll appreciate that."

"I'm sure you will." *J-I-H...* "It'll cool you off faster than skinny-dipping in an icy pond."

She shivered, not sure if it was from the image she'd used or the proximity of Rick Darcy as he played with her hand. "Don't worry, I'll keep you warm if it's too cold inside."

C-B-A. Withdrawing her fingers, she said, "I'll be fine."

"That dress isn't made for keeping anyone warm—except a man, of course."

She sent him a flirty little look. She couldn't help it. "Do you think so?"

He leaned across her and opened her door. She almost sighed as his arm pressed against her breasts. "I double-damn-near guarantee it."

She met his hot eyes for a moment longer, her gaze never leaving his as he withdrew. "You like this little number then?"

He clenched his fists. To keep his hands off her? she wondered. "I don't think that describes my feelings at the moment."

Feeling more confident, she smiled. "I'd suggest we stay and talk about it, but I don't think we'd get a lot of talking done."

"There are all kinds of ways to communicate, Silver, so we'll pick this discussion up later. You have my word on it."

Glory be, but she was playing with fire, she thought as she slid from the truck. She practically shouted with relief as her feet hit the ground. The man had a way of upsetting all of her plans and tying her emotions into knots, not to mention what he was doing to her physically. He was turning her into one big ache. She scarcely recognized herself. Managing to gather her poise, she led him to the front door of the restaurant.

Loretta's Burger Shack was an old railroad car that had been added to over the years. The architecture was as mismatched as the paint job, but the joint was jumping with happy people. It didn't matter to Loretta what the place looked like, Silver knew. All that mattered was it was hers. Loretta had worked her way up from nothing until she was a success—no more poverty and handouts for this lady, nosiree. In a town of unusual characters, she stood out, Silver mused as she and Darcy stepped inside.

Darcy blinked at the violent color combinations on the walls and in the booths—chartreuse vied with purple, red fought it out with pink—and cringed at the noise level as people enjoyed themselves at the top of their lungs. "Wow. This is..."

"Colorful?" Silver suggested.

"That wasn't what came to mind, but colorful will do."

"Wait till you get a load of Loretta," Silver said, her voice dry as dust.

The woman wasn't hard to find. She was standing over one of the young waitresses like a mother hen. Loretta's bright orange hair was fluffed into a puffball with pencils sticking out, vibrant red lipstick exaggerated her lips and her blue eyes were caked with so much mascara that Silver was always amazed she could lift her eyelashes. As Silver watched, she turned and conked one of the busboys on the head with her ever-present order pad.

"Gerry, you got lead in your shorts? Get a move on. We got customers waitin' to set themselves down."

Gerry glanced back over his shoulder, his thin, pimply teenage face creased in a grin. "Yes, ma'am, Loretta."

"Do people here get hazardous duty pay?" Darcy asked under his breath as Loretta turned and swatted another young man.

Silver laughed. "Being abused by Loretta is part of every teenager's maturing process here in Cecil." Her laughter got Loretta's attention. The woman turned and directed her eagle-eye stare at them, and when she spotted Darcy, her eyes brightened. Fluffing her hair, she headed in their direction, her sights clearly set on him.

"Protect me," Darcy murmured, cupping Silver's elbow.

She grinned at him. "Sorry, pal. When Loretta looks that determined, it's every man for himself." She turned back to face the woman bearing down on them. "Hey there, Loretta."

"Silver Braybourne, where you been, girl? I ain't seen you for weeks. I hear tell you got something else to occupy yourself with." Her eyes slid to Darcy and she cackled. "It do seem the gossip is right."

Silver took a deep breath as she remembered the downside of a conversation with Loretta. "I'm not sure what the gossip said, but if it said we have a new man working on our place, then it was right."

Loretta stared at Darcy. "And this would be your new man?"

Silver shifted. "He's not my man, exactly. Daddy hired him to—"

"Help Silver out," Darcy said, taking Loretta's bird-claw hand and practically bowing over it.

"Hmm," Loretta said, clearly not one to be overwhelmed by nice gestures. "You look like you might be up to dealing with Silver."

Darcy grinned. "Thank you very much."

Loretta tapped her lips with a fingernail that could double as a weapon, and studied him for a moment. "It ain't a compliment, boy. I've never known a more contrary girl in all my born days. I've known this one since she was in the cradle, and she was always the biggest pain in the behind you could imagine."

Darcy slid her a glance, which Silver tried to ignore. "You don't say," he murmured.

Loretta started to elaborate, going over every one of Silver's youthful indiscretions. Silver finally had to interrupt. "Loretta, I've been telling Darcy about your burgers and your fish sandwiches, so why don't we...?" She indicated a table. What was she thinking of, bringing him here? She could have chosen no better place to start tongues wagging. She'd forgotten to consider that.

After an assessing stare at Silver, Loretta nodded and waved to an empty booth. "You set yourselves right down and I'll bring you a couple of Shack Stacks."

"That sounds good." Silver grabbed Darcy's hand and pulled him across the room, smiling and nodding at people as she did so. "Sorry," she said as they slid into a booth. "You never know what she's going to say."

Darcy settled himself across from her. "I found it pretty interesting."

"Yes," Silver said, "I'm sure you did."

He grinned. "Especially the part where you galloped a horse through the gym at your high school."

"There was a reason for that."

"And that was?"

Frowning at the memory, Silver said, "I made a wager and I lost."

"And you always pay up when you lose, is that it?"

"That's right."

His amused glance sharpened. "I'll keep that in mind."

For some reason that simple comment made Silver a bit uneasy, but she wasn't sure why. She smiled as Loretta came back to their table, delivering their burgers personally.

Loretta slapped the food onto the table and snarled, "Here you go. You both eat up there, or I'll know the reason why."

Silver and Darcy glanced at each other, and knew better than to argue. Without another word they picked up the double-decker burgers and took a bite while Loretta stood over them and watched. She reminded Silver of a vulture looking for scraps. Finally, when Loretta was satisfied that they were going to do as she said, she bustled off to insult the rest of her customers.

"She's quite a character, isn't she?"

Silver smiled. "We're in racing country, so eccentricity is practically a requirement. However, in a town of eccentric characters, Loretta is more colorful than most. But she has the biggest heart in town. You should see her with her Little League baseball team."

"She's got a baseball team?" Darcy asked before biting into his burger again, his eyes lighting with surprise.

Watching his face as he chewed, Silver commented, "Fabulous, isn't it?"

"I've never eaten a burger like this before."

"What? You haven't? Where were you raised, on Mars?" Silver stared at him for a moment. "You haven't said much about your family. Do you have brothers and sisters?"

"No. I'm an only child." He cleared his throat. "And it's difficult to describe my family. They sure aren't anything like yours."

Silver laughed. "You should thank your lucky stars."

"No, you should. You've no idea what you have."

"What I have is people poking into my life every single minute."

"Maybe so, but I'm discovering it's a lot better than having them cold and distant. At least you know you're loved, Silver. That's a great thing."

Her voice grew gentle. "Didn't you know that, Darcy?"

He busied himself with his food, finally saying, "Uh, Silver, do you mind if we don't talk about this? It's very..."

"Oh, I'm sorry, I didn't mean to... Of course." She played with her fork, watching as he took another bite. "So what do you think of Loretta's special sauce? That's what gives it a kick."

"The sauce is great. I have to tell her." Darcy looked around for Loretta, but she was busy badgering another busboy. "Maybe I can get her recipe."

"You like to cook?"

"No, my ch—"

"Your what?"

Avoiding her eyes, Darcy took a gulp of his soft drink, then shoved a French fry in his mouth, speaking around it. "So tell me about her baseball team."

After a moment, Silver said, "It's made up of kids from social services. Those older ones who are stuck in the system without foster parents and not much hope of finding any. Loretta really makes them walk the line. She fusses over them, hugs them and runs their behinds ragged if they don't behave. She gives a lot of them jobs here, too—" she indicated the busboy Loretta had been picking on when they first came in "—like Gerry over there, for instance. She's been responsible for a lot of kids turning out well, I'll tell you." Silver arched a brow. "You'd better watch out or she'll recruit you to help."

"Do you help?"

Silver pulled a rueful face. "What do you think? I'm the third-base coach."

"Sounds like fun." Darcy smiled. "My grandparents would have liked her, I think."

"Most people do. After they look beneath the surface, that is." She took another bite of her burger. "Some people have trouble doing that."

"I know," Darcy said slowly, pulling his gaze from hers. "What you see isn't always what you get, is it?"

"No. You have to keep looking. Take you, for instance." The glimpse he'd opened into his past was so compelling she couldn't leave it alone. She wanted to know more about this man—and the lonely little boy he'd inadvertently described.

"Me?" Darcy met her eyes. "What about me?"

"I don't know," Silver said, nibbling on a French fry. "There's something that doesn't quite fit."

"You're imagining things."

"No, I don't think so."

"I know so," Darcy said, his brow lifting as his lips set in a firm line.

"One minute you're a flirt, one minute you're annoying and bossy, and one minute so haughty that I think I'm supposed to kiss your toes. Now that I know you're an only child, I suppose it makes some sense."

"Don't be ridiculous."

"You're a real puzzle, Rick Darcy."

"There's no puzzle, Silver. I am what I am. What I used to be doesn't matter."

"So there was something you used to be?"

"I...had this niche I operated in. Was tired of being there when I got this idea and decided to go with it. But it didn't quite turn out the way I expected."

"Financially, you mean? Or personally?"

Darcy shrugged, clearly uncomfortable. "Uh, yes, financially. That's it. I'm kind of broke at the moment."

"Let me guess—you went bankrupt, didn't you? Isn't that what you mean?"

"Bank—" He looked down for a moment, then fixed his eyes back on hers. "That's right. I went bankrupt a few months ago. It tore my life apart. Years of work, just wiped out. I decided it was time to change my life, move on and see what else is out there."

"Oh, Darcy." She reached out to cover his hand with hers, her eyes warm and sympathetic. The man looked so uncomfortable and guilty as he shared his secret that she ached for him. She knew what it was to have her pride and her belief in herself trampled. "It happens to the best of people. You needn't feel ashamed."

Darcy turned his hand so they were pressed palm to palm. "I...ah hell, Silver, I—"

"Well, I do declare, Silver, isn't this cozy." The woman's Southern drawl was so thick it practically oozed over them.

Silver looked up into the animated face of a very attractive brunette who was avidly staring at their linked hands. "My goodness, Silver, does John Tom know you're off here at Loretta's holding hands with another man? I declare, it's really brave of you. Seeing as how you two are almost engaged and all."

Bristling, Silver let go of Darcy's hand. "We are not engaged, Heather Lee. I'd appreciate it if you wouldn't help spread that rumor around."

"Well, Silver darlin', John Tom thinks you are, so the result will end up the same. You know how single-minded he can be." She turned her attention to Darcy. "Hi, I'm Heather Lee Ramsey, and I, on the other hand, am completely unattached."

Darcy smiled. "What's the matter with the men in this town?"

"Oh, not a darn thing, darlin'. I've been through most of them and I can honestly say, not a darn thing. So where do y'all come from?"

Silver ground her teeth as Darcy laughed. Heather Lee Ramsey was the biggest flirt—which was a polite way of putting it—in Cecil. Hell, in the whole state of Kentucky. As the other woman giggled, Silver wanted to ram her fist into that perfect little smile. "Darcy works with us at the farm, Heather Lee. He's working with the horses and helping manage the place temporarily."

"Ohh, I just love a man who works with his hands."

Darcy's eyes glinted as he gave her a long slow look—one that seemed almost second nature to him, Silver decided. "I know how to work with my hands."

"I'll just bet you do. I'll bet you know how to do that real well." Heather Lee's flirty look left no doubt that she wasn't referring to Darcy's manual labor skills. "I have some work that needs doing if you have a spare minute sometime. I could pick you up and—"

"Excuse me, Heather Lee, I'm here, too, remember? And we have to get going. As you've just reminded us, Darcy has work to do tonight." The nerve of the slut. Why didn't she just fling herself on the table and spread her legs?

Heather Lee sighed. "What a pity. Maybe we could—"

Loretta bustled up and shoved a carry-out bag into Heather

Lee's arms. "Now Heather Lee, you leave these two alone, you hear me? You got yourself in enough trouble with that Jimmy over at the Cadillac dealer. His wife boxed his ears good, I hear. So you just take your saucy self out of here and get this food on home to your daddy."

Heather Lee grimaced. "Loretta, you didn't have to—"

"Go on now, git." She hustled the young woman to the door as if she were directing traffic for a flock of geese. Then she turned and walked back to Silver and Darcy, who were sliding out of the booth. She shook a red fingernail under Silver's nose. "Now you listen to me, Silver Braybourne. You take this stud home to bed before one of those other young floozies gets her hooks in him, ya hear?"

Silver knew her blush must be deeper than Loretta's lipstick as the older woman changed tactics and poked her in the shoulder. "Loretta, please."

"Ya hear what I'm sayin' to you, young lady?"

"And you, boy—" she turned on Darcy "—you be good to this little gal." She looked him over. "Not that that should be a problem. You seem like you know what's what."

Darcy grinned. "You think so?"

"Yep. You've got a lot of the devil in you. But that ain't a bad thing. Not for a lover." Loretta patted her hair as her eyes took on a faraway look. "I buried five husbands, so I should know."

"I'll bet they died happy," Darcy said, impulsively leaning down to kiss her on the cheek.

"They sure as hell did." Loretta cackled as she waved them away. "Now you two go on and git. I got things to do so I can go have a good time myself later tonight." She winked at Silver. "And you bring Darcy to the next baseball practice, ya hear?" Then Loretta bustled off. "Gerry, don't you know how to wipe a table off without drowning the customers..."

Silver was shy about looking at Darcy after Loretta's comments, so she turned on her heel and made a beeline for the door. He caught up with her in the parking lot.

"Hey, where are you going in such a hurry?"

She reached for the door of the truck and yanked it open. "Um, nowhere exactly."

Darcy grinned. "Damn, and I was hoping you were going to take Loretta's advice."

7

THEY WERE QUIET on the way home, each lost in thought. Darcy pulled around the far side of the stables and parked his truck in his usual spot. For a moment they sat there, looking out at the night sky. Silver peeked at him from under her lashes, his last comment still vibrating in her mind. If he only knew how much she wanted to take Loretta's advice. Of course, if she did... She shivered.

Darcy looked over. "Cold?"

"No, not really."

"The air can get cool at night, even in the middle of summer."

"A goose must have walked over my grave—that's what my Granny Braybourne would have said."

"A goose? Why a goose?"

"I haven't the faintest idea. Granny used to twist the English language to suit her own purposes." As she met his amused gaze, she shivered again. His eyes were so compelling, they urged her to drop her barriers, to go for the moment. Those eyes were pure temptation.

"You're getting chilled." He moved over and wrapped his arm around her shoulder, one hand rubbing up and down her arm to create some friction. "You're one big goose bump."

"I'm fine, really," she said, her voice faint as the scent of his aftershave teased her nostrils. "You don't need to—"

"I know."

"It's still pretty hot outside. I'll warm up in a minute. It was the breeze from the windows when we were driving, th-tha—" she stumbled as her eyes looked deep into his "—that's all."

He lifted a brow, his eyes even more intent as they remained locked on hers. "Uh-huh, sure it was."

"It was."

His gaze swept over her. "Not the fact that my handkerchief could cover more of you than that dress does?"

"This dress is perfectly warm. Perfectly acceptable." When his eyes came back to hers, the tension grew until it was almost palpable in the soft summer night. The fingertips of his right hand continued to stroke her arm. If she closed her eyes right now, she thought, she could see them making love.

"Oh," he practically choked out, "that dress is more than acceptable. It damn near brought me to my knees when you stepped onto the porch." He lifted his other hand, fingering the straps that crossed behind her neck.

"Good." She knew she was playing with fire, but wasn't she a risk taker by nature, even when she knew it was insane?

His hand slid down from her neckline, skimming lightly over her breast to grasp her waist. "Is that why you wore it? To make me beg?"

"Are you begging?" One step closer to the flame.

"You'd better believe it."

"Then I'll have to thank the saleswoman who sold it to me."

"So will I."

Leaning forward, Silver whispered, "She said it would make a man crawl." Lord, it was hot. Her blood was beginning to boil.

Darcy moved closer until she could feel him along the length of her as they sat on the bench seat. "She was right. I'm lower than a snake's belly right about now. I have to make love to you, Silver. I know I shouldn't. But I can't help it."

"I know." She wanted to tell him she felt the same, but something held her back.

"Loretta was in favor of it."

"Loretta is a romantic at heart. After five marriages, she's dating Tater. The guys at the feed store are taking bets. Odds are even he'll become number six." She knew she was chattering to buy some time.

Darcy's eyes burned into hers. "My money's on Loretta."

"Mine, too," she whispered. What was she waiting for? Like Loretta, she wanted romance, not a merger. This was the man who could provide it. He was sexier than he had a right to be, but with just enough vulnerability to make their lovemaking more meaningful. Wouldn't it be thrilling to be swept off her feet, to have that fairy-tale moment when—

Darcy leaned over and nipped her ear. A shock of desire tore through her. She let her head fall to one side as he pressed little kisses on the soft area behind her ear. He caressed her lobe with the tip of his tongue before delicately probing the shell-like curve. His hand traced her jaw, then slipped into her hair, holding her still for the onslaught of his mouth on hers. His lips and tongue teased until she groaned and opened for him. Then, rather than take it deeper, he hesitated, his lips hovering over hers as he breathed, "Kiss me, Silver."

His voice vibrated in her soul. She wanted to refuse, but more, she wanted to accept. Plunging her hands into his hair and pulling his face to hers, she kissed him, taking the time to savor before she increased the pressure. She could feel herself sinking into him, unable to surface, wondering if she ever would. His lips were soft, so very soft. She could sup there forever and never be hungry. She drew back for an instant, but he stopped her from going very far.

"More," he whispered. "I want more."

"I need to breathe."

"No, you don't. I'm what you need at the moment. You're what I need."

Turning her head, she avoided his eyes. "I know, but it concerns me."

His hand brought her back around to face him. "Why? For God's sake, why?"

"Because I feel lost in you, and I don't like to feel lost."

"You're not lost, sweetheart, you're finding your way."

Her brows snapped together. "That sounds as if I need direction. I don't. I always know where I want to go. At least I did."

"And I'm just beginning to find out."

"I wasn't tempted to stray from my path. No one's been able to tempt me to do that before. Then you showed up."

His kisses were electrifying—a fact that excited her almost as much as it concerned her. She knew instinctively that much as she wanted him, he was a threat. His personality was too strong, too tempting. She could easily lose herself in him until he was all she thought about, all she wanted, all she needed, and that scared the living hell out of her.

"You know what I think, Silver?"

The rough edge to his voice got her attention. "No. What do you think?"

"I think you think too damn much. You have to learn to go with the moment and feel." He pulled her toward him and pressed his lips against hers. His hands slipped down her bare back, following the curve of her spine from the nape of her neck to her waist. His fingers slipped inside the material of her dress. His mouth was practically savaging hers, and his kisses seemed desperate as his hands moved to cup her breasts. Then he tore his lips from hers and dropped his head to rest against the red material that molded itself so enticingly to them.

"Ah, Silver, you're killing me."

"I know. And it's going to get more painful." Her voice was as agonized as his. "Much as I might want to make love with you at the moment, I don't really think I'm ready." She didn't mean physically, but emotionally. She wasn't ready for a man who had the power to make her go back on her vow to have nothing more to do with him. A man who goaded her into letting her pride take over so she teased him until he broke, then forced her to stare her desire in the face.

"You were ready yesterday."

"I didn't know you yesterday."

Darcy looked confused. "So, now you know me a little more. Earlier you said we should know each other better, remember?"

"That's the problem. Yesterday you were just the prospect of unbelievable raw sex." And heaven help her, on the surface he still was. "I didn't see anything wrong with that, but...today you're not. Not exactly." She knew she was making no sense.

She'd known the man for only two days and she'd not been thinking clearly for either of them.

"I'm not what?" If ever a man looked completely mired in mud, it was Darcy.

"You're not just a..." she waved her hands, trying to find the words "...a guaranteed orgasm on two legs. And I don't think—"

Grabbing her hands, he stopped her tirade. "Don't tell me you don't want me, Silver, because I know you damn well do. You can say as much as you'd like that you and me won't happen, but we both know it's not true. So it's time we stopped fooling ourselves."

"You're right. I do want you. But as I get to know you I find there's more to you than I thought. I'm not sure how I feel about that. And until I'm sure, I'm not going to leap into bed with you. I'm sorry." As she apologized, she leaned over to kiss him gently, which was a big mistake, one that seemed to push him over the edge.

He hauled her onto his lap before she had a chance to protest. His hands skimmed up her bare legs and under her skirt, finally cupping her buttocks as he pushed her down. He was hard. Very hard. As she pressed against him, his hips surged forward in an erotic movement. She gripped his shoulders, catching her breath as desire licked at her. She could never explain her sudden hesitation to him—she could barely explain it to herself. All she knew was the more she began to know Rick Darcy, the more real he became to her. The more she wanted him to stay. She wanted him to consider spending more time here, which was completely contrary to her plans. She didn't need him around as a manager, and that was the only way he could stay. He couldn't stay on as her lover, regardless of her desire.

She tore her lips from his. "Darcy, Darcy, we have to stop. My head is spinning."

He rested his forehead against hers. "Mine, too. I feel like a horny teenager on his first date. I can't get enough of you."

Silver chuckled. "I understand that."

He gulped, trying to find some air. "I've never made out in a pickup truck before. There's something about being outside under the stars with a beautiful woman in my arms that is very erotic."

They were silent for a moment, each trying to subdue the passion that only needed one idle movement to erupt again. After a moment, Darcy said, in a voice that seemed dragged from him, "I have a confession to make."

"What kind of confession?"

"I was supposed to give you a message from John Tom Thomas, telling you to meet him at the Derby Club at eight-thirty."

"The Derby? Why didn't you tell me?"

"I guess I was afraid you'd junk me and meet him."

"Why would you think that? A deal is a deal. Once I say I'm going to do something I don't welsh on it." She bit her lip. "At least I try not to."

"Well, just in case you did, I didn't want to think of you with that guy when you should be with me instead."

"You were jealous?"

"Yes. I know I have no right to be, but that doesn't change anything."

"You were jealous! Fancy that!" Small flutters in her stomach underscored her amazement.

"So jealous that I considered walking in with you on my arm, just to show him...." He trailed off, looking out into the night. Finally he said, "I know you'd said you had no plans, but he sounded as if you'd made a date earlier."

Silver chuckled, saying dryly, "John Tom practices that old sales tactic 'assumed consent.'"

Darcy nodded, then showed her how well he understood the concept. "So you can date me."

Silver tilted her head, considering him, wondering where he was going with this. "We just went out on a date."

"This wasn't a date. You told your mama that this was a neighborly act, remember?"

Silver considered their position—her legs still straddling his thighs, her breasts pressing against his chest. "This is a bit more neighborly than I'm accustomed to being."

Darcy chuckled. "Now that relieves my mind."

Silver chuckled in turn, her laughter stilling as her eyes met his. She could see the desire reflected there, and knew hers looked the same. It wouldn't take much to fuel the fire, she thought.

Darcy smiled, a grim smile that contained a warning. "I don't know where this is going, Silver, but we're going to have to play it out."

"I...I'd better go in," she said, fighting to keep the reluctance from her voice. "Five o'clock comes awfully early, and I want to get Lucky Hand over to the track."

"I'd like to join you."

"Well...okay. You can see what the horse is made of." *Get back to business*, she told herself. *Stick with business until you figure out what you're going to do about this.*

They sat in awkward silence for a moment longer, then Silver attempted to slide gracefully off his lap. Finally she gave up and just climbed off as if she was dismounting, turning around to reach for the door handle. "Good night, Darcy."

"Wait a minute." He scrambled for his own door, getting out and walking around the back of the pickup. "I'll walk you to the door."

"That's not necessary."

"I'm doing it anyway."

They walked in silence for a moment, listening to the sounds of the night. The chirp of the crickets, the whirling buzz of flying insects and that special kind of quiet that only occurs out in the country away from man-made noises. The peace was almost palpable. They climbed up the steps. At the door of the house, Silver turned to face him.

"We're here," she said, then mentally slapped herself. Of course they were.

"I had a good time tonight, Silver. One of the best I remember."

She smiled up at him. There was a wistful sweetness to his

voice that surprised her. "Me, too." And she had. Darcy was an enjoyable companion when he just relaxed and let his natural charm and intelligence come through, she thought.

"I meant what I said in the truck. Maybe we can do it again sometime, for real."

"I...I think I'd like that." Taking it slow didn't mean she couldn't take what she could. It meant she couldn't get any more involved. She was already too involved.

She reached behind her for the doorknob while Darcy hesitated, looking deep into her eyes. Silver tensed, both hoping he'd reach for her and praying he wouldn't. Finally he gave up his internal struggle and slipped his arms around her waist, molding her against his body. He kissed her gently, then firmly put her away from him.

"Sweet dreams," he said. He turned on his heel and struck out across the grass.

"Sweet dreams," she whispered as she watched him leave, knowing her dreams would be only of him.

A DENSE EARLY MORNING MIST hung over the fields as Darcy led Lucky Hand out of the horse trailer, guiding him carefully as he backed down the ramp. Darcy had seen a number of horses get excited and plunge off the side, and it was never really clear what set them off. Horses were a nervous bunch, especially Thoroughbreds. Their temperaments were more spirited and high-strung than many other animals, which was part of what made them so fascinating, he mused.

Almost as fascinating as the woman across the lot studying the track. He focused on Silver. In her ratty T-shirt, boots and old jeans, she didn't resemble the woman in the red dress he'd hungered over last night. And he'd hungered until he'd nearly starved to death.

After he left her, he'd gone back to his room and paced until he'd almost worn a groove in the floor. When his room became too confining, he paced the stables, all the time trying to work out his frustration and his confusion. Damn the woman. He might have known her for only a few days, but he felt as if he was dealing with a lifetime of yearning for this one female. He'd cast his mind over the many women he'd known. No one even approached Silver, not because of her beauty, but because of her total attitude. Loretta was right—Silver Braybourne was the most contrary woman he'd ever met. He wasn't sure what to do about her. She confused him and at the same time made him want to be better than he was. He couldn't understand it at all.

He was positive his cousin Nick would be rolling with laughter at the thought of him tongue-tied and stumbling in front of a woman. Not that Darcy was letting it be that obvious. After all, he had more experience than that—and one hell of a lot more pride. Too much pride, perhaps, which was a family failing. Not bad when it was used the right way, but stifling when it wasn't. Pride or not, he felt he'd already gone further trying to explain his feelings to Silver than he ever had with another woman. He wasn't sure why. Was she the most sympathetic listener he'd ever encountered? No, not at all. The most logical thinker? Not by a long shot. So what was it about her? Damned if he knew.

The only thing he could come up with was there was some strong invisible link between them. A sexual one, naturally—oh, man was there a sexual link! But more than that, a meeting of the minds that went beyond glib explanations. He knew Silver felt it, too, even as she tried to pretend their relationship was based on sex appeal. She had to know it was more or she wouldn't have shut down so fast last night. She'd told him that getting to know him—or at least as much as he could let her know—was now as much of an issue as not knowing him at all. But then Silver said a lot of things that her actions later contradicted. In some ways she was just like him. But better. A hell of a lot better. She had a purpose and determination that he admired.

He glanced at Silver as she stood slapping her gloves against her thigh in a movement that reminded him of a fractious horse. Perhaps he was making too much of the situation, reading too much into his response. It was time to step back and reassess. He studied her, trying to detach himself from his emotions. They hadn't bothered him regarding women before, so there was no good reason for them to start doing so now. He nodded, feeling more his old self. From now on when he looked at Silver he'd see what he had in the first place—a gorgeous woman with a hot temper who knew the score. He warned himself not to be taken in by her seeming confusion. It's what she wanted him to do. Too many women over the years had played this before, many more successfully than this pretty little Southern belle.

His mood a bit brittle, his resolve set, he led Lucky Hand over to Silver, noticing Tater coming from the opposite direction. "Hey, Tater, I didn't see you earlier. Silver was looking for you." Darcy looked around for his truck. "You just get here?"

Tater dug the toe of his boot in the dirt, saying in a terse manner, "I was a bit behind this morning. These old bones don't work too fast sometimes."

Silver tucked her tongue in her cheek as she said, "Don't fall for that, Darcy. Tater had a late date last night."

Darcy looked from Silver to Tater, whose face was turning red. "A late date?"

Ignoring Darcy's question, Tater glanced around at the other men and horses milling about, before shaking an annoyed fist at Silver. "Now you look here, girl. Ain't no need to broadcast my business to everybody in the place."

Intrigued by Tater's behavior, Darcy said, "A date with whom?"

Silver arched a brow. "Who do you think?"

Darcy's mind was too occupied with his own thoughts to consider Tater's social life. He thought hard for a moment, trying to run though the women he'd met since he'd hit town. "Let's see..."

Silver gave an impatient sniff. "Think red-haired and spicy."

Darcy stared at Silver, then remembered her commenting about Loretta the night before. He grinned at the older man, who now looked almost mad enough to spit. "Tater, you wouldn't be dating Loretta from the Burger Shack, would you?"

Silver nodded at him, as if he were her star pupil. "That's right."

Darcy whistled. "I'm impressed. I met her last night, and I'll tell you, I'd think twice about taking her on myself."

"There ain't no need for you to take her on, boy," Tater spat. "I've known Loretta for a long time. I just never been able to catch her between husbands to do anything more about it." He turned from red and annoyed to pale as he shifted from one foot to another, his words stumbling over each other in the rush to get out. "Not that I want to do anything about it, mind you. No, no, she's a fine woman, but I'm happy just the way I am."

Darcy clasped the man's shoulder. "That's when they sneak up on you, Tater."

Tater recovered with a vengeance. "She ain't turning my life upside down. There ain't a woman's been born yet that can do that."

Silver grinned. "Want to bet?"

"You're damn straight I'll bet, you saucy-mouthed brat. I ain't stayed a bachelor all these years just to get myself all tangled up in Loretta's net."

"I don't know, Tater. Loretta is doing some mighty big hinting about you lately at baseball practice."

Tater attempted to maintain some dignity. "Don't matter. A man will do what a man decides to do. And no damn-fool pushy woman is going to make me do otherwise." He pulled out his stopwatch and stalked stiff-legged and bristling to the fence that surrounded the track.

Silver laughed as she watched him. "Isn't he a romantic old fool?"

Narrowing his eyes, Darcy watched as Tater spat on the ground, then shoved a wad of gum back into his mouth. "I don't know if I'd describe him that way. More like a bear with a backache."

"He's lovesick, that's all. Loretta seems to have a way about her."

"From what I've seen of that carrot-topped powerhouse, I'd call it intimidation."

Silver chuckled. "Whatever it is, we should bottle it and sell it. We'd make a fortune."

"Women have enough weapons. They sure as hell don't need another one." He was positive his tone was sour, but he couldn't help it. This blonde had some nerve—and she was definitely jangling his. She stood there wearing beat-up clothes that were tight enough to be relics from her junior high school days, and she still stunned him. How was he supposed to concentrate on his job?

Silver wrinkled her nose. "Are you okay?"

"Why?"

"You look kind of funny. Like you ate a sour apple for breakfast."

"I didn't have breakfast."

"Me neither." She hesitated for a moment, then said, "We could stop at the Burger Shack for one of Loretta's farm-style breakfasts."

"No thanks. The mood Loretta's in, she might try to marry us off next. And I don't want anything to do with that."

"Then it's a good thing I turned you down when you asked, isn't it."

"Since I didn't mean it, yes, I'd say it was." He felt a twinge as he said it, especially after he got a look at her expression. He wasn't sure if she was ticked off or hurt by his comment. This was one topic he didn't want to probe too deeply, so he played it safe and changed the subject. "Besides, Lucky Hand will need a good rubdown after you work him this morning."

She flushed. "I know that. I wasn't suggesting we..." She let her words trail off.

Cursing himself for letting his tense mood affect the situation, Darcy fixed a smile on his face. "So, do you really think Tater is lined up for number six?"

Glancing back at the old man, Silver rolled her shoulders,

seeming to go along with Darcy's attempt to lighten the conversation. "Stranger things have happened. He's not getting any younger, you know."

"I'd say that's an understatement."

Silver sighed. "I'd love to see him with someone of his own. He's spent his life looking after the Braybournes."

"He's loved every minute of it, I'll bet." There were men just like Tater on WindRaven Farms, those who were more comfortable with the horses and the people they worked with than with any other close relationships.

"I'm sure he has, but still—"

"Whatcha waitin' for, Silver?" Tater called. "I ain't got all day to lollygag around here with you and this here horse of yours."

Silver yelled back, "I'm coming. You just keep your britches on." Then she made a face at Darcy. "With any luck he'll get a quick nap later, or else I'll have to lock him in the feed room until his disposition improves."

"Women have a funny way of souring a man's disposition." Darcy saw by her quick flush that his jab had gone home. "Take you, for instance. You've got me so windblown by your change in attitudes that I don't know which way is west and which is east."

She bit her lip. "I thought I explained."

"The only thing you explained was that you were too confused to explain. At least that's what I got from it."

"That's not what I said and you know it."

"I spent the whole damn night trying to figure it out—you and me, I mean—and I've come to a conclusion."

"What conclusion?"

"Silver Braybourne!"

Distracted, Silver turned her head again to look at Tater.

"The sun's gonna go down before you get that horse on the track. Get a move on."

"Tater, one more word and—ah hell!" Silver jammed the riding helmet on her head and buckled the chin strap. "We'll have to finish this later."

"That we will, sweetheart." How, Darcy hadn't the faintest idea. All he knew was that every time he got around this woman and opened his mouth, things he'd never intended to say came out. Scowling, he reached for Silver's knee to give her a leg up into the saddle. Then he was all-business as he walked beside her to the track. "How far are you going to push him?"

"First, I'll warm him up with an easy canter once around, then I'll give him his head. This track's a half mile, and the Rosemont is a mile, so I'm going to take him twice around."

"Have you run him that far before?"

"I've run him around our smaller track, and taken him for straight gallops, of course."

Darcy looked around. "It's still early. There aren't a lot of riders here yet. You can run him hard for a time, then maybe later we can start seeing how he does with other horses. That's been most of the problem, hasn't it? How he behaves when—"

"So Daddy was told." Silver looked down. "I haven't had him running with other horses so far, so I'm still not completely sure what the problem is."

Darcy laid a hand on the horse's rump, giving him a quick pat, ignoring the skittish response. "There's no better time than now to find out, is there?"

Silver leaned over to adjust her stirrups. "I guess not." She laid the reins across Lucky Hand's neck and turned him to the left to enter the track.

"Take him back a ways," Tater waved her toward the area where the starting gate would stand. "And start moving him forward."

"I'm going to warm him up a bit first," Silver repeated over her shoulder.

Tater walked up to join them. Hooking his heel over one of the fence rails, Darcy leaned his elbows on the top and watched as Silver started Lucky Hand in an easy trot before breaking into a canter. He watched the horse intently, measuring his gait, his stride, his balance, while doing the same to the woman who sat so lightly on his back. Never taking his eyes off the horse and rider, Darcy said, "So, Tater, what—"

"I ain't answering no questions, so you might as well not even—"

"Relax!" Darcy snorted. "I'm not asking about your social life. That's your business."

"Well, there's some Nosy-Parkers who wouldn't agree with you," he said, shooting a look in Silver's direction.

"I'm not one of them. I've got enough trouble with women, so I've no reason to worry about yours."

Diverted, Tater turned to look at him. "You wanna say any more about that?"

"No."

"Good, 'cause I'd rather not know."

"Good." The word burst through his tense lips as if it had been dying to escape.

Tater sent him another long, searching look. "It ain't hard to figure, though. So if I was you I'd watch it."

Darcy kept his eyes fixed on Silver as she trotted Lucky Hand around the track. "Easier said than done, Tater."

"I knew it was bound to happen—"

"Nothing's happened."

"You two been humming 'round each other like twin electric motors since you met."

Turning his head, Darcy hoped he looked reassuring instead of frustrated. "Tater, nothing's happened. Not what you're thinking, at least."

"Harden has his mind made up that Silver is going to marry John Tom."

Darcy shook his head. "Then Harden better have a serious conversation with his daughter. Silver doesn't seem committed to making it happen."

"I know. I've tried telling Harden, but stubborn doesn't describe that man when he gets a notion in his mind." Tater watched as Silver passed by the rail. "Truth to tell, Silver would ride roughshod over John Tom in a year."

Darcy grinned. He could just see her doing it, too.

"She needs a man she can't control so easily. Harden thinks John Tom is it, but he ain't. I've known that girl since she was a little bitty handful and she needs strong, loving hands to bring her to the starting gate." His voice lowered until he almost seemed to be talking to himself. Darcy leaned closer to hear. "John Tom thinks he'll wear her down by not listening to her and trying to move forward the way he wants them to go. She might give in on the surface, for good manners and her daddy's sake, but she won't like it. If she marries him I'm afraid Silver'll end up like some of them other rich young wives, with not enough to do except buzz around like social bees. That wouldn't be enough for my little gal." His expression troubled, he heaved a great sigh and grabbed hold of the railing to steady himself. "I gotta tell ya, Darcy, it's been worrying me some."

Darcy shifted, not sure what to say. He was tempted to tell Tater not to worry, but knew he had no basis for doing that. He had no right to interfere. In a few weeks his adventure would come to an end and then it wouldn't be his problem anymore. Not that it was now, but still he couldn't help but... But what? Stop her from making a mistake?

Who was going to stop him from making one? From going back and picking up his old life?

Darcy watched as Silver leaned low over Lucky Hand's back to whisper something into his ear as she swept around the backstretch. The right man for Silver would have to be a horseman, someone who could understand Silver's passion for animals and who could help get the farm back on its feet. It was a pretty tall order, Darcy thought, looking at the woman trotting toward them. The poor bastard would not only have to take on Silver, he'd have to take on every person and beast in her life, and sometimes take a back seat while he did so. The man who got mixed up permanently with Silver Braybourne would have to be pretty damn confident in who he was in order to deal with it all. Which effectively left him out, he thought, in what was an uncharacteristic moment of insight for him. He was coming to realize that much of his confidence was based on his birthright and financial attributes. It wasn't something that formed a rock-solid foundation.

If his grandfather were still alive, would he be wondering who Darcy was and what he was made of? His grandfather would have provided the guts and the purpose, because his parents, unfortunately, were jet-setters who didn't look beyond the surface of their lives. Reviewing his own recent lifestyle, Darcy suddenly wondered if he was actually more like his parents than he wanted to believe. Like a fist, the thought slammed into his gut.

Fate had a real sense of humor. Darcy acknowledged that he'd begun to face the truth about how he wanted to live the rest of his life, but he'd never expected it to happen while he was standing in the middle of a dew laden field on the outskirts of Cecil, Kentucky.

But first things first. First there was Silver—and Lucky Hand.

Darcy looked out over the track. The mist was still hanging low, just starting to rise. He glanced at his watch. It was going on 5:30 a.m. As Silver approached where he and Tater were standing, he said, "Let's get a move on, Silver. Let's see how fast this horse runs."

"You'd better stand back then, 'cause he's going to blow you away."

"It takes a lot to blow me away."

Silver grinned. "We'll see."

Darcy and Tater watched as she walked the horse back to the track area. She turned him in a slow circle, bringing him to a stop, steadying him as Darcy dug a handkerchief out of his pocket. Silver crouched low over her horse's neck. After nodding at Tater, who was lifting the stopwatch, Darcy extended his arm, and with a flourish dropped the white cotton. The instant the hankie left Darcy's hand, Tater clicked the watch. Silver and Lucky Hand were already moving. They thundered past Darcy as if the devil himself was racing at their heels. The stallion's noble head jutted forward, his great chest extended, his long legs ate up the ground under his hooves.

"What do you think?" Darcy asked Tater as horse and rider took the sweep into the first curve.

"He's a pretty runner, I'll say that for him."

"Does he want to win, do you think? Or is it the rider?"

Tater sent Darcy a glance. "You know it don't matter who's riding or who's training, much as we like to think so. The horse has to be bred to race. It's in his genes and nothing anybody does can change it. That's the way it is." He pulled his attention back to the track. "I guess only time will tell with this horse."

"Tater," Darcy said impatiently, "I already know it's one part genetics and one part black magic, so quit feeding me that bull. I asked you what you think!"

Tater and Darcy watched as Silver passed them and started on the second lap. "Well, sir, I reckon he wants to win when he's by hisself. When he's in a race? Now that's another story." He shook his head. "Some horses are just too damn independent."

Like some women, Darcy thought as he watched Silver.

Tater suddenly grinned at him, his eyes knowing and amused. For a moment Darcy wondered if he'd said the thought aloud. "That can be both a good and a bad thing for everyone involved, boy—independence, I mean."

Giving Tater a rueful grin, Darcy said, "Some things are worth working for."

"And some things won't drop into your lap no matter how hard you work."

Meeting Tater's wise old eyes, Darcy hesitated before saying, "I guess time will tell." He turned back to the track as Silver approached the homestretch. "Ready, Tater?"

"Yep." He clicked the watch. "Got it."

As Silver slowed her horse to a walk, Tater stared at the face of the stopwatch with wonder in his eyes.

"Well, I'll be." He held the clock out to Darcy. "Look at that time."

Darcy whistled. "Not bad, not bad at all. What do you say we find him another horse to work with and see if he can duplicate it?" Silver, still mounted, walked Lucky Hand over to the fence. "You up to another round, Silver? This time with another horse for company?"

"You bet." She leaned over and patted her horse's neck. "And so's my partner here."

"You think so?" he asked, taking a moment to study the black. In spite of his hard run, Lucky Hand still seemed riproaring and ready to go.

"He has to be. If he isn't, he's going to have to learn."

Darcy glanced up at Silver. "I agree."

"Thanks so much. Glad you approve."

Darcy stared into her eyes, and she stared right back. Independent, contrary, prickly, mercurial, but rock solid underneath it all, with a determination that blew him away. All that and more described Silver. Life with this woman sure as hell would be a challenge. What man would knowingly stick his head in the noose?

A gambler, that's who. The answer popped into his mind as she sent him an impudent smile, one full of daring and mischief.

"Why don't you go find me a horse to race?"

"I can do that." Tater jerked a thumb in the direction of the old barn near the track. "That looks like Boone over there with John Tom's little filly Teardrop. Be right back." A few minutes later, Tater returned accompanied by a pretty roan filly and a slim man around Darcy's age.

Darcy indicated the horse. "That's a very pretty lady you've got with you."

Boone smoothed a loving hand down his horse's face, chuckling as she leaned to give him a fond bump with her nose. "Teardrop is the best. She can run, but we think more of her breeding potential. She's from a pretty impressive line."

Tater nodded. "Breeding's the big moneymaker in the horse business, not racing."

Silver shook her head. "Not for a stallion. A stallion has to race so he can prove his genes are solid."

"You're right," Darcy agreed. Stud fees and breeding were the key to WindRaven Farms' success. He glanced back at

Lucky Hand. He'd put in another call to his manager today to see what he'd found out about this horse's lineage so far. Darcy couldn't deny that Lucky Hand might prove to live up to his name if he could handle the stress of the racetrack—both physically and mentally. From the restless look of the black as he eyed the little filly, the mental discipline would be their biggest obstacle.

Darcy nodded at Silver. "Ready?"

"Totally."

Her expression set and determined, Silver turned her horse and headed to the starting area. Boone followed right behind her as Darcy and Tater walked to the rail. Leaning over, Darcy picked up his handkerchief. He glanced at the two riders, then at Tater, before raising his arm. He could feel the tension. For Silver and Braybourne Farm this could be a defining moment. He opened his fingers. The white square caught the slight breeze and fluttered to the ground as the dirt exploded underneath the horses' hooves.

Lucky Hand was behaving well. His nose was forward and all of his attention was focused on the track stretching before him as they took a long sweep into the first turn. An old memory teased Darcy as he watched. "That horse is too close to the rail. He's going to feel crowded." He thought back to the horse he suspected could be Lucky Hand's sire. Take a Chance never liked to be sent to the rail too early. Somehow, Darcy knew Silver's horse was the same.

"You sound like you know this horse."

Darcy met Tater's curious gaze. "No. I've got a feeling about this, is all."

Tater pulled his attention back to the track. "Ah hell, the black's gettin' riled up."

Darcy followed Tater's pointing finger. Lucky Hand's focus was no longer straight ahead. The black was deliberately moving to the right, seeming determined to bump Teardrop. Was it sheer temper and lack of control, or was he looking for an open path, for the broad sweep to the right that Take a Chance always preferred when breaking away from the pack? Silver was firmly keeping him on the inside as she fought to avoid the other animal. Dashing around the last curve, she seemed to be losing the battle.

"Sweep him right, sweep him right," Darcy yelled. But it was too late for Silver to respond. Lucky Hand lurched and plunged as Silver pulled up on the reins. The alarmed roan increased her speed, roaring past Tater and Darcy. His heart in his throat, Darcy watched Silver try to control Lucky Hand, then raced out onto the track to catch hold of the stallion's bridle. "Damn it, why didn't you listen to me and sweep him right like I was telling you?"

Silver, face white, arms trembling, barely kept her seat as Lucky Hand reared.

"Because he likes the left. He likes the rail."

"No, he doesn't. He just likes to start there. Anybody with sense could see that."

"Are you saying I don't have any sense?" She yanked on the reins to stop the stallion from his agitated dancing. "You have a hell of a lot of nerve."

"You've been working this horse for a month, so you ought to know how he's thinking."

"I'm training him to rethink."

He snapped right back at her. "You can only train so far and then the horse's natural inclinations have to take over. You can't fight them."

"And you think I'm fighting them?"

"Yes," Darcy said, his lips drawn into a straight line. "You're damn lucky you didn't get yourself killed."

Temper flared in her eyes. "I had it under control."

"Oh yeah, it looked like it."

"He went after Teardrop with no warning. I couldn't anticipate that."

"Look, it's very simple. Pay attention." He knew that comment was going to tick Silver off, but he was completely ticked off himself. This damn woman must have taken twelve years off his life, and his blood was still racing. "This horse needs to sweep to the right, to get to the outside with no competition."

"It's a harder way to win."

"But it's the horse's way."

"I'll lose if I let him do that."

He stared at her. "And that's what it's all about, huh? You have to win."

"Yes. I have to win."

"No matter what it takes?"

Silver hesitated. "No matter what it takes—as long as it's not illegal."

"Silver, that isn't the way to handle this horse and you know it. You're only saying it so you don't have to admit I could be right."

"Oh, you think you know so much, don't you? You think you know all about horses and about me, right?"

"No, but I know enough." He stared at her vivid face, at her sparkling eyes, her lips, then at the way she held her body upright in the saddle, her lines fluid and graceful but full of power. A power that almost brought him to his knees every time he looked at her. As angry as he was with her right now, he'd like to lock her in his bedroom for the next six months.

"Do you know how badly I want you off my farm? Away from my horse?"

"I've got an idea." He stared at her, easily reading the conflicting emotions in her eyes—desire mixed with anger, pleasure mixed with pain. Yes, he had a good idea how much she wanted him gone, how much she wanted to remove his special brand of temptation from her path. She wanted him gone almost as badly as he wanted to stay.

"No, you have no idea. It's more than taking my place, it's—it's...you confuse me. I don't know myself when I'm with you. God, if I could just—"

"Get rid of me? I'll tell you what, Silver," he said, in his slowest, most dangerous drawl. "I'll make you an offer."

Eyes wary, she asked, "What kind of offer?"

"Do you play cards? Poker?"

A disdainful expression crept over her face. "What do you think?"

Darcy cupped the palm of his hand around her calf, where the trembling muscles pressed against the horse. "Okay, here's the deal. We'll play for it. For all of it—me off the farm, away from Lucky Hand, away from you."

"Play for it," she repeated, her tone skeptical and hopeful at the same time.

"That's right. If you win, I leave. If I win..."

"If you win?"

"I stay out the month. I manage the farm with no interference from you. I actively help train this horse." His hand slipped up to her thigh. "And I make love to you."

Silver stared at him for a long moment before plucking his hand away. "All I have to do is win and you're going to pack up and walk away?"

Darcy smiled. "Win by my rules and I'm gone."

"*Your* rules? I don't think I want to—"

"Scared?" She would never let him get away with calling her a coward.

Silver glared down at him. "You should be so lucky."

"Yes, I should." He knew she couldn't resist the dare. "Well, what do you say?"

With a sharp, quick nod, she gave her response, her words as much a warning as an agreement. "You've got a deal, Rick Darcy."

"I'll see you in the stables tonight at ten. My room."

"No, the manager's office," she said over her shoulder as she started to walk Lucky Hand to cool him off.

Darcy nodded. "Don't be late."

8

AFTER DINNER, Darcy spent the rest of the evening in his room cursing himself and wondering if he'd just lost every brain cell he'd been born with. Why had he made Silver such a reckless offer? Just because she goaded him constantly, often through no fault of her own, was no excuse. There was no way he'd just up and walk out on this family when they needed him, regardless of what he'd told Silver. Even if he'd spent more time playing around in college than studying, he actually had a business degree, and it was coming in handy. During the last few days, he'd learned how many management details and opportunities were being overlooked because of the lack of personnel and time. He was finding that very challenging, and satisfying. So he couldn't lose this poker game tonight. He'd have to find a way out, a way to make it impossible for Silver to play. He thought for a moment. He'd said they'd play by his rules—meaning that he'd choose the terms of how many hands declared the winner. Now he'd have to make the game a lot more unappealing. He wasn't sure how.

When his room became too confining, he stepped into the corridor and paced up and down the stables again, with only the horses to keep him company, instead of the woman he craved. The woman he kept provoking.

Oh man, you've got it bad.

After paying a visit to each animal, he finally ended up nose to nose with a beautiful little mare named Rosie Red. She'd foaled that summer, and the little guy, Red Devil, had the look of his namesake. He might be one to watch, Darcy thought, if Braybourne Farm lasted that long. He'd had his banker do some checking. Harden Braybourne was in a tight spot at the moment. No wonder Silver was pinning such hopes on Lucky Hand.

Darcy cupped the palm o

the trembling muscles presse

the deal. We'll play for it. For

from Lucky Hand, away from y

"Play for it," she repeated, her

the same time.

"That's right. If you win, I leave. I

"If you win?"

"I stay out the month. I manage the

ence from you. I actively help train th

slipped up to her thigh. "And I make love

Silver stared at him for a long moment b

hand away. "All I have to do is win and you

up and walk away?"

Darcy smiled. "Win by my rules and I'm gone

"*Your* rules? I don't think I want to—"

"Scared?" She would never let him get away w

her a coward.

Silver glared down at him. "You should be so lucky

"Yes, I should." He knew she couldn't resist the dare.

what do you say?"

With a sharp, quick nod, she gave her response, her wo

as much a warning as an agreement. "You've got a deal, Ri

Darcy."

"I'll see you in the stables tonight at ten. My room."

"No, the manager's office," she said over her shoulder as she

started to walk Lucky Hand to cool him off.

Darcy nodded. "Don't be late."

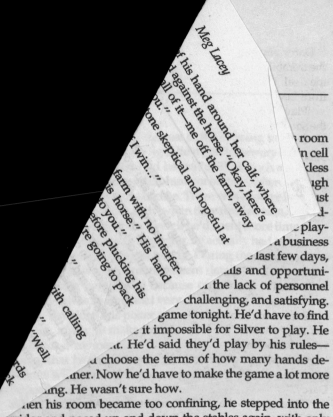

Meg Lacey

f his hand around her calf, where
d against the horse. "Okay, here's
all of it—me off the farm, away
ou."
one skeptical and hopeful at

I win..."

farm with no interfer-
is horse." His hand
to you." His hand
fore plucking his
're going to pack

ith calling

Well,

rds
k

room
n cell
kless
gh
st
d-
play-
business
last few days,
lls and opportuni-
the lack of personnel
challenging, and satisfying.
game tonight. He'd have to find
it impossible for Silver to play. He
t. He'd said they'd play by his rules—
choose the terms of how many hands de-
ner. Now he'd have to make the game a lot more
ing. He wasn't sure how.

en his room became too confining, he stepped into the
orridor and paced up and down the stables again, with only
the horses to keep him company, instead of the woman he
craved. The woman he kept provoking.

Oh man, you've got it bad.

After paying a visit to each animal, he finally ended up nose
o nose with a beautiful little mare named Rosie Red. She'd
oaled that summer, and the little guy, Red Devil, had the look
f his namesake. He might be one to watch, Darcy thought, if
raybourne Farm lasted that long. He'd had his banker do
me checking. Harden Braybourne was in a tight spot at the
oment. No wonder Silver was pinning such hopes on Lucky
nd.

Darcy strolled over to the black's box and looked over the door. The horse turned his head and gave him an inquiring stare—free of the temperament and arrogance Darcy had usually seen. It was as if he was saying, *I'm not that bad, I've just been misunderstood and mistreated.* Darcy smiled, imagining that the horse gave him a look of approval in return.

"You can be the winner Silver wants you to be, you know," Darcy whispered, watching the horse's ears prick forward. "You've got the right stuff, the right breeding—maybe not the right owner until now, but that's in the past. The future is dead ahead. All you have to do is run toward it."

If Lucky Hand could actually win some races and then set up for stud, the horse would be worth some big bucks. Every indication was that the black had been bred at his farm from Take a Chance and Mistress Mine. If things went well, racing-wise, Darcy could even put a value figure on the stallion's future worth, thanks to his farm manager's phone call. He and his manager were beginning to piece together what had happened to this horse since he was sold from WindRaven Farms.

The scrape of the stable door over concrete attracted his attention. He turned and squinted in the dim light. Silver stood inside the doorway. She hesitated for a moment, then walked toward him, reminding him of a lamb on its way to becoming a lamb chop. Not that Silver could remotely be considered a lamb. She was much too bold for that. Still, there was a naiveté about her at times, an innocence in her belief that she could make things go her own way if she wanted them badly enough and worked hard enough. A lump of tenderness welled in Darcy's chest. He wasn't sure how he could ever walk away from this woman. Then, as she came toward him, he suddenly knew how he could make her concede the poker game. He smiled at the prospect of springing it on her.

"Not scared, are you?" he asked.

Silver stared at him as he strolled toward her. "That's the second time you've asked me that." Scared? Hell no. She wasn't scared. She was terrified.

"And?" He stood with his brow lifted politely, waiting for her answer.

Broadening her stance, fists on her hips, she thrust out her chin. "Let's play cards." She hoped her bravado would eventually calm her quaking insides. Until it did, she'd play the role as she felt it needed to be played.

Darcy walked over and held the office door open, gesturing her inside. "*Mi casa es su casa*. That is, if you're really lucky tonight."

Giving him a cocky stare, Silver swaggered past him. "Start packing, amigo."

Parading over to the desk, she yanked a pack of cards from her pocket and slapped them onto the surface. "We might be playing by your rules, but we're playing with my deck."

"You think I'm going to cheat?"

"Let's say I'm not going to take a chance."

"I thought you lived to take chances."

She sent him a tiny smile. "Only when I can predict the outcome." Which wasn't true in this case, but she hoped she had enough skill to get around that little detail.

Darcy sat in the chair behind the desk. "That sure of yourself, are you?"

Silver remembered what had happened the last time he'd sat in that chair, with the stables dark and deserted around them. A little flicker licked at her insides.

"Something wrong?" Darcy asked, his eyes keen as he expertly shuffled the cards, then placed them in front of her.

"Not a thing." She sat in the straight chair opposite him, praying as she cut the cards that her uneasiness hadn't been apparent in her voice.

"Not worried that your father or Tater will interrupt us?"

"They both go to bed early."

"That's good news."

"Besides—" she shrugged "—we're just playing cards."

Darcy peeled off a card. "Did I mention this is a game of strip poker?"

Silver erupted to her feet. "What?"

"Strip poker, five card stud. Win the majority of five and you take the prize." Darcy grinned. "My rules, remember?"

"I didn't agree to stri—"

"If that makes you uncomfortable we can just say I win and forget the whole thing."

"Oh, you think so, huh?"

"I'm merely offering it as an option."

She glared at him. He expected her to say no. Concede without a fight? Who did he think he was talking to? She sat down again and leaned back in her chair. "Deal the cards."

He did so, snapping the cards onto the table, then placed the rest of the deck in the center. Silver scooped up her cards and fanned them in her hand, cautiously rearranging them by suit and color. She had very little to work with. She peeked up to see Darcy with his cards folded into his hand, looking very much as if he had every good card in the deck.

Putting his hand down, he picked up the deck. "How many?"

All of them, she wanted to shout. But she managed to keep her poker face and say with a laconic gesture, "I'll take three."

Darcy dealt the cards and slid them in her direction. Then, taking none for himself, he put the deck down and picked up his cards again. He smiled a little teasing smile that made Silver grit her teeth.

He's bluffing, she thought. *His hand isn't that great—he's just playing a mind game. Don't fall for it.* She glanced down. She had a pair. That was better than nothing. She threw it down. "Pair of nines."

Darcy smiled as he laid his cards face-up. "Sorry. Three queens." Then he looked up at her expectantly. "You do understand the rules of strip poker? Or would you like me to review them?"

Who did he think he was, Edmond Hoyle? She scowled. "There's no need to speak to me as if I'm a three-year-old. I understand perfectly. You lose, you strip."

Darcy closed his eyes, his expression pained. "Please, you remove only one item of clothing per loss. You don't *strip* unless you're not wearing that many clothes to begin with. In which case I suppose..." His eyes opened, and Silver could see they were brimming with laughter. She wanted to kill him.

"Oh, shut up." She was wearing a peach-colored, sleeveless shell and matching cardigan, along with her grandmother's pearls, but she'd added jeans and her old boots so he wouldn't think she was dressing up for him. Making a big deal of it, she toyed with the top button of the cardigan. "Don't you want to hum some stripping music?"

Shocked, he grabbed his chest. "Silver Braybourne, what would a nice Southern lady like you know about stripping music?"

Keeping her eyes fixed on his, she licked her lips as she slowly pushed the top button of the cardigan through the buttonhole. Then, inch by inch, she slipped the cardigan off her shoulders and down her arms. "Maybe I'm not as nice as you think I am."

Eyes wide, Darcy grinned. "That sounds promising."

"My turn to deal." She reached for the cards and took her turn in a quick, efficient manner. They played the next hand in virtual silence. She'd thrown the gauntlet and had obviously intrigued and surprised him. Now it was time to concentrate and to pray the luck of the draw was in her favor. She smiled. "Well, well, well, would you look at that. I have a straight. Isn't that nice? And what do you have, darlin'?"

Darcy looked up, folding his hand. "Looks like you're going to win this one, sweetheart."

"I think I'd like you to remove that shirt so I can sit here and stare at your manly chest while I kick your butt." A glint in Darcy's eyes warned her she was playing with fire, but she didn't care.

"The rules don't say you can tell the other person which item of clothing to remove."

"There's no rule that says you can't."

Darcy shook his head and stood up. "Never let it be said I'd disappoint a lady."

"I'm sure you wouldn't." That was an understatement.

Nothing about Darcy could be termed a disappointment. She practically choked as he faced her like a Chippendale dancer standing center stage. She could scarcely keep her eyes off him as he unbuttoned his shirt. He made sure it took him a long time to push each button through the hole. Then he mirrored her previous movements by slipping it over his shoulders. Letting his arms hang down straight, he allowed the fabric to slip off unaided.

She knew his body; she'd smoothed her hands over it already. But it was different when she sat back as a voyeur. Her gaze roamed over his shoulders, then proceeded south, touching every ridge and valley along the way. He had a horseman's body—long limbs, lean hips, sinewy arms and a chest with enough sculpted muscle to control a wild stallion...or a woman. Silver's breath came a bit quicker at the thought. She'd like to—

"Those kind of thoughts could get you in trouble, Ms. Braybourne."

Silver could feel the blush flooding up her neck and onto her cheeks as Darcy gave her a smile that had a bit too much satisfaction in it to suit her. Retrieving her control, she forced a cool comment through her lips. "If you're finished with the show, the score's tied and I'd like to get on with it."

Darcy sat down and shuffled the cards. "My deal, I believe." They played intently, each focused on the cards, each trying to second-guess the other.

Silver glanced down at her cards. "You might as well fold, Darcy. There's no way you'll beat this hand."

"I'll take my chances." With a flourish he laid down a pair of aces and a pair of jacks. "Beat that."

Hesitating, Silver glanced at her cards again, then plunked them on the table facedown. With a disgusted sigh she pulled her shell over her head and flung it aside, not bothering to add any finesse whatsoever. She was left sitting there in a brief scrap of lace that barely contained her full breasts. *Relax. Don't think about the fact that you're sitting here in your bra and your pearls,* she told herself. *After all, you bare more than this at the beach*. Then she looked up and saw Darcy's expression, and all thoughts of relaxation flew out the window.

"You...you—" he cleared his throat "—you, uh, didn't ask me..."

"I don't have to, remember? You said so."

"And then you said—"

"I don't care what I said. I don't want to play that way anymore. I lost the second game. I removed my top. End of story." She knew she sounded like a snotty little girl who wanted her own way or she'd go home, but she couldn't help it. The longer this game went on, the more dangerous it was becoming to her peace of mind, not to mention her libido. She could feel his gaze on her breasts as strongly as if it was a kiss. Wetting her lips, she hunkered down in her chair and reached for the cards. They played again. This time the loser was Darcy.

He stood.

Silver's gaze journeyed up his body, ending at his smiling lips. "That seems to be your favorite position for removing your clothes."

His fingers toyed with the buttons on his jeans. "I thought you might appreciate the view."

Would she ever! She tried not to, but her gaze kept going back to his jeans as he opened the first button, then the second, then his hand hovered over the third...until he removed his watch and placed it on the desk. Silver felt the disappointment down to her boot heels, but she couldn't help giving a short laugh.

"Very nice move there. Completely unexpected. Yes, very smooth."

He bowed. "Thank you, thank you. A bit of suspense helps build the tension, don't you think?"

The tension was high enough, she thought, but she just nodded and pushed the cards in his direction. "Final round. How's your luck hanging?"

"Hanging tight." As he dealt the last hand, he asked in a very polite voice, "How's yours?"

"I guess we're going to find out, aren't we?" Fanning the

cards in her hand, she said a quick prayer before looking down. Nothing. She was holding absolutely nothing. She debated trying to bluff him, but that hadn't worked too well the last time. "Give me five." She slapped down her old cards and accepted the new. That was more like it. She shuffled the suits, pleased to see a hand top-heavy with matching picture cards. She almost chuckled, but swallowed it as she looked up to meet Darcy's steady eyes.

Why does he look so calm? What does he have?

"I'll call you."

Just like that. He'd given her no warning. She now had no way of psychologically building things up, of mentally convincing him to throw in the towel. No—just a bold, sure statement from the cool customer sitting across from her. The man she never expected to see again after tonight, given the promise of her winning hand.

She threw it down. "Two kings, two jacks. Read them and weep."

He let out a breath. "Not quite, sweetheart." He fanned his cards across the desk. "Full house."

"It seems this is your lucky night." Horror and joy warred within Silver as she stared down at the two kings and three queens. Her gaze lifted to meet his. "Funny. I thought it was mine."

"That's what keeps people believing. Sometimes you get on a roll and you believe in Lady Luck even more."

"True." Silver was still trying to come to terms with her loss. But she was a Braybourne and Braybournes always paid their debts—somehow.

"But you can't control the lady," Darcy continued. "She's fickle. She makes love to one person, then another. The only thing you can do is roll with her when you've got her." He hesitated for a moment before finishing in a low voice, "I'm sorry, Silver."

Silver stood and walked around to his side of the desk. He swiveled to face her as she studied him, seeking some sign of the arrogance that would anger her enough to make her walk out the door. There was none, only a gentleness and a humility that winged straight to her heart. "Don't be sorry. A bet's a bet and a deal's a deal. You win. So you stay, train Lucky Hand—"

"We train Lucky Hand. I can't do it by myself."

"And..." Her voice faltered.

He didn't make her say it, but finished the sentence for her. "And I make love with you." He cupped his palms on her forearms, caressing her skin. "That's the only reason I started this in the first place, you know."

She placed both hands on the arms of the chair and leaned down to him. "Not your burning desire to work the Braybourne Farm?"

"That, too. I like it here. But strong as that desire is, something burns hotter." His eyes were intent on hers, searing into her until she could feel the embers stir. "I tried not to let it happen, but it was no use. You were always there. Always in my mind..." He slipped his arms around her waist and leaned forward to press a kiss on the skin just above the waistband of her jeans. Then he pressed a kiss higher on her abdomen.

Silver unhooked her bra and straddled him, feeling the erection she suspected had been growing bigger as their game proceeded. It felt so good against her. She settled herself fully on him, enjoying his hardness rubbing against her as he automatically responded to her bold move. She slid her hands down his chest, taking her time to lean forward and press tiny kisses in their wake. She pressed her breasts against him, her stomach clenching as his chest hair scraped her taut and tender nipples. A bolt of desire spiked her groin. Her fingers slipped inside his partially unbuttoned jeans and lingered there. Then she undid the last button, teasing, "I hope you don't mind my doing this. You seemed mighty attached to these jeans a few minutes ago."

"Not so attached that I won't rip them off faster than you can say—"

"Take me?"

"Oh, bless me..." He groaned. "Take me's good."

She leaned forward and licked his chest, pulling his nipple

between her teeth, rolling it with her tongue. "All during the game, I was watching you. And I kept getting hotter and hotter."

He groaned again as Silver lifted her head and cupped the outline of his sex with both hands, her thumbs and fingers kneading and stroking. Then his lips claimed hers, the hunger almost knocking her into the next universe.

"I'll bet you can't get these jeans off before we both explode." She lifted her hips, then rocked hard, as she whispered, "Because I'm way too close as it is."

"I'll take that bet."

His hands went to her jeans. Seeking the zipper, he slid it down with more haste than finesse and began working her pants off her hips. Only able to get so far with her on his lap, Darcy stood and sat Silver on the desk while he pulled her boots off and slipped her jeans down her legs. Then he froze, awestruck by her magnificence as she sprawled on the old oak desk, eyes smoky with arousal, breasts high and tight, legs wide and welcoming, the only barrier between himself and satisfaction a tiny scrap of white silk. He fingered the lacy trim, sliding his finger under the edge.

He smiled as his finger teased her. "I like your taste in underwear, sweetheart."

"I'm glad," she whispered, lifting her hips as he stroked her skin.

He trailed his fingers over the scrap of silk barely covering her womanhood. "Thong bikinis are my favorite."

"Mine too. I always wear them."

"You do?" he breathed, his fingers pressing a bit harder.

She licked her lips. "I don't like to be too constrained."

He grinned. "Now that's a thought that's going to keep me rock-hard for the next month."

She smiled a temptress's smile as she focused on the hard bulge that was straining to burst free. "It's going to be a bit difficult to ride then, isn't it?"

"Oh, I don't think so. For the first time in my life, I'm planning to get saddle sore." She chuckled, the little sound ratcheting his desire up one more notch. He leaned over and kissed her, lips closing over the silk. Then he slipped his finger under the fabric, teasing her until she moaned. "My God, you're gorgeous," he murmured.

She reached for him, arms greedy, her breathing fast and shallow. "Hurry."

"Not too fast. I want this to last." He slipped her thong off, continuing to caress her while he freed himself. He was so enthralled with the heat of her, he never wanted to stop touching her and watching her respond.

"Please," she gasped, her head moving from side to side, "please." She pressed her hands against his, holding them against her.

"You're so wet."

Unable to stop, he fingered her, the heel of his palm pressing hard as she arched. He watched, stunned, when she turned to quicksilver under his hand, her orgasm taking him by surprise. She let out a long low cry, and he could feel his blood rushing, pulsing, hardening him to pure gold. Now urgent, desperate, he broke free, pulling her toward him, her bare buttocks sliding over the desk. She clasped her legs around his waist and reached for him. He pressed against her, muttering, "Hot, so hot..." as he entered her inch by inch, burying himself deep in her heat. Slowly, carefully, he started to move, feeling her contract around him as he paced himself, not wanting it to end.

"Let go the reins," she coaxed, voice husky with desire, tongue caressing his ear. Her fingers dug into his back. Impatient now, she nipped his shoulder, hips rocking as she demanded, "Damn you, Darcy, let go."

His vision blurred and his need took over. He couldn't hold himself in check any longer. With a small cry, he cupped her buttocks, lifting her even higher, and plunged, a stallion wild with lust, frantic to mate. He rode her, rode her hard, her legs clamped tight around him as she met him thrust for thrust. Never in his life had he been so out of control, so focused on satisfaction—not just his own, but hers. His senses were flooded with the slick feel of her, the musky scent of her, the taste of her still on his tongue. She was all there was. All he could see. She filled his world as fully as he filled her.

Without considering any possible consequences, he poured himself into her, his mouth on hers swallowing her scream as she came again. Breathing harsh, muscles weak, the room still spinning, he collapsed on her. For long moments the only sound was the loud ticking of the clock on the wall. When he could breathe again, he lifted himself on his elbows, removing his weight from her, but not withdrawing completely, unwilling to break their intimate connection.

"Silver," he whispered.

She said nothing, just squeezed her eyes more tightly shut and breathed deep, her chest rising and falling, drawing air into her lungs as if she was suffocating.

He couldn't resist pressing his lips to her breasts, first one, then the other, before asking, "Silver, are you all right?"

She shivered at his touch, then rolled her head from side to side.

"Come on, darling," he coaxed, a hint of laughter in his voice as he ran his fingertip over her lips. "Say something, or I'm going to think I killed you."

"Dear God."

"No." He grinned. "You're giving me too much credit."

"Dear God. What have we done?"

He stared down at her. "Somehow that's not what I hoped to hear."

"What *have* we done?"

"Had hot, mind-blowing sex."

"Mind-blowing sex. Whew—it was that all right." She reached up with both hands to cover her face. "Dear God!"

Did he miss something? He was silent for a moment, somewhat confused. After all, they'd just shared one of the most satisfying experiences he could remember. He stared down at her, feeling completely out of his depth. What was it with women? Why didn't they react the way they were supposed to react? He examined her more closely. Could she be feeling shy? He wouldn't have thought she had a shy bone in her body after the passion they'd just shared, but women were funny that way.

"Silver? Look, there's nothing to be embarrassed about. This was natural and good—better than good, great even."

When she didn't respond, he decided to overcome the awkwardness by appealing to her competitive instincts. "If it helps, you won the bet." Those instincts ran as strong in her as they ran in him. He was sure they'd come bounding back in full force the minute she caught her breath.

She dropped her hands from her face, eyes popping open as she lifted her head to look at him. "What bet?"

"You bet me that I couldn't get my jeans off before we exploded. Well—" his voice roughened as he remembered the sheer glory of her "—I didn't."

"Oh, dear God," she wailed, and covered her face again.

"You were unbelievable," he whispered. Just thinking about it had him stirring again. He shifted his hips.

"What are you doing?"

Surprised at her sharp tone, he stuttered, "I...I—"

"You...you can't."

His eyes gleamed as he rocked forward. "Oh, I assure you, darling, I can."

She placed a hand on his chest, even as her body began to respond. "I don't think we should do this anymore."

Stunned, he stared at her. "What?"

Why the hell couldn't women just be rational and do what felt good without thinking about it all the time? Obviously she needed help to understand. He decided to ignore her comment and listen to his body instead. "Of course we should."

"You're breaking our verbal agreement."

"What agreement?"

"One time, and one time only."

He leaned over her. "That's old news, Silver, and you know it. Besides, we were interrupted by your father without fully completing that agreement, so it's void. But this time we made a bet. Which I won."

She watched as he leaned closer, then she rushed to speak

before he kissed her. "Okay, you won. You said you'd make love to me. Love—that's singular—as in once—not plural."

"Let's discuss it." He dipped his head, pressing a quick kiss on her lips, then lingered to press another, this one more intimate. Lifting his head, he looked at Silver, satisfied to see he'd rendered her speechless.

Staring up at him, eyes wide and smoky, Silver tried to speak, but nothing came out. She licked her lips, shook her head and tried again. "That's how you discuss it?"

"Nonverbal communication." Darcy smiled, feeling quite proud of himself, sure he'd gotten around her as he did with most women when he made a concentrated effort. "Works for me."

Unfortunately, Silver Braybourne wasn't most women.

She crossed her arms over her breasts with the modesty of a virgin and stared at him. "From now on, we use words."

His smile deepened as he dipped his head again. "Whatever you say."

The palm of her hand flat against his chest stopped him. "I say we should stay away from each other."

"What? Why?"

Her green eyes hardened, the diamond-bright glow almost feverish, as she nailed him with her comment. "So this type of thing doesn't happen again."

His desire waned as rapidly as it had begun. Drawing back, he straightened up and adjusted his jeans, straining to slip the buttons through their holes. Finally, he looked up and said, "Staying away from each other is going to be a bit difficult, isn't it?"

She came up on her elbows, her jaw set, her expression resolute. "No. Because we're going to use firm discipline and work on our self-control."

Darcy lifted a brow, considering the woman lying in front of him. Slow as a hot lazy afternoon, his gaze passed over her as he allowed himself the pleasure of focusing on each tempting inch of skin. Even though she was rejecting him, she responded to his gaze. It was impossible for her to control the reaction of her nipples and the slight twitch of her hips. Her mind, however, was a different story.

He met her determined eyes again. "Are you sure this is the way you want it?"

Silver stared at him for a moment, wondering if she really did mean it, or if she was just being a coward in wishing to stay away from him. She was used to men she knew how to handle. And although Darcy was definitely her fantasy come true, she had a feeling that she was out of her depth in attempting to control him. Which naturally made her determined to try, even as she wondered if she'd lost her mind.

"Surely we're both capable of exercising self-control."

"I'm sure we are," Darcy agreed. "But why should we?" His fingertips skimmed over her. "What damage can we do?"

She could fall in love with him. As Silver met his eyes, she knew she was already more than halfway there.

He continued, his tone reasonable. "Why shouldn't we enjoy this while it lasts? Who are we hurting?"

"There's John Tom...."

"I thought you said there was nothing between the two of you."

"There isn't. He just won't believe it."

Darcy smiled. "Maybe I can help with that."

"No."

His hands gripped her waist as he bent over her. "Are you ashamed of me? Of this?"

"No, but my father needs to be told that—"

"Are you planning on being upfront with your father about what happened in here?"

"Good God, no. I'm truthful, not suicidal. I meant I need to tell Daddy I'm not going to marry John Tom, not about this." She waved her hand, indicating the two of them. "Daddy wouldn't understand this. Even I don't understand."

In a way that was the truth. Her behavior with Darcy was so uncharacteristic she wondered if an alien had taken over her body. But maybe it went deeper. Lately, even as she knuckled down to perform what she considered her life's work, she'd been feeling confined. Like the foals they raised, she wanted to run wild and free, to feel the rich grass under her feet, to kick up her heels and frolic—no worries. Perhaps that explained her instantaneous attraction to Darcy. She sensed some of the same needs raced through him, beckoning her with an unseen bond that was as tempting as it was dangerous.

"What's to understand?" He shrugged. "I'm a man, you're a woman."

"Somehow I don't think Daddy will buy that." Silver's voice was dryer than drought-baked dirt.

Darcy nodded, a slight smile lifting the corner of his lips. "Actually, I don't think he will, either."

"So maybe we should just forget about this attraction between us." Which was a pretty mild word for what was happening as she lay in his arms. She struggled to sit up. He let her go but didn't move back to give her any space. Instead he just gave her a cool, taunting look.

"I never figured you for a coward, Silver."

Stung, she replied, "I'm not a coward."

"What are you so afraid of? This?" His lips teased hers, followed by his tongue. He drew her emotions to the surface as he forced her to face herself. To face her desires. To give him the honest response he was asking for.

She wrenched her mouth away. "I'm afraid of me, goddamn it. Of what I could feel for you."

"That makes two of us."

She could sense his fear lurking behind his desire. It only made him all the more compelling. She ran a fingertip over his bottom lip. "Don't you think we should play this smart, Darcy? Wouldn't it be better if we didn't allow this to happen again?" She was almost pleading, but prayed he'd disagree.

"Better for whom? I think it would be very unhealthy for me." He grinned. "And it wouldn't do you any good, either. Do you know what happens to people when their frustration builds up? They go berserk. No. I think the best thing to do is to get so much loving out of each other that we get sick of it."

She laughed and locked her legs around his hips, running

her hands over him, thrilling as she saw his uncontrollable response. "And what are the odds of that happening?"

He snatched her up in his arms and headed for the door. "We'll never know until we try. Why don't we go talk about it in my room?"

She slipped her arms around his neck. "Real talk, or your interpretation of talking?"

Holding her high, he hurried through the stables and into his bedroom before he answered. He placed her on the bed as if she were a precious jewel. Following her down, he said, "Let's play it by ear."

They did. Two more times.

EXCEPT FOR THE FAROFF NICKER from one of the horses, Darcy's room was quiet as Silver struggled to open her eyes. She'd been having a lovely dream, of she and Darcy racing free over the fields.

Darcy.

Eyes now wide, she turned her head and studied the man sleeping next to her. He wasn't a dream. She smiled. He was a dream come true. Her eyes memorized every detail—the dark slash of his eyebrows, the long black eyelashes, the straight, aristocratic nose, the high cheekbones and...his mouth. Oh, she'd dreamed about his mouth—hot, hungry, demanding, the lips full and oh-so-skilled at seduction. She'd reveled in his mouth as he'd tasted her, as he'd sent her into a world unexplored and uncharted.

What she'd told Darcy was true. She'd have to tell her father there was no way she could marry John Tom. The thought of making love with another man after Darcy was impossible. Which was the very thing she'd been afraid of.

A month, he'd said. She had a month to talk herself out of being in love with him. Or to convince him he was in love with her. *I'm in love with him? How did that happen?* Last night she'd suspected she could be, and now, without any fanfare, she was. Why? Because he was a superb lover? No, it was more than that. She knew it was much more. It was the way he looked at her when he didn't think she was aware. The tenderness in his voice that came through at the oddest moments. The innate understanding he seemed to possess of her feelings and her confusion about them. The bold way he pushed her to take a chance. It was because he was Darcy.

But what about *him?* What did he feel? Could he have made love to her the way he had last night if he didn't feel something? He'd practically admitted to her that he did. He just hadn't told her what. She held her breath, almost afraid to whisper the word in her mind. Could it be love?

Darcy rolled over to his side. Even in his sleep his body sought hers as he draped his arm over her waist. She stilled, afraid to awaken him, enjoying having him entirely to herself. She could pretend he was in love with her. That theirs was a permanent relationship like her parents'. While he slept, she could indulge herself with thoughts of Darcy helplessly in love, even though she knew that her hopes of convincing him he was in love with her were foolish. Trying to put a rope on Darcy would be like trying to chain a wild stallion. There was a restlessness about him he hadn't yet resolved. He'd only stay when he decided to stay. He'd made that clear without ever really saying it. And so had she. From the beginning she'd convinced herself, and him, that he wasn't wanted, so he might as well not even consider anything permanent.

Wait...what are you doing, giving up without a fight? That's not the Braybourne way.

Darcy stirred. Keeping his eyes shut, he ran his hand up and down her back before pulling her closer to him. "I think there's someone in my bed."

She leaned over and kissed his nose. "Anyone you know?"

"Let's see." His hands roamed over her body. "My, my, my, what have we here? And here, and..." his hand slipped between her thighs to caress her most secret place "...here."

"Umm." A small moan escaped her.

"I love that little noise you make in your throat just before you slip over the edge." Opening his eyes, he looked deep into hers. "I've been dreaming about you."

She licked her lips as his finger slipped inside her. "I've been dreaming about you, too."

"I've been dreaming about all the things I still want to do to you."

She pulled him on top of her and nipped his lower lip, taking her time releasing it from between her teeth. "Then you should stop dreaming and start doing."

He nipped her back, then soothed her with his tongue. "You're the boss."

"Flattery, flattery..."

His knee spread her legs farther apart. "...will get me where I want to go."

She arched her hips. "And where do you want to go?"

He thrust inside her, his aim straight and true. "Right across the finish line."

Clasping her legs around his waist, she lifted to meet him, gasping, "I'll race you for it."

9

OVER THE NEXT WEEK and a half they worked together, butting heads less often as the days went by. Lucky Hand was making great strides in both speed and control. And *they* were making great strides, too, Darcy thought, as he and Silver led Lucky Hand out onto the training track near John Tom Thomas's farm.

"Go on, Silver, take him back to the gate. And watch that gelding you're running with. Tater said he looks slicker than spit."

Silver grinned. "You got it. Don't go away now, you hear?"

"Dynamite couldn't shake me loose." His need rose, practically choking him with its strength.

"Good. That's just what I wanted to hear."

"Stop looking at me like that. You're going to get us in trouble."

Silver leaned down, pretending she was adjusting her stirrup. Lips pouting with promise, tone provocative, she whispered, "I plan on us getting in trouble later."

Just for an instant, Darcy slipped his fingers over her hand. Then he stepped back. "Go on. Get in position."

Silver gave him a little salute and headed toward the starting gate as he headed toward the railing where Tater was waiting.

"She okay this morning?" Tater asked, his voice a bit suspicious as he pointed at Silver.

"Both she and Lucky Hand are chomping at the bit."

One of the other trainers dropped a flag and the four horses were off. Darcy watched Silver handling the black stallion as if he were an extension of her body. Their communication was total as Silver moved him into position to overtake the field of horses. On the sidelines, Darcy whispered encouragement. "That's it. That's it. Not too soon. Hold on just a bit... Now!"

"Damn me—look at that," Tater said as Lucky Hand swept right, to the outside of the three horses he was racing against. Tater glanced at his watch as the black edged out a bay, then the two others. Silver crossed the improvised finish line, and Tater clicked the Stop button. He checked the time, then whistled. "Way under a minute. This here horse might amount to something, after all."

Darcy pounded on Tater's back as Silver slowed the black to a walk. "He's got the stuff. I'm telling you, Tater, he's got the stuff to go the distance."

"Yep, if we can hang on that long."

Darcy snapped him a glance. "What do you mean?"

Looking a bit flustered, Tater swiped his hat off his head, then jammed it back on. "Nothing. Forget I said anything. It ain't my place."

"Tater, what're you—"

"Did you see him?" Silver broke in, leading Lucky Hand behind her. Her voice was so high with excitement that Darcy thought she might float away. "Did you see how he was running? It was like riding the wind. I just tried to sit there and go along for the ride. It was..." She looked from one man to the other. "What's wrong?"

"Not a thing, missy."

After a quick glance at the older man, Darcy leaped in. "Tater is still in shock over the time. Show her, Tater."

He shoved the watch at her. "Lookee that—fifty-eight seconds."

"You're kidding." She grabbed the watch, peering at it. "Good Lord, he could win the Rosemont Cup with this time."

Darcy grinned. "That's the point, isn't it?"

"Yes, but... This better not be a fluke just to get my hopes up."

"It's not," Darcy said, pointing at Lucky Hand, who seemed to have an aggressive, satisfied gleam in his eyes. "Look at him, Silver. Can't you see the difference? He's got the will now, and more important, he's got a taste of it. He'll keep running as long as you keep racing him."

"Then I guess I'll have to keep racing him."

"Braybourne Farm rises again," Darcy said, even though Tater looked a bit strained at her comment.

"That's welcome news," John Tom said as he joined them. "Hello, darling. I saw your black run. He's looking better."

"He looks great, you mean," Silver snapped.

"You've done a good job with him, considering."

"Considering what?"

"Some of the limitations you have to work with. But don't worry. That'll all change after we're married, of course. You'll have complete access to the right training facilities, the best that money can buy."

"That's not going to get me to the altar, John Tom."

"We'll see." He laughed. "I think that horse is the way to your heart."

Darcy studied John Tom out of the corner of his eye. The man had a mighty satisfied look, which made him wonder just what was going on.

"Hey there, John Tom." Harden came across the field from the parking area. "Your manager told me you were down here. That new bay of yours is a beauty."

"Wait till you see him run. Real Thing is lightning on four legs. I'm entering him in the Rosemont Cup. I think he'll win it hands down."

"I wouldn't be so sure of that, if I were you," Silver said.

"You'll feel differently after we win, darling. Wouldn't you like to be in the winner's circle?"

"Yes. And I will be." She patted Lucky Hand. "With this beauty right here."

"You're entering the black? Really?" John Tom turned to Harden. "But I thought we'd...uh, never mind, darling. Harden, when you finish here, why don't you stop by and have a closer look at my horse? Then you and I can talk."

"I'll do that."

"See you later, darling," John Tom said to Silver.

Silver barely nodded before she turned her attention to her

father. "Daddy, you should have seen Lucky Hand run today. He was something, wasn't he, Darcy?"

"Yes, sir. I think you've got yourself a winner."

"You've done a good job with him, Silver. When we got him I wouldn't have thought..." Harden sighed. "Anyway, you've done a good job."

"Thanks, Daddy, but I didn't do it alone. Darcy has been a huge help." She sent Darcy a look that had his toes curling. He hoped her father wasn't paying any attention. Although he knew Tater was, and it was obviously troubling him.

"Daddy, I know we still have a way to go," she said, stroking her hand down her horse's neck. "Thank heaven we have a bit more time."

Darcy watched the older man closely as he smiled and nodded at his daughter. Harden didn't look very well, Darcy thought. Underneath his ruddiness was a pasty quality that Darcy found disturbing. "Are you feeling all right, Harden?"

"Never better," the man snapped.

Silver whirled to face her father. She stepped closer to the fence. "What's wrong, Daddy? Is your leg hurting, or your arm?"

"No."

"Harden," Darcy said, as much to rescue his boss from his daughter's attention as anything else, "why don't I take you—"

"Are you sure nothing hurts, Daddy?"

"Nothing's hurting except my ears." Harden turned to Tater. "Call these two off, will ya?"

Tater rubbed his hand over his chin as he studied his old friend. "Well, now I think on it, you do look kind of peaked. Might be you're getting that bug that's going—"

"Oh, yes." Silver picked up on Tater's remark and added to it. "One of the stable boys told me about Essie Montgomery feeling ill at the club during lunch the other day. Everyone was talking about whether she had the flu or was pregnant."

"The stable boy told you all that?" Suddenly Darcy wondered what the boys at WindRaven had been saying about him all these years. He decided he didn't want to know.

Harden turned a shade paler and rested a hand on the railing. "Damn town gossips too much, if you ask me."

"Even so, Harden, you do look—"

"I'm not paying you to look at me, Darcy. I'm paying you to get your work done."

Darcy grinned. "Yes, sir." That sounded more like Harden, even if it was a bit forced. If there was a problem beyond a possible flu bug, he'd pry it out of Tater once he got him alone.

"Then get to it." Harden turned to Tater. "You come along with me. I forgot to, uh, add something to that feed store list I gave you last night."

"What list? You didn't give me any—" Tater gasped as Harden clasped his shoulder and shook it hard. "Oh, that list. I remember now."

"Don't you get senile on me now, Tater," Harden said as they walked away.

Silver led her horse off the track as the two old men took the path toward the barn. She turned to Darcy. "What do you think that was all about?"

"I don't know." But Darcy didn't have a good feeling about it. Obviously something had happened that had shaken Harden's equanimity. If Darcy had to guess, he'd say it was his finances. Given Harden's current financial shape, his behavior didn't seem promising. Darcy decided he'd better find out what was going on.

"Would you like to stick around and watch that bay of John Tom's run?" Silver asked.

"I'd better get Lucky Hand back to the stables. Let me know if Real Thing is the *real deal*, okay?"

Silver glanced around to see if anyone was watching, then stepped closer and slipped her hand into his pocket. "I know the real deal when I see it."

He slapped his palm over his pocket to keep her hand from delving farther. "You keep it up and you're going to see it faster than you think."

"I like the sound of that."

"Me, too. Too much." He was lucky he could get any work done at all. He wanted this woman with a raw need that stunned him. But that hunger was tinged with guilt. Ever since that night at Loretta's, Darcy had wanted to tell Silver the truth about himself, but he wasn't sure how to go about it. All he knew was he couldn't let this situation go on for much longer. He was getting more involved than he'd ever thought possible. If he didn't call a halt to it soon—

"I thought that was our goal, remember?" Silver whispered. "To get so much of each other we'd be sick of making love."

He laughed. "It's not working. Maybe we need to up our schedule."

"Better yet," she purred, "we could just stay in bed all day."

"Believe me, if I didn't think your father would come after me with a shotgun, I'd consider it." Darcy plucked her hand from his pocket. "Now behave."

"That's no fun."

"Keep teasing, Ms. Braybourne, and you're going to get the spanking of your life."

Silver chuckled and threw out a challenge. "By you and who else?"

"Maybe John Tom will help." At her grin, Darcy scowled and muttered, "Why does he still act as if you two are getting married tomorrow?"

"It's his way of ignoring the truth."

"Has your father accepted that you're not going to marry the boy next door?"

"I haven't quite told him. I meant to, but every time I tried, something came up to change the subject."

"Keep it up, Silver, and you're going to end up married to the guy." Stupidly, Darcy felt hurt that she was dragging her feet. In her position he'd probably do the same. But he still didn't like it.

"Don't be ridiculous," she snapped, as she tried to settle Lucky Hand, who was getting bored with the inactivity.

"Maybe it wouldn't be such a bad thing," Darcy said reluctantly.

Much as he hated the thought of Silver and John Tom, he was beginning to believe that in the long run it might be the best thing for her. Passion like theirs wouldn't—couldn't—last. In his experience it never did—beyond tales of long-ago Kristof relatives who fell madly in love at first sight and then built a life together. But these modern times were different. There were different pressures on men and women today. Besides, Darcy thought, even if finding one's true beloved was some sort of family legend, it had sure passed over his father, whose relationship with his mother seemed to be based more on their passion for the same clothing designers than for each other. But John Tom and Silver had a history, a history they could build on if Darcy was out of the way.

And he would be soon.

His time here was coming to an end. He needed to be in Virginia before long, anyway. His trustees were meeting in three weeks to discuss the ramifications and responsibilities of Darcy coming into another trust fund. Instead of sending Nicholas to deal with them as usual, Darcy intended to be there in person. It was time he started behaving like an adult.

"No, maybe it wouldn't be a bad thing at all," Darcy repeated.

"What are you talking about?"

"You and John Tom. The guy's obviously nuts about you."

"In his own way, I suppose." She jerked on her horse's bridle to stop him from dancing into her. "Will you settle down?"

Darcy gripped her arm with one hand and took the reins with the other. "You could do worse, you know."

"I don't want to talk about this, Darcy. Not when you and I are—"

"Look, Silver, there's something I have to tell you."

Silver threw up her hand, stopping him. "Wait—tell me later. Tater is waving at me. I've gotta go. He looks upset." She started to run toward Tater, calling over her shoulder, "I'll see you back at the farm."

SILVER POUNDED UP THE STAIRS of the farmhouse two at a time. She practically ran into her mother, who'd just turned the corner, ready to descend the steps.

"Mama. How is he?"

"Damn fool man. I told him not to go out this morning, but did he listen to me? No. He said he had to go see John Tom about something and off he went."

"What's wrong with him? Is it a heart attack?"

"No, no, honey lamb, nothing like that." Her mother's face set into serious lines as she said darkly, "Although if he doesn't slow down for a while..." Then she saw the fear Silver was trying to hide, without much success, it seemed. "You put that thought right out of your mind, Silver Braybourne. Your daddy is too mean for a heart attack. That stubborn old mule has a touch of that flu bug that's been going around." She shook her head. "Something had been bothering him yesterday, so I didn't worry about him eating hardly a thing at dinner last night. But when he got up this morning and refused any breakfast, didn't even have his cup of coffee, I knew. He looked kind of funny to me, but said he had a bit of a headache and hadn't slept well. So I tried to convince him to go back to bed, but no—out he went." She folded her arms. "Damn fool. Thank goodness Tater was with him and could bring him home. John Tom said he'll bring your daddy's car by later."

"Can I see him?"

"Of course. I'm on my way downstairs to get him some tea. Why don't you stop in and make sure he doesn't need anything else?"

"Okay." Silver started up the hall, then hesitated and turned back. "Mama, do you remember how you told me you wanted me to find someone who was right for me?"

"Yes, I remember."

"How do you think Daddy will take it if I have?"

Aggie chuckled, but a shadow passed over her face. "You know your father, Silver. He's bound and determined that everything go his way, and he had definite ideas of what that way should be. Fate doesn't always cooperate, though. Take your brothers, for example. At one point or another, Harden made plans for each one of them to take this place over someday and carry on. And now..." She sighed. "Now he's trying to find a way to hang on to it so he *can* have something to hand over to someone. That isn't easy on a man's pride."

"No, I suppose it isn't." She hadn't thought of it like that before, although she should have. Pride and Harden Braybourne went hand in glove.

"You go see him." Aggie shook her finger. "And you tell that man to stay put in that bed or I'll tie him down and lock him in the room."

Silver chuckled at that and went to her parents' bedroom. She paused in the doorway. Her big strong father lay in the center of the bed, but he didn't look so big and strong. He looked shrunken and defeated. Silver gasped. She'd never seen him like this. Frightened, she stepped forward. Reaching the edge of the bed, she leaned down and whispered, "Daddy?"

"There's no need to look at me as if I've cocked up my toes, Silver."

Silver sank onto the mattress. "Damn you, Daddy, you scared me to death just now."

His brows snapped together. "I was resting. Can't a man rest without people getting all riled up?"

Silver studied her father's glazed eyes. "So you caught that flu bug, did you?"

"I wouldn't dare catch anything like that. Your mother wouldn't let me."

Silver giggled. "You'd better watch out, she'll be coming up here with the disinfectant spray any minute."

Harden smiled back at her, but Silver sensed the smile was forced and that his attention was elsewhere. She covered his hand with hers. "Something's wrong, isn't it?"

"That depends." He tried to prop himself higher in the bed, and Silver leaned over to push a pillow into position. "You're getting mighty friendly with Darcy, aren't you, for an almost engaged woman?"

Silver rolled her eyes. "I'm not an almost engaged woman. I'm heart-whole and fancy-free."

"Silver, you know John Tom wants to marry you. He's been waiting to formally ask you, but he has spoken with me and I've—"

"He's talked to you? Why?"

"Because that is the proper thing for a gentleman of good breeding to do, that's why."

"I appreciate that." How like her father to focus on tradition, even when it was outdated. "Still, it's not as if you have anything to do with my decision."

"I'm sure John Tom feels you'll be guided by my judgment."

"Excuse me, Daddy, but if he really thinks that, he's one brick short of a load." She ignored her father's sputtering. The time had come to take a stand on this issue, and by God she was going to do it. "Naturally I love you and respect your opinion, but that doesn't mean I'm going to follow it."

Harden raised his hand, palm out. "You're not too big to get turned over my knee and walloped, young lady."

"You're the second person who's told me that today." Of the two people who'd threatened, Silver would put her money on Darcy to carry it out before her father did. Her dad blustered and threatened, but in Silver's experience it was generally her mama who doled out the occasional swats.

"Well then, you must need it."

Grinning, she leaned over and kissed his forehead, but was alarmed by the heat under her lips. "Daddy, you're burning up."

"It's all these blankets your mother piled on top of me. It's the middle of summer and she's bundled me up like a pig in a poke." He tried to push back some of the covers.

"Stop that. You stay put."

"I've got to get up. I have things to take care of."

"Darcy has everything well in hand. That's what you hired him for, remember?"

"That's right, I did. What I didn't hire him for was making eyes at my daughter."

"Well, what if I tell you that I'm making eyes right back?"

"It won't do, Silver. I like Rick Darcy, but he's not for you. You've got the right man in your pocket just waiting to pop the question. And I've got to tell you, from my point of view, he'd be welcome to do so. John Tom's got the background and the money to make this a going concern, to bring us back to life. Without it...well, I'm afraid..."

"Daddy, I know our finances have been pretty tight for the last six months. But we'll work our way out of it. We always do."

Harden hesitated, then faced his daughter head-on. "The bank has called our notes. Fred Waring came to see me yesterday afternoon. Came personally to tell me. He thought I should hear it from him, and hear how he tried to keep it from happening."

"But the First National has been our bank since the beginning. They're the backbone of most of the businesses here. They know horse farms and farmers. They know we'll come out of this, so why would they call in our notes?"

"First National was bought out. Absorbed into this big bank in New York. Their only concern is the bottom line, not the people involved. And our bottom line isn't looking too good. Hasn't for years. Not to mention I've been borrowing from Peter to pay Paul when it comes to managing the money."

"But Daddy, I've been looking at the books and I know it's bad, but not that bad."

"I kept some things kind of private." He looked toward the window, where the lace curtains stirred with the summer breeze. "I didn't want you and your mother to know. I thought I'd be able to turn things around and you wouldn't have to find out."

A feeling of dread came over Silver. "Find out what?"

"A few years ago I sold John Tom's father an interest in the farm."

"You what?"

Harden set his jaw tight. "He wanted our south pastures. They adjoin his and he was looking to expand his operation. It was an under-the-table deal between gentlemen. Money in exchange for a handshake and the promise our two families would join."

"Our two families would join? Join how?"

"Well, you and John Tom."

"Me and—" Silver's jaw dropped as she gaped at her father. "Marriage? Are you talking marriage?"

Harden flushed, saying defensively, "It was a good idea. It still is. You were always sweet on John Tom. He was sweet on you."

"Never at the same time, Daddy. Besides, it was a teenage thing. I outgrew it."

"Well, it might be that John Tom grew into it. Anyway, it was his father's last wish before he died, and John Tom is bound and determined to honor it."

"This is absolutely medieval. I'm not a piece of merchandise you can sell to the highest bidder."

"It's not like that. I know it sounds like that, but it's not. I'm only thinking of you and what's best for you."

He tried to take her hand, but Silver snatched it away. "I'm not going to do it. No way, no how. So you can tell John Tom—"

"John Tom is going to finance the rest of the money to pay off the banknotes so we can keep the farm. Without his backing we're going to lose it, Silver. No more Braybournes at Braybourne Farm."

"Daddy, you don't understand. I'm in love with someone else."

Harden was silent. His face paled as he fixed his gaze on a spot on the wallpaper. Finally, he said, "I know you might think you are, but it can't happen, honey. Not if you care about your family."

"Daddy," she wailed. "That's not fair. You can't just throw this on me like that."

"I don't know what else to do."

As Silver stared at her father, she saw the truth of his statement. The father she'd always admired and adored seemed suddenly every minute of his sixty-nine years. "Daddy, what if I use my inheritance? The money Grandma Sweet left me."

Harden sighed. "It would be a drop in the bucket."

"I'm talking about using it to take the pressure off. To give us a few months. Let us get through the Rosemont Cup."

Harden groaned. "Silver..."

"No, hear me out. I know horses, and I've never seen a horse like this one. I know he's going to win. I just know it. And it's a big purse. The money would do a lot. And wouldn't it convince the bank to stick with us until we can race him some more and then put him up for stud?"

"He's not going to be able to command big stud fees. We don't have his registry or any other papers. Hell, I don't even know why I took the damn horse. Except the man disappeared and I had nobody to give him back to."

"Darcy's already working on tracking down his papers. I know this horse has a pedigree, but it doesn't matter, because he's got something better. He's got heart. And so do I. I'm not giving up on anything I want—*anything!*—without a fight."

Harden looked at her, his expression authoritative, his gaze sympathetic. "Silver. I know it's not fair, and I'm sorry about that, but for all of our sakes you need to marry John Tom. I know you'll see that when you calm down and start looking at it in a realistic way."

"Damn you and John Tom's father and John Tom—damn you all. I'll show you. I'll show all of you."

"Silver." Her father's voice floated after her as she stalked angrily out of the bedroom, down the steps and out into the yard, where she could breathe. Though she was seeing red at the moment, pain and anguish would come later, she knew. She loved this farm. She'd wanted to make it her life. And now... Her thoughts scattered as tears threatened. Now what? She blinked furiously as she walked through the gate and instinctively headed across the yard toward the stable complex.

She stepped inside the double doors. The atmosphere welcomed her, as always. But there was a different quality, or so it seemed to her. Now it seemed to be waiting. Waiting for her to do what? Come to the rescue? Ride up on her black horse and rescue the damsel in distress?

Except I'm the damsel.

She needed to think it through. There must be a way. Failure was not an option. Her stomach muscles clenched with fear even as her mind toughened with determination.

She passed Lucky Hand's stall and looked in, smiling when the horse welcomed her with a soft nicker. The black's coat gleamed to match the cocky look in his eyes. Darcy had obviously washed him and rubbed him down. He looked every inch the champion Silver was sure he could become. "Hey there, fella. It's you and me all the way. Are you up to it? 'Cause I am."

I hope.

The insecure part of her, the little girl who lived deep beneath the confident exterior, craved reassurance. She needed to touch and be touched by someone who believed in her, who could make her believe in herself. Who could help her through the rough spots. She needed Darcy. Urgently. She glanced around. Seeing no sign of him on the main floor, she started searching all the areas where he could be. Finally, she climbed the ladder to the hayloft above the stables.

She stepped off the last rung of the ladder onto the scarred, wide-planked floor that supported the loft. The double doors to the outside were open a crack and the dust particles were visible in the streaks of sunlight, forming lovely patterns across the loft. Her mind filled with carefree childhood memories as she breathed in the sweet smell of timothy hay. She remembered playing up here with her brothers. Then as a teenager, escaping up here to brood over events, or to read, or to dream of her future. Her future? She stared across the loft, and there was Darcy. He had his back to her as he steadily pitched his fork into the bales and twisted to toss the hay down the chute to the feeding stall. Yes, she'd thought a lot about her future, but never had she considered it would contain anyone like Darcy.

He stopped for a moment, wiped his damp forehead on his

sleeve, then stripped off his shirt, tossing it to the side. Silver froze, watching the muscles in his back and arms ripple as he resumed his activity. His tan skin gleamed like polished copper as the sunlight played over his shoulders. His jeans rested low on his lean hips as he stood, long legs firmly planted in a competent yet inherently graceful stance.

With quiet steps she crept up behind him, aching to be closer. She yearned to touch him so badly she thought she'd go mad from it. She stepped closer still, her fingertips skimming his shoulders, barely touching him, just enough to tease and reassure herself that he was real. That he was here. That he was hers. She followed her fingertips with the tip of her tongue, tracing the same path, the tangy taste of his slick skin a counterpoint to the sweet feelings he stirred inside her. She raised on her tiptoes to blaze a trail to the sensitive spot behind his ear, before nipping his earlobe.

Darcy exhaled, but beyond that made no other sound as her tongue continued to trace the curve of his ear, and her fingers slipped from his shoulders to track the tense muscles that spanned his back. Her mouth left his ear and nipped his shoulder as her hands gripped his waist. She pressed against his back. She could feel the heat of him against her breasts. Her nipples firmed, the peaks so sensitive that as she slowly rubbed back and forth she could feel the heat begin between her legs. She moved her hands over his hips and around to his front, where she slipped them into his jeans pockets so she could knead him into hardness. Not that it took much effort. He rocked as her fingertips stroked him.

"I warned you what would happen if you did this again."

"Yes, you warned me," Silver breathed, closing her eyes as she rubbed herself against his firm buttocks in rhythm with her questing fingers. "Do you want me to stop?"

He groaned as his hands came over hers. "Yeah, in about ten years."

She withdrew her hands from his pockets and moved them to his zipper. She slipped it down a half inch at a time as she whispered, "You think we'll have had enough of each other by then?"

He took her hand and plunged it into his open fly. "I doubt it," he gasped as her fingers slipped inside his briefs to find him.

"I need you, Darcy. Make love to me." She took him in her hand and pressed harder against his back, her lips caressing his shoulders as she slid her hand up and down his shaft.

"Oh, Silver." He reached behind her to cup her buttocks and paste her against him, while his hips moved in time to his own inner music. She wanted to give him pleasure, to send him to the edge of reason along with her. She could feel the hard seam of her jeans rubbing against her, feel the way her womanhood swelled and turned wet at the pressure on her flesh. Darcy's hands dipped into the back of her jeans, his hard fingers gripping her cheeks, before he swore softly at his inability to reach the treasure between her legs.

With an abrupt movement he slipped his hands from her pants and reached around to grab her fingers, stilling them as they caressed his rock-hard length. "I'm going to come right now if you don't stop." He turned his head to look over his shoulder at her. "And I'd rather come inside you."

He turned, slipping an arm around her waist, his other hand making short work of unzipping her jeans and spreading the opening to reveal her taut lower stomach. He angled his body so his freed erection jutted against her flesh as he rocked his hips. His hand slipped inside her pants to cup her mound, his fingertips searching, probing for treasure. With her arm around his waist, she gripped him hard for balance as she moaned and thrust herself against his hand. Her other hand fingered his velvety tip, whispering her approval at the moist drop that formed in response to her touch.

"Silver, sweet Silver," he gasped, as her fingers squeezed him. His words trailed off as he kissed her.

She stepped closer, pulling his erection against her, lifting and locking her leg around his hips as she continued to writhe against his hand.

With a gentle movement he swept her other foot out from under her, and they fell back onto the straw. Darcy took care not to fall on her with his entire weight, but Silver wouldn't have cared. As far as she was concerned the only thing that existed was Darcy. He was her escape from all that threatened her.

Darcy jerked at her thin knit top, pushing it up over her breasts and undoing the front clasp of her bra. Then his mouth was on them, his lips teasing and tasting, his tongue circling each tip before pulling the hard button into his mouth to suck. At the same time his hand continued to stroke her, his shaft pressing against her hip as he shared the excitement.

Then he rose to his knees between her spread thighs. He looked down at her, but she was so deep in a haze of pure emotion and desire that she could scarcely focus on him.

She licked her lips. "I need..."

He bent over her, one hand pushing her jeans down her body. She helped first with hers, then with his. "Need what?"

"Please, I need...*you.*" She gasped as his fingers pressed deeper. "It could be the last time."

His mouth replaced his fingers, his tongue seeking and probing her heated flesh. She moaned softly and then cried out when he lifted up and thrust inside her. His hardness melted into her heat, and she came as he erupted, thrusting deep within her before he collapsed on her, his breath rasping in and out of his lungs.

Long moments later Silver stretched, her arms rising above her head, her legs extending, her torso twisting and arching with satisfaction. Darcy could feel himself respond instinctively as her body moved against his. He glanced down. "Keep it up, sweetheart, and we'll be here all day."

"I'd like that," Silver whispered.

Darcy smiled, removing himself from temptation by shifting to stretch out by her side. "So would I."

He studied her, his gaze caressing her hair, pale and luminous as a moonbeam, her beautiful face, at turns mysterious and revealing, and her luscious body. He could lose himself forever in her and never care. It was getting harder and harder to think about leaving her. Each day he was falling deeper and deeper. Each day he stepped closer to the edge of no return—the moment when he would be forced to admit that he loved her. But if he admitted it, wouldn't he have to do something about it? Like marry her? Well, why not? Why couldn't he marry Silver? Suddenly the idea of marriage didn't seem so horrible. It was damn appealing, as a matter of fact. All of his earlier thoughts about her and John Tom flew out of his mind. After what they'd just shared, he couldn't let her go.

Darcy opened his mouth to ask her, for real this time, when her words of a few moments before slammed into his gut. Gently, he shook her shoulders. "Silver, what did you mean, it could be the last time?"

"My father..." She glanced away, her mouth trembling.

"How is he?" By God, he'd forgotten about Harden. "Tater told me he'd be out of commission for a few days. Is it the flu or something more serious?"

"That depends on what you consider serious," Silver answered, her tone slow and heavy. "Although he does have the flu, too."

At her worried look, Darcy smoothed her hair back from her face. "Silver, sweetheart, what's wrong?"

She bit her lip before saying in a matter-of-fact voice, "The bank has called in our loans. We don't have the money to pay them."

"When did this happen?"

"Yesterday afternoon, I think."

"Well, there must be something we can do to buy some time." Damn, he'd been afraid something like this might happen. But he hadn't expected it so soon.

"Yes." Silver nodded. "I've been thinking about that. I have an inheritance. It's not huge, but if I can convince the right people, it might be enough to take the pressure off for a few months until...until I can find a way to..."

Darcy frowned. "A way to what?"

Eyes huge, Silver exclaimed abruptly, "Oh, Darcy, Daddy

sold part of our farm to the Thomases a few years ago. Our land. Braybourne land. On the agreement with John Senior that John Tom and I—that we... All this time, John Tom knew, and I had no idea. I thought he wanted me. But no, I'm just a part of the deal. How's that for the old ego? Sold like a piece of beef on the hoof. Do you believe that? In this day and age? Do you believe anyone would have the nerve to—"

Darcy grabbed her shoulders and made her look at him. "You're supposed to marry John Tom because your fathers arranged it as part of a deal? Are you telling me your father...that old son of a bitch sold you out?"

As his harsh words registered, Silver jumped to her father's defense. "Daddy was desperate." It was one thing for her to condemn him, but she hated hearing anyone else do it. "He did it so we could keep the farm."

Darcy took a deep breath and got himself back under control. Alienating Silver wouldn't help, but he couldn't help saying in a bitter tone, "Naturally, he had a good reason for selling his daughter's affections." There was nothing new in that. In his very rich world, having money or property attached to a marriage agreement was common, a way to keep wealth and power in the family. But he didn't like thinking about it with Silver.

"John Tom is handsome, kind. I've known him forever, so I suppose I could do worse."

Darcy's eyes flashed with temper. "Who are you trying to convince? You or me?"

She dashed her hand over her eyes. "My father wasn't trying to hurt me, he just—"

"Did what he thought best, regardless of anyone's feelings?"

"I guess."

"Does your mother know all this?"

Silver shook her head. "I don't think so. Daddy said he'd kept it quiet from both of us."

Darcy gave her a mirthless smile. "He probably did. I can't see your mother going along with this."

Silver sniffed as she sat up, beginning to adjust her clothing.

"No, me neither. She probably would have boxed his ears if she'd known."

Darcy yanked up his jeans and briefs. "So what now?"

"Now? Now I'm going to make sure Lucky Hand is ready to win the Rosemont Cup. The money's more important than ever."

He leaned on his elbow. "I'll buy him from you. That should help. Then when you win the first race you can buy him back."

Silver laughed. "You'll buy him? With what? I thought you were broke!"

Damn. He'd forgotten about that. All he'd thought about was taking the pressure off Silver, putting a smile back in her eyes. "That's true, but I still have connections. I'll bet I can raise some money."

Taking him by surprise, Silver leaned over and kissed him. "I appreciate it, love, I really do, but I can't take anything from you. Braybournes got themselves into this mess, and Braybournes have to get themselves out."

"How?"

"Beyond Grandma's money? I don't know yet, but I'll come up with something."

He let the subject drop as he stood up and pulled her to her feet. "Well, standing here worrying isn't going to help, is it? I'll get back to work and I suggest you do the same."

"I have to go to town. I'll see you later."

"Tonight?"

"No...I have some decisions to make. I hope you understand."

"I understand." He had things to take care of, too. "I'll see you tomorrow."

"Yes, okay, tomorrow sounds good." Silver gave him a little wave and tried to keep her chin high as she walked over to the ladder. She swung herself onto a rung, then looked up at him as he walked toward her.

"Silver?" He wanted to tell her he loved her, but wasn't sure now was the time.

"Yes?"

He squatted down to her level, hoping she could see the love in his eyes. "Try to relax. It'll all work out."

She smiled, the distress in her own eyes nearly breaking his heart. "Of course it will."

"I'll see to it," he said under his breath as she left the loft.

Darcy waited until he was certain Silver had left the stables. Then he went down to the office and called his cousin. He told Nick to buy all the outstanding loans for Braybourne Farm and to settle all bills or credit liens against them. He also asked Nick's advice about the situation with the Thomas family, and what legal ramifications there might be, if any.

Then Darcy hung up the phone. *Whether you want it or not, Harden, you're about to get a silent partner,* he thought. After all, he couldn't have his bride-to-be's family homeless.

Now his only problem would be figuring out how to tell Silver the truth.

10

THE NEXT AFTERNOON, Silver shoved a check in her pocket and marched down to the stables to find Darcy. She was waylaid by the sight of Lucky Hand pacing in his stall. She leaned over the door.

"What's the matter, boy?"

Lucky Hand flattened his ears and backed toward the corner of the stall. Intrigued, Silver lifted the latch and slipped inside. "Easy, easy now," she soothed as she approached him. Lucky Hand began to whinny and paw at the ground. He butted his head toward her. "Hey now, what's the matter with you?" She tried to reach for his bridle, but the stallion slipped sideways and started to rear.

"Whoa! Wha—?" Silver squeaked in alarm as Darcy grabbed her from behind and lifted her back toward the doorway.

"What the hell are you doing, Silver?"

"What am *I* doing?" She tried to look over her shoulder. "What are *you* doing?"

"I'm keeping you from getting trampled by that damn horse."

She struggled, forcing him to put her back on her feet. "I had the situation under control."

"It looked like it."

"I don't know what's wrong with him. Maybe he's getting sick or something. I'd better call the vet."

"He's protecting his new friend."

"What? What new friend?"

"Look."

Lucky Hand had his nose down in the straw, rooting around until Silver heard a small, annoyed meow. A ginger kitten emerged, obviously a bit upset at having his nap interrupted.

Lucky Hand only nosed the kitten affectionately, bumping and sniffing so hard that Silver was surprised the kitten was still standing when the horse finished. The kitten didn't seem to mind, though. He rubbed up against the horse's leg.

Silver could swear Lucky Hand was grinning. "Oh, look at them. How cute."

Darcy gave her a quick squeeze. "Your horse didn't want you to bother his new stable buddy."

Silver smiled. "A horse likes having a buddy." She snapped her fingers. "That's it! We'll call him Buddy."

Grinning, Darcy sent her a sly look. "I think that he's a she. What about that?"

"Women can be buddies, too, you know."

"I know." But the hunger on his face reminded her that it was much more fun to be lovers.

Much as she'd like to take him up on his obvious invitation, she had other reasons for tracking him down. She glanced up at him. "You're making quite a habit of this, aren't you?"

"A habit of what?"

"Rescuing me."

"I didn't want that lovely body of yours trampled into a pancake."

Although Silver smiled, she was serious. "I wasn't talking about that."

Darcy's eyes turned wary. "What then?"

"My mother told me what you did."

Darcy looked uncomfortable. "I didn't do anything. I just made a phone call to someone who could take the immediate pressure off. That's all. No big deal."

"I'm sure it was easier said than done."

Darcy shrugged. "I just wanted to help. I hated to see you wipe out your inheritance if there was another way. I told you I had some contacts, so I used them."

"Thank you." She knew the words were a bit terse, but she couldn't help it. Accepting help was always a bit difficult for her, but in this situation more than her ego was at stake. Her family had needed the help to survive. She couldn't remember ever having been in that position before.

Darcy grinned. "You don't sound as if you meant that."

"I do. It's just…" Searching for words, she dug the tip of her boot in the dirt, partly embarrassed and partly resentful. "Please don't misunderstand, I do appreciate what you've done, but…"

"But?"

She looked up and met his gaze. "I wasn't looking for a Prince Charming or a bold knight to come riding up on a snow-white horse to rescue me. I know it doesn't make sense, but I guess I was hoping to rescue myself. To prove myself."

"Prove yourself how?"

"I thought if I could find a way to buy us some time, then make something of Lucky Hand, it would prove once and for all that I could do the job here."

"I know you can do the job here, Silver, and do it much better than I ever could. This place is in your bones, your blood. Since I've been here I've discovered how important that is. What it means to build something and help it grow. I've decided it's what I want to do, too, when I get back…." He glanced at her, then at the ground, before meeting her gaze again. "On my feet, that is. This place has so much to offer. I respect what you're trying to do here. You've just gotten stuck with some bad luck, that's all."

"Well, thank you. But even so—"

"You find it hard to accept help, right? Should I apologize?" He rubbed his chin. "The etiquette book is kind of hazy on this point, isn't it?"

Silver never meant to deny what he'd done, or hurt him for stepping in. "That makes me seem totally ungrateful, and believe me, I'm not."

Darcy laughed. "Listen, if riding to the rescue is what it takes to make you look at me like that, I'll saddle up every day."

"That's not what I want from you."

"What do you want from me?" he asked, his expression hard to read.

Silver wasn't sure how to tell him, so instead of seizing the moment, she hedged. "What do you want from *me?*"

Darcy shook his head. "I asked first."

He stepped closer, and she put her hand on his chest, unconsciously rubbing the firm muscles under her fingertips. *I'd like you to love me as I love you.*

He leaned down to nuzzle her hair, and when he didn't say anything, she stepped back and shoved her hand into her pocket. She pulled out the cashier's check. "I want you to accept this. I cashed out some of my funds. At least let me compensate you for—"

"No way." He pushed her hand away as she tried to give it to him. "You're making too much of this, Silver. This didn't cost me anything more than a phone call. Honest. All I did was call some people I know and tell them about the potential of Braybourne Farm...and you."

"And just like that they wanted to bail us out?"

"Yes."

Silver snorted in disbelief. "Then they're either nuts or have money to burn."

He leaned back against the wall. "Does it matter?"

"No, I guess not." Then a thought hit her. "But it depends on the terms, doesn't it? What good is it if we're going to be joined at the hip for life to these people?"

Darcy smiled. "I don't think you'll have to worry, Silver. I'm sure the terms will be very generous, and fair. You'll have the time you need to get back on your feet."

"I don't know. What about John Tom?"

Just the thought of John Tom and his involvement made the situation seem even stickier. She wanted to resolve the problem without creating an enemy. John Tom was her friend, even if he drove her nuts. They were neighbors with a long-time family connection. For her father's sake, she'd have to come up with something—something besides marrying him. She couldn't marry one man while she was head over heels in love with another.

"Silver, relax. John Tom's being taken care of. So let it go and concentrate on getting Lucky Hand ready to race."

Silver rubbed her hands over her eyes. "Daddy told me this morning that he'd already half promised to sell Lucky Hand to John Tom."

Darcy grabbed her hands, the pressure reassuring. "They haven't signed any papers yet, have they?"

"No."

"Then you keep working him, okay?"

"Yes." She nodded. "Yes, I will." Her mind grew calm for a moment as she looked into his eyes. She'd never appreciated this man more. For all the wildness and danger she sensed, there was also a core to him that reached out to steady her, to make her believe when she was having trouble believing.

"That's settled, then."

"Darcy, I love you," she blurted. At his look of complete shock she forced a smile to her face and added, "For what you did. I don't know how you managed it, but I promise I'll find a way to make it up to you."

From Darcy's stunned expression, she'd obviously revealed her true feelings too soon. But she felt as if she'd been holding in the words forever. However, she didn't want him to think her declaration of love was merely gratitude. With an effort, she kept her smile in place, even though she wanted to run and hide. She'd just discovered that saying those three simple words aloud was more revealing than making love with this man could ever be.

He hesitated, then muttered, "Silver, I keep telling you, it wasn't a big deal."

"It seems like a very big deal to me. Besides, I know it was. Mama gave me the full scoop this morning."

Darcy flushed. "My actions weren't that noble. There was self-interest behind it, believe me."

"I don't."

"Silver—" he inhaled deeply "—I'm not what you think I am."

She touched his cheek. "I know. You're more."

"No, I'm not. Look, Silver, I have to tell you a few things about myself, my situation. Why I came to Cecil."

"I don't care about your past."

"You will. Believe me, you will. Let's find a place to sit down." He led her to the manager's office and was backing her into a chair just as Tater burst into the room behind him.

"Darcy, you gotta come with me, quick."

Darcy turned. "What's wrong?"

"The fence broke through over in the yearlings' pasture, and them damn youngun's have taken off in all directions. We gotta track 'em down, then fix the rails."

"Where are Billy and Ed?"

"Ed's sick today, and I already sent Billy for supplies to fix the damn thing."

"Okay, I'll be right there."

Tater hesitated, looking from one to the other before dashing out again, saying over his shoulder, "See you outside."

"I have to go. We'll talk when I get back, okay?"

"Of course. Don't worry. I'm not going anywhere."

He gave her a steady stare. "Me neither."

Waving her hand, Silver said, "Go before those horses run to the Tennessee border. I've got plenty of things to do."

"Right," he said, then gave her an abrupt kiss. He looked as if he wanted to say more, but shook his head and strode from the room instead.

She sat in silence for a moment, enjoying the familiarity of her environment, an environment she'd thought she might lose. Her gaze roamed the office, taking in the scarred floor, the old pine walls, the serviceable furniture. She knew every inch of this place, knew every inch of this farm. She could recognize every sound, every scent, every sight, but now it seemed different. Now there was Darcy. He was part of it. He'd even said he wasn't going anywhere. Silver glanced at the door and chuckled. That's what he thought. He was going to the altar if she had to drag him there. From the look in his eyes before he'd left, she didn't think he'd mind too badly. Or was that just wishful thinking?

The phone rang and she grabbed it. "Yes."

"May I speak with Darcy Kristo—uh, Rick Darcy," a deep voice said.

She snapped back to life, reaching for a pen and message pad. "I'm sorry, Darcy's not here right now. Can I get your name and—"

"Ask him to call Nick. He's got the number. Thanks."

Puzzled, she stood up and stared at the receiver. What was that all about? Who was Darcy Kristo? He had another name? Now, why would Darcy not use...?

She reined in her imagination, which was rapidly sifting through wild scenarios. *What's the big deal? He told you he'd had some problems, so maybe he changed his name. It's a free country.* She bit her lip. Was it Kristopher, maybe? Darcy Kristopher? No, something about Kristopher didn't seem right. She thought for a moment longer. Kristo rang a bell, if only she could remember where she'd recently seen something like that. Silver squeezed her eyes tight. *Where?* A magazine. She'd been in the house reading a magazine.

She whirled and ran for the door, yanking it open to race through the stables, across the yard and into the house. She practically skidded into the living room and headed right for the magazines piled in an old basket by the fireplace. She tossed aside one, then another. Finally, she found a recent issue of *Gracious Country Living* magazine. She flipped through it, fanning the pages until she found what she sought. With a sinking heart she stared at the headline: Gracious and Glorious.

She skimmed the article about the Kristof family, the multimillionaire industrialists with their fingers in every big financial undertaking of the last century. The interview had taken place at WindRaven Farms, their country home in Virginia, which was just one of many they possessed.

She paged through the article, which featured pictures of the house, Darcy's parents, and one of Darcy as he watched a horse running on the track. Stunned, she peered at the picture.

Idiot. Why didn't you realize this before? Before you fell in love with him? Tears formed in her eyes and she furiously blinked them away. Rising to her feet, she threw the magazine across the room as her despair was rapidly replaced by anger.

"You son of a bitch. You sneaky, untrustworthy, manipulative... Why? Why would you do something like this? A joke? A sick little rich-boy joke?"

She could feel her heart splinter. Of course it was a joke. What else could it be? All of it—the laughter, the lovemaking, the promises—all a joke. Eyes narrowed in pain, mouth tight, body shaking, she walked over to the fireplace and grabbed the magazine. She spun on her heel and stalked to the front door.

Her mother was coming down the stairs. "Silver, is something wrong?"

"Don't worry. I'm going to fix what's wrong right now."

Ignoring her mother's plea to wait, Silver slammed out the door and strode to the stables. She stopped and forced herself to take a deep breath before she entered. She looked around for Darcy, but not seeing him, she figured he was still chasing the horses. Still, she checked the horse stalls and the office to be certain before she stopped at the door to his room. Finally, with a bold movement, she turned the knob and stepped inside. No Darcy. She gazed around the room where she'd spent so much time observing the small touches he'd put on the room—an old poster he'd unearthed from somewhere, a book topped by reading glasses with black wire frames. She didn't know he used them. There was a lot she didn't know about Darcy, it seemed.

Her lip curled. How about the fact that he was a multimillionaire playboy, for starters? Oh yes, there was a lot she didn't know about the man she'd fallen in love with. At least knowing his real identity explained all of Darcy's inconsistencies, which she'd overlooked as she became more and more comfortable with him. However, there was one thing she'd never been confused about—his appeal to women. That was a given from the word *go!*

Her blood burned as she thought of him, of the last time he'd touched her. She tried to keep her focus off the bed, where she'd found love and passion in his arms. The bed he'd probably be bragging about to his friends. She could hear him now, saying, "I remember when I played this great trick on a little country girl. Why, I even lived in the stables for a while. We used to make love in there. She was so gullible. Easy pickings, really. Too easy."

Too easy, was right. She'd fallen into his hands like a ripe plum. The pain threatened to overwhelm her, but she forced it back, summoning anger instead. With determined steps, she walked to the closet, searching for his luggage. She extracted the duffel bag and began to pack his clothes. When she'd finished, she threw the bag to the middle of the bed, then walked over to the corner to sit in a chair to wait.

DARCY WAS IMPATIENT to find Silver so he could continue their discussion. He peered first into Lucky Hand's stall, then the office, but there was no sign of her. "Damn."

He wanted to take her in his arms and tell her how much he loved her, then tell her the truth about himself. God, she'd stunned him when she said, "I love you." Oh, she'd tried to cover it up, but Silver's poker face wasn't always as good as she thought. She loved him, and he was going to make sure she knew it wasn't a one-way deal. He started to plan how he'd fold her gently in his arms, drop a tender kiss on her lips and whisper his total and unwavering devotion to her. Then they'd make love like they'd never experienced it before. Darcy could see his future as clear as if it was happening in that instant—he and Silver in church, he and Silver with their children. He couldn't wait to find her.

In high gear, he opened the door to his room and headed straight for the bathroom to grab a towel to wipe his sweaty face and filthy hands. He stopped halfway, surprised at the sight of Silver sitting motionless in his only chair.

"What the—? Silver!"

Darcy tried to recapture his composure. "Sorry, I didn't see you."

She said nothing, only looked at him, her eyes dark and stormy.

"Tater and I had to chase one of those horses through the creek. I thought we'd never catch that little..." His words trailed off as she stared a hole through him. A bit uneasy now, he brushed at his jeans. "I slipped in the mud. We got him, though." Why wasn't she saying anything? "Tater and Billy are repairing the fence now."

Her sudden movement surprised him. All he could see was a blur coming through the air at him. It hit him in the chest. A magazine. Automatically, he pulled it against him so he didn't drop it.

"Page forty-two."

Darcy glanced down at the magazine, his heart sinking as he recognized the title. The words he wanted to say stuck in his throat as he turned to the right page. He'd forgotten about this article. The story actually focused mostly on his parents, so he'd paid little attention, beyond his mother mentioning it to him a number of months before. He glanced up at Silver. Her eyes were as cold as winter as she stared at him. He opened his mouth to say something, anything, but she stopped him cold, freezing him out before he could form the words.

"And so—" she indicated the magazine "—with all that sumptuous living in his back pocket, I have to ask myself what is a man like Darcy Kristof doing on Braybourne Farm in little old Cecil, Kentucky?" Her eyes narrowed. "And you know what? I can't find any reason for an international playboy to be here at all—except some type of elaborate joke to make a fool out of me and my family."

Finally finding his voice, Darcy jumped in, hoping to smooth over the situation. "It wasn't a joke. It was a bet." He watched as her expression grew even colder.

"A bet." Fury leaped into her eyes. This was an anger deeper and richer than any he'd ever seen. His heart sank even further as he nodded, still hoping to explain.

"Uh-huh, a bet with my cousin Nick," he stated, rushing to make her understand. "Harmless really, no big deal."

"Nick. Would that be the 'lawless' cousin Nick you mentioned? The one who called today and asked for you?"

"For me?"

"For Rick Darcy. But your cousin made a little bitty mistake before he got the name right, you see."

I'll kill him. I'll damn well kill him, Darcy thought. His gut tightened as he wondered how to make her listen. He tried reason. "Nick's also my lawyer. He's helping me with some business transactions."

It didn't help. Silver ignored his comment and kept traveling down her own road. "Thanks to Nick, I started wondering. It took me a moment, but then I remembered the little story about the wealthy and powerful Kristof family and their million dollar hobby farm."

He tried to smile. "Silver, you're taking this all wrong—"

"Oh, I don't think I'm taking this wrong at all. So, did you call Nick at night and laugh about this place, laugh about me? Was that supposed to be part of it? Fun and games for the high society set. Was that it? And why me, anyway? Why did you pick me?"

"You're wrong, all wrong. I was bored, so I picked a place out of the blue. Then I borrowed a groom's pickup and hit the road. I met Tater and he told me about your dad and the farm, about your needing someone to help out." He shrugged. "Here I am." As he told the story aloud he realized how absurd it seemed.

She looked at him, the disdain in her eyes piercing. "That's right. Here you are."

"And there you were."

"Bonus points, was I?"

"Yes. I mean no. You were a bonus, yes." He stumbled over himself, trying to get his feelings out, trying to salvage this mess, knowing as he did that he was only making it worse. "I didn't mean that the way it sounded—the bonus points thing. You know that's not true."

"I know nothing of the sort. My social set doesn't run to disgustingly rich guys and their preferred mode of behavior."

Under the anger, he could finally see a glimmer of the hurt she was trying to hide. Tossing the magazine aside, he stepped toward her, trying to take her in his arms. "Silver..."

She slapped at him and moved away, putting the width of the bed between them. "Don't touch me. Don't you dare touch me."

"Silver, please, let me explain."

"How dare you play me for such a fool? All along I thought I mattered to you, and you were just using me and my family to amuse yourself. A practical joke that you'll repeat back at your country club or wherever you hang out."

"No." He watched as she paced. "It might have started as something like that but—"

She whirled to face him. "You're pathetic. Was your life so empty that you had to dream up this elaborate masquerade just so you could pass the time? Is that what it was, huh? A way to add a bit of kick? A way to escape your poor-little-rich-boy existence?"

Her words stung. "Yes, it was a way to escape. To escape a life I was beginning to find tedious."

"Oh, tedious, was it? Oh, my, what a problem. How nice it must be to have so much money that life can become *tedious*."

Darcy could feel the color rush to his cheeks. He didn't blame her for her biting scorn. He'd sounded like a spoiled three-year-old, even though that wasn't his intention. "Look, Silver, I wanted a month. One month to prove I could be ordinary. It was the adventure of it, don't you see? That's all it was."

"Oh, please, spare me. Poor little thing, you wanted to be like the rest of humanity. Stuck right down there in the muck along with everyone else!"

His lips thinned. He deserved it, he knew, but still he resented her making fun of him. "Maybe I really wanted people to see *me.* I wanted to prove to myself that I could be liked for who I am, not what I am or what I have."

"How could you expect anyone to react to the real you when you were pretending to be someone else?"

"I know. I realize now it sounds stupid. I didn't mean to hurt anyone. I wanted to tell you, Silver, I really did. So many times I started to, but—"

"But you didn't want to interrupt your fun. Not to mention your hot new sex life with the little country mouse, is that it?"

Darcy laughed; he couldn't help it. He gave her a quick once-over. "I can't imagine anyone less resembling a mouse."

Silver practically snarled at him. "Shut up. Don't you dare make fun of me."

"I wasn't trying to. I care about you, damn it."

"You care about me, Darcy? You care about yourself, period. You don't give a damn about me."

"That's not true. I do. But I couldn't tell you how I felt until I told you the truth about myself."

Her voice was bitter. "Well, I spared you the trouble, didn't I? So now you might as well just—"

"I love you."

Silver stared at him for a long moment. "I don't believe you."

"You have to believe me."

Her chin lifted. "I don't believe liars."

"My God, I don't believe this," Darcy said, his frustration barely contained. "You don't believe liars? Your own father lied to you."

"Not for his own self-interest," she said hotly. "He lied to protect his family, to protect his farm, yes. He didn't lie to expand his ego and have a joke at someone else's expense."

"Silver, please let me explain." Again Darcy tried to take her arm, but she avoided him. "Please, let's start again. Let's pretend you and I are just meeting for the first time."

"I won't listen to any more of this. I want you to leave. Now." She walked to the bed, picked up the duffel bag, and threw it at him. "Get out."

He caught the bag. "What happened to our building something together for the future?"

"It was a fairy tale. Not a good foundation to build on."

"It can be if you'll give me a chance."

"I'd rather face the future alone."

Darcy knew there was no way he'd get through to her at that moment, but he gave it one more try. "I love you, Silver."

She walked to the door. "You dishonor the words. You're just saying them so I'll say them back and then you can go away and gloat. Well, forget it. There's no way I'm going to be the butt of a joke for some spoiled rich boys to laugh about over drinks one night." She turned the knob, yanking open the door. "Now, get off this property."

Darcy stared at her, at the love he'd lost because he didn't have the guts to tell her the truth when he'd first suspected he was falling in love with her. He opened his mouth, but shut it just as quickly. Perhaps it would be best for him to leave and give her some breathing room. "This isn't over," he said as he stood in the doorway.

"Yes it is. I never want to see you again." She slammed the door in his face.

Darcy hesitated, tempted to break the door down to get to her, to make her listen. If he could just get her in his arms... Then he shook his head and walked away. He stopped by Lucky Hand's stall. A tiny smile escaped as he saw the huge black stallion lying down, the kitten curled up beside him. He said a silent farewell before moving on. No one was around when he emerged from the stables. He walked over to his truck and flung his bag inside, then turned to study the farm.

My grandfather really would have liked this place, he thought. Would have told him it was a good place for a new beginning. And what had begun here would have to be finished. The only problem was, he didn't have the faintest idea how.

"Best if you was to go on out of here, Son."

Darcy turned as Tater's hand fell on his shoulder. He searched for something to say. However, Tater only smiled as he gave him a brisk pat. "Ain't no need to say anything. I heard it all. I'd just come into the stables when Silver started. Bless the girl, she sure ain't quiet when she's riled up, is she?"

Darcy felt a smile threatening to break. "Then you know who..."

"Yep. Thought there was something odd about you right off, something that didn't fit, but it didn't bother me none. Sometimes a man's got to forget his past. I seen it before." Tater lifted his hat to scratch his head before jamming it back down. "I always figure a man's reasons is a man's reasons."

"I never meant to hurt anyone," Darcy rasped. "Least of all Silver."

"I know that, boy. Now you'd better git on down the road before Silver comes out and starts throwing things at you."

Rubbing his chest, Darcy chuckled. "She already has."

"Girl's got a good arm. I taught her myself."

Darcy climbed into his truck and started the engine. He leaned out the window to shake Tater's hand. "Tell Harden and Aggie that I—"

"Don't you worry none, I'll tell 'em. And good luck to ya."

Darcy nodded as he backed out. Then he hit the brakes. "One more thing."

Tater stepped closer. "What's that?"

"You tell Silver Braybourne this isn't over by a long shot."

"I'll do that," Tater said with a chuckle. "You take care of yourself, Darcy."

"I'll see you again. Soon."

"Damn me." Tater laughed, slapping his thigh. "I'm countin' on it, boy, I'm countin' on it."

TWO WEEKS LATER, Darcy sprawled in an armchair at Wind-Raven Farms, clicked off his cell phone and stared at his cousin across the room.

"Well?" Nicholas asked.

Dumping the phone onto an end table, Darcy scowled. "Goddamn stubborn woman still won't speak to me."

Nicholas was sitting at a desk putting finishing touches on some formal documents. "Well, if it makes you feel any better, she answered the phone when I called yesterday to speak with her father, and she refused to talk to me, too."

"You're lucky *I'm* talking to you."

Nicholas held up his hand. "Don't start that again. I didn't slip up on purpose. I was just trying to wrap up your financing arrangements for Braybourne Farm and needed to ask you a question."

Seeking peace, Darcy held up his own hands. "I know, Nick. I know. I'd like to blame it on you, but it wasn't your fault. It was mine. I should have told her the truth the first time I touched her." He shoved his hand through his hair. "How the hell did I know I was going to fall in love with her?"

"You're sure about that, Darcy? I mean, you're absolutely sure? It would be a crime to want to marry her just because she's playing hard to get and you don't like to lose. At least you won our little bet." Nick came around the desk and handed the papers to Darcy, pointing to a dotted line. "Sign here. This completes the final financing arrangements for the Braybourne Farm credit line. Since you're going to underwrite this woman to the tune of a million bucks, you'd better be damn sure this is the way you want to go."

"I am damn sure." Darcy scribbled his name. "And you're wrong about Silver. She's not playing hard to get. And even if she were, I'd still propose. I love her, Nick. I didn't understand what that meant before, but I do now."

"Man, I hope so, because your parents are going to raise a stink. They've practically got you married off to someone else."

"Then you'll have to marry her instead. Because I'm going to marry Silver Braybourne if it's the last thing I ever do."

Nicholas laughed. "From what you've told me of Silver's temper, it might be."

"You're right there," Darcy agreed, laughing right back.

"So what are you doing sitting here? Why don't you go get her?"

"I'm going to."

"What are you waiting for, then?"

"I'm leaving tomorrow. Tater told me she's still running Lucky Hand in the Rosemont Cup, and I intend to be there when she does."

"Are you going to give her the pedigree papers and title to the horse at the same time?"

"I think I'll save that as an engagement present. Funny how things work, isn't it? Who would have thought that one of our horses would link us together before I'd ever met her?"

Gathering his papers, Nicholas walked back to the desk and placed them neatly inside his briefcase. "We're lucky we found the horse at all. He was stolen from the first owner, who died unexpectedly, then the horse's name was changed and the records destroyed. Then he was stolen again. Then he was lost in a poker game." Grinning, Nicholas shook his head. "That's not what I'd call a good track record. If I was a superstitious man, I'd say anyone who touches this horse is taking a big chance and is going to need all the luck she can get."

Darcy grinned. "I hear you. However, I think Silver believes in making her own luck. She can't resist a challenge. So she's the right owner for this horse. She would be even if I wasn't going to marry her."

Nick poured himself a drink. "Sounds like someone else I know."

Darcy stood. "You think so?"

Lifting his glass in a toast, Nick said, "Tell the Braybournes I'll see them at the wedding."

THE DAY OF THE Rosemont Cup, the sky was still gray as Silver stood in the chilly dawn mist outside the stables at the Kearney Racetrack. The silence was broken only by an occasional sleepy chirp from a bird and the rustling of horses, the sounds of a barn beginning to wake up. She choked back a sob. That was the problem with the night, she thought—it gave you too much time to think. Too much time to yearn, to imagine what might have been. She'd expected to stand here on this day with Darcy by her side. Instead she was alone. Even her horse had his

Buddy to share his stall, and what did she have? Nothing. Except anger and pain.

"Hi there, honey." Her father's quiet voice came out of the darkness behind her.

She turned to smile at him. "Hi. You're down here mighty early, aren't you?"

Harden shrugged. "I couldn't let our first Derby winner start his career without showing up, now could I?"

Silver whistled. "The Kentucky Derby? Those are big dreams."

"Didn't you tell me this horse is a winner? Well, that's what I expect from a winner. He might not make it, but at least he'll run his best race." He cupped her chin and kissed her cheek. "We'll all run our best race. That's what it's all about. I'm damn proud of you, darlin'."

She choked back another tear. "Thanks, Daddy."

Awkwardly he patted her back. "Don't you fret, it's going to work out fine."

"I know it will, Daddy." She smiled up at him. "Are you going to join Mama for breakfast? She's probably wondering where you are."

"Your mama is already entertaining a good-looking young buck, so I'd better get back there and—" He shut his mouth with a snap.

"Who?"

"Never you mind, Silver, you just see to that horse. And you tell that damn jockey I want a win today."

Diverted, Silver said, "Will you stop calling Hectoire 'that damn jockey'? He's the best in the business. How we ever got him to ride Lucky Hand, I'll never know."

"He rides the WindRaven horses, of course."

She knew Darcy had a hand in it somehow, but preferred to ignore that fact. "Go on, Daddy. I'm fine. You know how grumpy you get if you don't eat breakfast."

"Silver..." He hesitated, then said, his voice a bit rough, "You don't want to let your pride stand in the way of what you really want. That's no good. I know because I've been doing it all my life."

"Do you have any regrets, Daddy?"

He smiled. "Lord love you, girl, who doesn't have regrets? The point is, are any of my regrets so huge that I can't live with them? To that I'd have to say, almost. Yes, sir, they almost were, but not quite. Not anymore. Things have a way of working out the way the good Lord intends, I guess. And we can thrash around all we want and we won't change destiny. You need to let go of the past, Silver. Look at the future." Harden exhaled. "Damn me if that isn't the longest speech I've ever made to you."

Silver threw her arms around him. "I love you, Daddy."

He kissed her forehead. "I love you, too. Now you remember, Braybournes are winners. You go in there and make that damn horse understand that."

Silver let him go. "Yes, sir."

After a bracing look at her, Harden strolled away. Silver now knew there was no friend of a friend who'd made a call to a banker. It was Darcy who had put himself on the line financially. Silver still had mixed feelings about it, but thanks to Darcy's financial string-pulling, both her parents looked years younger. It was hard to hold a grudge against a man who had given her a gift such as that.

But she was still trying.

Silver walked into the stables, wandering the aisle until she reached Lucky Hand's stall. She entered, whispering a greeting to her horse and to the kitten who'd become his constant companion. Funny how animals could bond like that. Simple, uncomplicated love and friendship could make the difference between happiness and... As always, her thoughts shifted to Darcy.

"Damn you, Darcy," she said, the words half a curse, half a caress. She sighed and tied her horse to the post, smoothing the grooming brush over his back before reaching down to pet the kitten pestering her ankles.

Then she straightened back up and resumed grooming. Her

brush strokes hardened as her emotions took over. *Why can't I forget you? I want to forget you. Honest. I want to.* She remembered laughing with him, swearing at him, loving him. Every time she closed her eyes he was there. The tears brimming in her eyes overflowed as she began to sniffle. Her strokes over the horse intensified, and Lucky Hand stomped and shifted, restless under her hands. Realizing the horse was picking up her mood, which could jeopardize his chances in the race, she apologized and started to hum a tune to calm him down.

After a moment, she paused and rested her forehead against her horse's shoulder. "God, I miss you, Darcy."

"I've missed you, Silver." Darcy's voice echoed her words.

Stunned, Silver looked up and saw him standing in the shadows by the gate. Her pulse leaped. She knew her love was in her eyes, but she couldn't hide her feelings any longer. Finally she whispered, "What are you doing here?"

"Please, just give me a few minutes," Darcy begged. "Listen to what I have to say. Then you can decide whether or not to throw me out."

Silver gulped. Throw him out? She was having trouble keeping herself from throwing her arms around his neck and kissing him senseless. She met his anxious gaze and nodded. "All right."

He opened the gate and stepped inside the stall. "I'm in love with you, Silver."

Her jaw dropped as she listened to him. He stepped closer. "You're the only woman for me. The only one I'll ever want. Damn if the Kristof legend wasn't right—love at first sight. I took one look at you and I haven't been the same since."

"Neither have I," she whispered.

"Everything always came too easily to me, Silver. But not with you. Even if you'd known who I was from the beginning, you still would have made me prove myself. Except for my grandfather, who died way too young, no one's ever given me that type of challenge. I'm a better person because of you."

She couldn't stop her smile. "You are?"

He smiled back. "I am. Believe me, I am. And I'll get even better if you promise to take me on."

"Take you on? Hmm, that sounds like quite a responsibility. I'm not sure I—"

He grabbed her wrist. "Silver, I was a complete and total idiot. Please give me a chance to show you how much I love you! How much I need you!"

Judging by his hollow cheeks and the slight shadow under his eyes, these last few weeks had been as hard on Darcy as they'd been on her. Compassion stirred, along with love. She stroked his cheek, her breath catching as he turned his face to press a kiss in her palm.

"Please give me another chance."

She couldn't think of a good reason not to give him one. She loved him. If she'd ever doubted it, his absence had confirmed it. Her heart swelled.

"Silver?"

She wouldn't give in too easily. Everything came too easily, he'd said. So she had to make him suffer a bit more first. Retribution, then reward, was the trainer's philosophy.

Her brows lifted. "Are you being humble? I didn't think you knew how."

His lips quirked at her light tone. "I didn't. I had to buy a book."

"What kind of book?"

"A book explaining how to swallow your pride and beg for forgiveness."

"I see." She pretended to consider his statement, attempting to hide the smile that threatened to break. "Aren't you going to kneel?"

"Kneel?"

"You'd be a lot more convincing if you knelt while you were begging."

Darcy glanced around the stall. "Absolutely not. These are brand-new pants."

She laughed as she stepped forward and threw her arms

around his neck. "Thatta boy. I knew you couldn't be humble for long. It's completely out of character."

"I'll make you a bet."

"A bet? Okay, let's hear it."

He slid his arms down her back and cupped her buttocks, pressing her against him. "I'll bet if I kneel at your feet, I can give you an apology you'll never forget."

She shivered at his sensual tone, rubbing against him, feeling the power of his erection through his pants. "Hmm...I like the sound of that. But you might get too busy 'apologizing' to remember one tiny detail."

He rained kisses over her face, ending at her lips before asking, "What tiny detail?"

"Aren't you going to ask me to marry you?"

He grinned, pulling her tighter, as if he'd never let her go. "That's a very forward thing to say, Miss Braybourne. Not what I'd expect of a well-bred young woman like yourself."

She grinned, then drew his lips down to hers for a long, satisfying kiss. "Get used to it. When we Southern belles see something we want, nothing stands in our way."

Epilogue

SILVER STOOD BY THE RAIL at the track, too excited to stay in the owners' box with her parents. The minute Lucky Hand had swung to the right and pulled ahead, she'd run up the steps to get as close as possible to the horses, with Darcy pounding along right behind her.

"Look at him, Darcy, my God, just look at him."

Standing shoulder to shoulder with her, Darcy gripped the rail with one hand and her hand with the other. "He looks like a winner to me."

"Of course!" She snapped him an incredulous look. "I told you he was."

He chuckled. "And you're never wrong, are you?"

"Nope." Grinning, she pulled him close for a kiss. Then she caught a flash of movement and started screaming, "He's going to do it. He's going to do it." Her horse lowered his head, stretched his neck forward and lit out for the finish line as if frenzied hounds were snapping at his heels. Silver pounded on Darcy's shoulder. "Oh. Oh. Oh. Oh!"

"Ouch."

"Sorry, but oh my God." She bounced like an out-of-control rubber ball as her horse nosed over the line. "I can't stand it! I think I'm going to die!"

"Hang in there, sweetheart." Darcy laughed. "I'm not losing you now."

She flung her arms around his neck. "You'll never lose me."

Darcy pulled her close, holding tight. "You're damn well right I won't. Kristofs don't like to lose."

"Neither do Braybournes."

He grinned. "Lord help our children."

"Our children?"

Eyes gleaming down at her, he growled, "I want a lot of them."

Intrigued, she studied the sexy, devil-may-care, testosterone-laden, two-legged stallion holding her so tight she couldn't breathe. Her nerves, already inflamed by Lucky Hand's win, were practically a conflagration as she met Darcy's focused stare. "How many?"

"Five."

Silver was a bit stunned. "*Five?* Then maybe *you'd* better have them."

He winked. "I get to have the fun of making them, remember?"

"No, *we* get to have the fun. This is an equal partnership."

He smoothed her hair back from her face, tucking it behind her ear. "So I'm getting a wife, a lover and a partner—someone who can share my life. That's a pretty good deal."

Silver nodded, cupping his cheek with her palm. "Do you want to go to the winner's circle with me, partner?"

"As long as we're together, I don't care where we go."

She flashed a grin. "Remember that when I'm in my twentieth hour of labor."

"On second thought—"

"No backing out. Partners, remember?" Silver grabbed his arm and pulled him toward the circle, where the winning horse, jockey and officials were crowding around. Lucky Hand looked very pleased with himself as Silver walked up and stroked his neck. "I'll bet you are the greatest horse that ever lived."

Glancing at the stallion, Darcy paused. "I'm not sure we know enough to back that bet, sweetheart."

"Since when are you so cautious?"

Darcy laughed, grabbed her by the waist and whirled her around. "You want to go out on a real limb? What do you want to bet we live *happily ever after?*"

"No one lives happily ever after. That's not realistic," Silver teased. A flirty little smile curved her lips.

"Maybe not, but word of a Kristof, we're going to give it a try."

HARLEQUIN®
Temptation.

It's hot...and it's out of control!

This spring, the forecast is hot *and* steamy!
Don't miss these bold, provocative, ultra-sexy books!

PRIVATE INVESTIGATIONS by *Tori Carrington*
April 2002
Secretary-turned-P.I. Ripley Logan never thought her first job
would have her running for her life—or crawling into
a stranger's bed....

ONE HOT NUMBER by *Sandy Steen*
May 2002
Accountant Samantha Collins may be good with numbers, but
she needs some work with men...until she meets sexy but
broke rancher Ryder Wells. Then she decides to make him a
deal—her brains for his bed. Sam's getting the better of the
deal, but hey, who's counting?

WHAT'S YOUR PLEASURE? by *Julie Elizabeth Leto*
June 2002
Mystery writer Devon Michaels is in a bind. Her publisher has
promised her a lucrative contract, *if* she makes the jump to
erotic thrillers. The problem: Devon can't write a love scene to
save her life. Luckily for her, Detective Jake Tanner is an
expert at "hands-on" training....

Don't miss this thrilling threesome!

HARLEQUIN®
Makes any time special®

HARLEQUIN®
Temptation.

Look for bed, breakfast and more...!

C O O P E R ' S   C O R N E R

*Some of your favorite Temptation authors are
checking in early at Cooper's Corner Bed and Breakfast*

In May 2002:

#877 *The Baby and the Bachelor*
Kristine Rolofson

In June 2002:

#881 *Double Exposure*
Vicki Lewis Thompson

In July 2002:

#885 *For the Love of Nick*
Jill Shalvis

In August 2002 things heat up even more at
Cooper's Corner. There's a whole year of intrigue
and excitement to come—twelve fabulous books
bound to capture your heart and mind!

**Join all your favorite Harlequin authors
in Cooper's Corner!**

HARLEQUIN®
Makes any time special ®

If you enjoyed what you just read,
then we've got an offer you can't resist!

Take 2 bestselling
love stories FREE!

Plus get a FREE surprise gift!